THE
MAH JONGG
MURDERS

By

LINDA PIRTLE

Venture Galleries, LLC

Copyright © 2015 Linda Pirtle
Venture Galleries LLC
1220 Chateau Lane
Hideaway, Texas 75771

ISBN: 978-1-937569-48-8

Book Cover Design: Laura Gordon
(www.thebookcovermachine.com)

Manufactured in the United States of America.

The Mah Jongg Murders is a work of fiction. Names, characters, places, and incidents are either the product of the author's imagination or are used fictitiously. Any resemblance to actual persons, living or dead, or events is entirely incidental.

To my husband, Caleb,
who has been my inspiration and
who has always encouraged me,
no matter what kind of project
I have attempted.

And
To my son, Josh

Chapter 1

THE MOMENT LILLIAN Prestridge saw the standard poodle running up the hill, she tuned out her husband who was reading from their current devotional book. She stood, walked to the railing of the front deck to get a better view, and wondered why the owner would ignore leash laws and allow his dog to run loose in the neighborhood. Then, she quickly chided herself. Perhaps, the dog simply got away from his owner. She whistled, and the dog changed direction and ran toward her house. He stopped at the end of the driveway and waited for her. The dog whimpered softly as she approached him.

She chuckled at the sight of the dog, leash in his mouth, walking himself. That is, until she spotted the hair on his face and chest. Both were smeared with blood.

She knelt in front of him. "What's wrong, buddy? Where's your owner?"

Immediately, the dog began barking. He turned and trotted a few paces away. Then he stopped, looked over his left shoulder, barked, ran back to her, wheeled around, ran another few feet, stopped, barked, came back.

Lillian looked up at the deck. Her husband Bill was peering over the rail. The dog continued to bark.

"Come out here," she commanded. "I think this dog is trying to tell me something. Let's follow him and see what's going on."

Bill yelled down from his perch on the deck. "What? What did you say?"

"Don't ask questions." Lillian realized he could not hear her over the louder and more frantic barks of the dog, so she beckoned for him to come down toward her.

"Oh, okay I'm coming."

When Bill reached the end of the drive, Lillian motioned with her head. "Look, there's blood on him."

The dog repeated his barking, running away, returning and barking again.

"See. He is trying to communicate with us." She looked down at the dog. "Okay, buddy, let's go."

The dog took off in a dead run. Lillian and Bill struggled to keep him in sight. He led the couple down the hill and toward the dam at the end of the small fishing lake. He began to whimper again. He dropped down and low crawled toward a figure lying near the edge of the lake. He sat up and howled.

Both Lillian and Bill pulled up short at the sight of a woman's body. She was on her stomach, face turned away from them. A pool of blood seeped from beneath her chest. Lillian walked around to see the woman's face and knelt by the body. She reached out, picked up a limp wrist to check for a pulse. There was none.

"Don't touch her, Lil. I'm going to run back up to the house to call security. You stay here with the dog and try to comfort him."

"Okay, I will."

She didn't touch the body again but began to look around the area in search of clues that might tell her what had happened. She found no traces of a struggle. There were numerous footprints, including hers and Bill's, but since the dam was part of a popular trail where people came either to fish from the pier or to hike, footprints didn't help much.

She led the dog over to a bench near the pier and sat down to wait for help to arrive. She pulled the dog close to her and looked at the tag on his collar. "So, your name is Eli. I'm so sorry, Eli, that someone you love has been hurt. Don't worry, buddy. I won't let anyone hurt you."

As she and Eli sat side by side on the bench, it suddenly occurred to her how quiet everything was. She concentrated on the sounds she should be hearing, sounds of nature. Nothing. Usually, during the early morning, she could hear the harmonious symphony of the cardinals, blue jays, house wrens, and mockingbirds that gathered around the lake.

Lillian sighed. She stroked the dog's head which he had placed on her knee. She looked at the lake. Perfectly still. Not one wave rippled toward the bank. Then she saw them, the dreaded evil turkey buzzards. Circling. Circling. Descending slowly on the other side of the lake. Lillian shivered.

"I just hate those things."

Eli looked up at the birds and emitted a low growl.

"I understand, Eli. You don't like them either."

Lillian was relieved to see Bill.

"Emergency should be on its way," said Bill as he joined Lillian on the bench. Exhausted from his run up the hill, he took a deep breath. "That hill gets steeper every time I walk it. I guess I'm out of shape."

"No, dear," Lillian said, "you are in great shape, but as I recall, this is the first time you've ever run up the hill instead of climbing it leisurely."

Sirens could be heard as security and the ambulance hurried to the scene. Now, all of Leisure Lake knew that something was amiss in an otherwise peaceful community.

* * * * *

GRANT PERRYMAN, LEISURE Lake's Chief of Security, enjoyed his slow-paced job. Once, he had been in excellent shape. He had played college football for Sam Houston State University where he received his degree in Criminal Justice. After college, Grant had joined the Dallas Police Department. He had grown weary of the politics of the city's judicial system and had returned to East Texas and secured his current position.

Now, Grant was more than a little overweight, and his thick black hair showed streaks of gray. He scowled when he saw Lillian sitting on the bench. *Should've known she'd be right in the middle of whatever's going on.*

Grant heaved himself from his patrol car and trudged over to the dam. He walked straight to the body and squatted down, and without touching the corpse, he visually examined it for foul play. Grant took a small notebook from his front shirt pocket and began to write.

Jane Doe.
Approximately 5'4"
Brunette.
Weight: Approx.100 pounds.
Left earlobe ripped. . . Pierced?
Note: Check to see if earring is in other ear.
White blouse.
Torn sleeve.
Designer jeans.
Gold chain around neck.
Could there have been a pendant?
No shoes.

The local paramedics arrived on the scene less than five minutes after Grant. He looked up and recognized the older medic Thomas Matthews.

"Hello, Tom. You must have been close by to get here so soon."

"We came as quickly as we could." Tom said as he walked toward the body.

"We have a Jane Doe," Grant said.

"Yes, sir, I see," said Tom Elder who drew up short when he realized her condition.

"Have you called the justice of the peace, yet?"

"He's on his way. Should be here in less than thirty minutes. When I called him, he was on his way to his son's little league game."

"Good. We'll be glad to help you anyway we can while we wait."

"Ten-four. Two of my security guys are on their way." He glanced up at the onlookers who were beginning to congregate on the road at the entrance to the path leading down the hill to the scene. "But it will take them at least ten minutes to arrive." He nodded toward the group. "Could you make sure they don't enter the trail. Need to contain the area."

"Yes, sir." The two men headed off to comply with his request.

Grant put his hands on his hips and gazed out at the lake. The rays of the sun pranced over the tops of the waves as they sashayed their way to the pier and introduced themselves to its support beams. He took a deep breath, turned around, and studied the face of the beloved mother of his childhood friend, Jake. When Grant's mom died at the early age of forty-five after a long fight with cancer, it was Lillian to whom he had turned for comfort. When he reached the bench where she waited, he sat down and took her hand in his.

I see that far away look in your eyes and I know what you're thinking.

He spoke gently. "Lillian, are you okay?"

She nodded and looked at him. Grant recognized the pain in her eyes. Those clear blue eyes revealed more. They were resolute and determined. He was overwhelmed with a dread that was almost palpable. He understood Lillian would not rest until the mystery of the woman's death was resolved. *I don't know how in the world I'll be able to keep you out of the investigation. I'd never forgive myself if I allow you to be hurt.*

"Have you or Bill touched anything?"

Lillian responded in her most businesslike voice, "I touched her wrist to check for a pulse, and then Bill ran back up to the house to call you. I see the ambulance came, too, but I think it's too late for the ambulance, don't you?"

Grant ignored her question and continued with the informal interview, "Do you normally walk the lake at this time of day?"

"Usually, we sit on the deck early each morning while Bill reads our daily devotional. Today, the text was from Romans. It was about not doing any harm to one's neighbor, and just think, someone did just that right here in our community. I just can't believe it."

"Lillian, calm down. You didn't answer my question."

"Forgive me. What was it?"

"I asked if you and Bill normally walk the lake this time of day."

"No, we don't. And, for your information, I am calm. Furthermore, I'm angry, angry that someone would do such a thing to one of my neighbors. He will live to regret it."

"Lillian, like I said, calm down. I'll take care of the person or persons who did this. All you have to do right now is answer my questions."

"Sure."

Grant knew that her 'sure' was her way of making him think she would do as he asked. He forged on. "If you and Bill don't normally walk around the lake, then what caused you to do so today?"

Lillian pointed to the dog.

"I noticed Eli; that's his name. I read it on his tag. I looked at it so I could identify his owner but saw only the name of the dog. The tag is one of those cutesy tags, not one from a veterinarian."

"What caused you to pay attention to the dog?"

"He interrupted our morning."

"How?"

"He came walking down the street holding his leash in his mouth. I thought it was cute, so I whistled to him, and he came running, barking, and making circles. You know, like he was trying to tell me something. Then I noticed the blood on his face and chest. Anyway, I called Bill, and we followed him here. Does that answer your question?"

"I believe it does. Do you have any idea who the lady might be?"

"No. In fact, I've never seen Eli in the neighborhood either."

More sirens blared as two Leisure Lake security vehicles arrived. The officers relieved the paramedics of their guard duty and quickly sealed off the area with yellow crime tape. One of the officers instructed the onlookers.

"Okay, folks, this is a crime scene. You'll have to move farther back onto the road."

His partner set up barriers, thereby establishing parameters for the crowd that had gathered.

Howard Bernard, Justice of the Peace for the precinct parked his car on the side of the road. He shoved his way through the crowd and walked down to the scene.

"Sorry to interfere with your watching Bobby's game," Grant said.

"Don't worry about it. My son knows I'm on call twenty-four seven." He completed his paperwork, signed off, and looked at Grant. "Do you have everything you need here? If so, I can release the body to the paramedics."

"No, Sir. I need photographs of the scene. My men should be able to do that in thirty minutes or so."

"I understand. FYI: I called the county sheriff. He should be arriving with his detectives any minute now. I'm sure he'll want photos as well."

"Jake will. Do you need to wait on him?"

"No. In fact, I'll let the paramedics know that Sheriff Prestridge will release the body."

"Thanks. You go on. I know your son is anxious for you to be at his game."

"If you need me, give me a call later. I won't mind coming by your office first thing tomorrow."

"Ten-Four."

Sheriff Prestridge arrived just as the justice of the peace was leaving. Grant noticed Bernard lower the window on the passenger side of the car as Jake approached. The two men shook hands, and the justice drove away.

Grant waved a greeting to Jake and turned back to the crime scene.

Lillian looked up when Jake approached. She stood to greet him, but he motioned for her to stay put. He walked past her and nodded to Grant.

"Thanks for coming out," Grant said.

Jake nodded an acknowledgment and walked around the body. He then joined Grant. They stood, talking, with their backs facing the park bench.

"Bring me up-to-date." Lillian heard Jake say.

Grant pulled his notebook from his shirt pocket and thumbed through the pages to his notes and read them to Jake. But as her son turned to glance at her, Lillian knew they were discussing more than the body lying before them. *You two think you can keep me out of this business, but be forewarned, I will find the culprit who murdered that woman with or without your cooperation. I heard Grant tell you it was your dad and mom who found the body.*

Bill spoke, "Grant, Jake, do you need us anymore?"

"Yes, Dad, I'd like you to tell me why you and Mom decided to hike down the hill this morning." Bill confirmed everything Lillian had told Grant.

"Have you seen the woman before this morning?" Jake wanted to know.

"Never," responded his dad. "I've never seen the dog before either."

Grant pulled his cell phone from his pants pocket. "Well, I guess I'll call the animal shelter to pick up the dog."

"You can't do that."

"Why can't Grant make that call, Mom?" Jake asked.

"I promised Eli that I would protect him."

"People don't make promises to a dog," Jake shook his head. "Why am I not surprised to find you right in the middle of whatever's going on here?"

His mother ignored his comments and stood her ground.

"I do. And as you know, I always keep my promises."

Grant sighed and explained. "He will stay at the shelter until we know where he belongs. The victim may have family members who will want him."

"He can't stay there. I promised Eli that I would not let anyone harm him. I'm taking him home with me." She stood and squared her shoulders.

"Come on, Eli. Let's go."

Bill walked over to stand behind his wife. He put his hands on her shoulders as if to restrain her. Eli growled and moved between them.

"Sit, Eli. Bill won't hurt me."

The dog obeyed but kept his eyes on Bill who put his hands in his pockets. "Now, Lillian, you can't interfere with Grant doing his job. He knows what's best. Besides, Jake agrees with him."

Grant just nodded. He knew it wouldn't do any good to argue with Lillian, the flamboyant matriarch of the neighborhood.

He looked at the gentle, loving woman and tried to decide how to phrase his next statement.

"Lillian, I just thought of something that would help us solve this mystery."

"What?"

"The blood on the dog's hair could be critical evidence."

"Oh, I hadn't thought of that."

"So, I think it best that you don't take him with you right now. The medical examiner will need to cut some of his hair with the blood on it for DNA analysis."

"How long will that take?"

"Not long. In fact, I won't call animal control. I'll transport him to the shelter myself if that will make you feel better."

"Yes, it does. Thank you."

"I'll call you when it is okay for you to come down to the shelter. You'll need to complete the necessary paperwork before you take him home with you."

Lillian reached up and hugged Grant and looked over his shoulder to her son. "It's good you're here. I think Grant is going to need all of our help."

"Mind you, this will be only temporary until we find a relative of the victim. Are you okay with this?" Grant asked, ignoring her last remark regarding the "help" he would need. *Hope Jake can help. . .help keep you out of this mess.*

Lillian nodded, bent down and patted the dog on his head, and reluctantly turned Eli over to Grant. "Eli, you're going to be cared for. Grant's your friend. I'll see you as soon as I possibly can. Be a good dog, now."

He led the dog over to his cruiser. Before Eli leaped into the backseat, the poodle turned and looked at Lillian as if to say, *You promised.* Grant closed the door, made sure that the windows provided fresh air for the dog, and returned to the scene. He, Jake, and the detective shook hands.

"Thanks for the head's up on this, Grant. I'll take over now so you can drive to the shelter. We will be here a while. Come back by if you want or call me first thing tomorrow morning, and let's set up a meeting time to go over our findings."

"Will do." Grant climbed the small hill to the street and opened the door to his cruiser. He plopped down behind the steering wheel and glanced back to watch Jake giving his detective orders.

As usual, ole buddy, you think you're the quarterback and I'm just your backup. Just like our games in high school and college. But don't get ahead of yourself. Remember, this is my community.

* * * * *

LILLIAN WATCHED GRANT lower the back seat window half-way. Eli poked his head through the opening and howled. *That is so sad. He hates to leave his master lying there in the red East Texas dirt. Both of them look lonely. I have to help Jake and Grant identify her.*

"Just think, Bill, somebody lost a loved one today and knows nothing about her death."

Soft-spoken Bill, a sixty-five-year-old recently retired investigative journalist, turned to Lillian and stated, "My dear, let's not hang around here any longer."

"I just wish we knew more about her. We could help Grant."

"We can help him by minding our own business," Bill stated. "Someday, perhaps, you can slow down and enjoy the kind of retirement you've dreamed of having."

"I don't know how you can say that. You're not retired yet even though you say you are."

"Now, Lil, you know my writing is a hobby."

"I guess you will include this scene in one of your novels."

"Probably, somewhere down the road, I might." Since "retiring," Bill had successfully produced a syndicated column for more than two hundred small town newspapers. "I promise you one thing," he continued, "I won't put anything about this in any of my blogs on my website."

"Oh, why not? Some of your fellow writers might find it entertaining."

"Don't be sarcastic. No, I don't think it's appropriate. But, maybe after the case is solved. . ."

"Don't worry, dear. We'll let Grant work this case. After all," Lillian reasoned, "we have plenty of things to do right now. Let's go exercise and try to forget this horrible morning."

Lillian and Bill sold their house in the city and moved to the lake. She was not ready for the rocking chair – her description of retirement. Lillian kept her 5' 8" body at a precise 135 pounds by working out each day.

"Good idea, but I know you. Keep your concern about today to yourself and don't gossip about it with the person who is on the treadmill next to you."

As they entered the gym, Lillian looked around to see who was there. Could one of her neighbors possibly be a murderer? She shivered at the thought.

Chapter 2

LILLIAN HEARD THE telephone ringing as she and Bill entered their back door upon their return from the gym. Bill ran and picked up the receiver.

Lillian walked on through the kitchen to the master bedroom to shower and freshen up for the challenge of solving the crime.

"Hello. Yes, I'll tell her. Can't believe the medical examiner is finished with them already."

"Who was that on the phone a few minutes ago?" Lillian asked as she stepped out of the shower and saw that Bill had entered their bedroom, waiting for his turn to shower.

"Grant. He said you could go to the shelter and pick up the dog. . .what's its name?" Not waiting to hear her response, he slammed the shower door and turned on the water.

"Eli. His name is Eli. I'll get dressed and drive downtown and pick him up before they close for the day. I don't want him to stay there overnight. After all, I did promise him I'd get him ASAP." She shook her head, knowing that her husband hadn't heard a word she said.

But she was wrong. She knew otherwise when she heard him muttering above the drum of the shower, "I guess we'll have a dog now. She needs something else to mother."

"I heard that." She laughed. "Don't worry. I won't ignore you, my dear." Fifteen minutes later, Lillian headed for the kitchen to grab a bottled water to have in the car on her drive into town.

* * * * *

LILLIAN PARKED HER SUV as close as possible to the entrance of the Tri-County Rescue Shelter. Her first stop had been at the local pet store to purchase items she considered necessary for a responsible pet owner to have.

She walked out with a doggy seat cover, a harness for the car seat to prevent his falling forward if she had to slam on her brakes, a dog bed large enough for a big dog, three or four squeak toys, dog food and treats, and a retractable leash. Smiling, she checked to make sure she had the back seat ready for her new friend.

She entered the shelter and greeted the young lady whose name tag had volunteer in all capital letters with her name just below the shelter's logo. Lillian glanced at the name tag and said, "Good morning, Ms. Walters, how are you today?"

"I'm doing well, thank you. Can I help you?"

"Yes ma'am, you can. I'm Lillian Prestridge, and I'm here to pick up Eli. He's a white standard Poodle."

"Oh, yes. We've been expecting you." The receptionist handed Lillian a clipboard containing an application to complete. "You'll have to fill out these documents before I can release the dog to you."

Lillian took the documents and scanned them. "I'm sure I don't need to do this. Didn't Grant Perryman tell you that I would be here to pick up Eli?"

"Yes ma'am, he did."

"So, why do you need any paperwork from me?"

The volunteer looked at Lillian and explained, "Mr. Perryman informed us that you would be taking temporary custody of Eli."

"That's correct, but I expect my caring for him will be a long 'temporary' situation."

"Of course, it may very well become permanent, but in the meantime, we will consider your home as a foster home for Standard Poodles. We need to know how to stay in touch with you just in case his owner contacts us."

"I promise you that won't happen."

"Oh? What makes you think we won't hear from Eli's family?"

"Because his owner is dead, and we don't know anything about an extended family."

"I'm so sorry to hear about Eli's loss, but that doesn't change our policy. We need you to complete the foster application, please."

Lillian decided to cooperate and to lighten the mood. She laughed and said, "I've mothered a son, a stepson, and all of the critters they brought home during their growing-up years and never once thought of myself as a foster mother to any of them."

The volunteer laughed with her. "I guess you'll have a new title after today," she said as she handed a pen to Lillian.

"And one I don't mind at all." She took the ballpoint, turned away from the desk, walked over to an empty chair, and sat down to complete the application. After making sure that all of the questions were answered, she returned the paperwork to the receptionist who reviewed the document.

She looked up and said, "Wait here. I'll bring the dog to you."

Five minutes later, she returned with Eli. Lillian could tell he was distressed. His head drooped and his tail was tucked between his back legs. When he saw her, his body language morphed from a sad dog to a happy one. His head perked up. His tail wagged back and forth. He let out a yelp and began to sprint toward her.

"I can tell he's excited to see you," said the volunteer as Eli dragged her across the reception area in his anxious attempt to reach Lillian.

"No more than I'm happy to see him." Lillian smiled. "Come on, big boy. We're going home." She removed the shelter's leash and clipped on the one she had bought.
"Thank you so much, Ms. Walters."

"You're welcome. Let us know if we can help you in any way."
"I will."

The new foster mother and her charge left the shelter. She walked Eli to her SUV and opened the door to the back seat. He jumped in. Lillian secured the seat harness to him and walked around to the driver's side. As she sat down behind the wheel, the dog reached over the back seat and planted a big, wet doggy kiss on her right ear.

"Oh, I already love you, too, you pretty boy. I think you and I are going to be friends for a long time."

Eli responded by placing his chin on her shoulder and letting out a long sigh.

Instead of going straight home, Lillian drove to the edge of the lake. She attached a leash onto Eli's collar and gave him the other end. "Go home, Eli. Take me to your house."

Eli trotted off with Lillian following as closely as she could possibly walk without running. Eli turned right at the dam, walked up to Horse Shoe Circle, turned left on Pecan, and stopped in front of the third house on the right which was situated on a sloping lot. It was painted red and had a gray-tiled roof. The front yard was meticulously landscaped. The dog walked around to the back of the house and entered an open gate. Lillian followed, careful not to touch the gate. She took note of the back yard. It, too, looked as though a professional had created it. There was a patio at the basement level, covered by a deck that protruded from a set of patio doors on the first floor of the house. Next to the ground level patio was a figure-eight swimming pool. She reached down and patted the dog, taking the leash from his mouth.

"Good boy. Let's walk around and peer through the windows."

They circled the lower level with Lillian stopping at each window. Unfortunately, all of them had plantation shutters that were closed. Finally, with Eli following close behind, she climbed the steps to the deck and peeked through the French doors that opened into what appeared to be the family room. It was neat, everything in place, except for an overturned table at the base of a stair case leading to the next level. A vase had fallen to the floor, and its flowers lay sprawled across the carpet. She could not see beyond the family room and could not determine if anything else looked out of the ordinary.

"I wonder what happened in there to knock over the table," she said to Eli. She looked down at him. He had begun to paw the bottom of the glass and whimper. "Come on, big boy, let's go home. You need to get away from here. It's too sad for you."

Chapter 3

THURSDAY MORNING, THE county sheriff sat at his desk reviewing the report the medical examiner had given him earlier. He frowned when the phone on his desk buzzed. He picked up the telephone receiver, pushed the intercom button.

"Yes, Nora?"

"Sheriff, there is someone here to see you," his secretary, announced.

"Who?"

Nora looked up and winked at the tall, stately woman who smiled back. "She says she's your mother."

Jake took a deep breath. "Send her in." Knowing how doggedly his mother would try to solve the murder at the lake, he did not look forward to the challenge of fending her off the case.

Lillian, with her long, gray hair pulled back in a ponytail, walked in leading the poodle who, upon seeing Jake stand and walk toward them, positioned himself between the two in a protective stance. Teeth barred, he let out a low, menacing growl.

Instead of hugging her son, Lillian stopped three feet away from him and blew him a kiss. She then reached down, patted the poodle.

"Eli, this is Jake. He's my son and a good friend to you. Say hello to him."

On command, the dog wagged his tail and sniffed the hand that Jake extended. Then the sheriff bent down to scratch Eli behind his ears and, looking up at his mother, said, "I knew you would show up here sooner than later."

He turned and walked back to his desk, sat down, and closed the file folder labeled *Jane Doe*. He motioned for his mother to sit in one of the blue leather chairs facing him.

She got right to the point. "Has Grant called you? Have you received anything from forensics or the medical examiner?"

"Yes, I've heard from both of them. Grant, Will Ogburn, and I have a meeting scheduled for one-thirty this afternoon."

"Good. How long do you think it will last? I need to meet with you two boys to discuss the case."

"No, Mom. You don't need to meet with us."

"What if I have some information that might help you identify the woman who was murdered?"

Jake decided not to take the bait. "Mom, I know the incident at the lake will have your brain in overdrive trying to help me and Grant solve the crime, but I want to go on record right now. Stay out of it."

"You sound just like your father."

"Please take our advice. There's a murderer loose at Leisure Lake, and I don't want you to become the next victim." Jake sat still. He gripped the armrests of his chair and braced himself for her to argue with him.

When she didn't, he asked, "I can tell you're thinking about your comeback to what I just said, so go ahead. State your case, but understand this: It won't do any good to argue about it. I'm ordering you to stay out of it and let me handle finding the culprit."

Lillian looked at him and with a sly smile, said, "Let's forget about that right now and start all over with this conversation."

Jake laughed. "Okay, but only if you promise me you will not put yourself or Dad in danger."

"I will do my best."

Jake looked at her, nodded in agreement, and began a new conversation.

"Hi, mom. To what do I owe the pleasure of your visit today? I hope it's to take me out to lunch."

Lillian played along with him.

"Hello, Darling, yes, let's do lunch. My treat. Where would you like to go?"

"I don't care. Just something quick. I do have several meetings scheduled this afternoon."

"What about the new Corner Bakery that's just opened? It's within walking distance, has healthy food for me, and hamburgers and fries for you."

"Sounds good to me. And, one additional feature you will love, Mom, is that the owner of the bakery is considerate of customers who walk their dogs."

"How so?"

"He's provided a space beneath a wide awning that covers the sidewalk in front of the bakery where pets can wait for their owners. And, there's a water bowl and a place where you can attach Eli's leash. They've thought of everything, haven't they?"

"Well, Eli, what do you think about that?" Lillian asked the dog. Both she and Jake laughed when Eli responded with a doggy snort. "That settles it. Let's go."

As they exited the building, Jake decided to cut to the chase and try again to dissuade his mother from getting involved in the case. He stopped walking to look her in the eye as he cautioned her.

"Mom, as I said before, I know you are going to try to get information from either me or Grant or both of us about the body you and Dad found."

He held up a finger to stop her from interrupting. "So, before you begin, let me say this: I don't know anything yet. Grant, the M.E., and I will meet this afternoon, but in the meantime, until this case is solved, I want you and Dad to be alert and aware of everything and everyone you come in contact with at the lake."

"Son, don't you think that we may have already thought of that?"

"I'm sure you have, but I just wanted to express my concern. That's all." He took her by the elbow as they resumed their slow pace down the sidewalk and continued their conversation.

"To be honest with you, when your father and I were at the gym yesterday, I could hardly concentrate on my exercise routine. I kept looking at everyone, wondering if one of them could be guilty. I even considered old Mr. Simms," said Lillian.

"Simms? Your imagination must have been in high gear. Poor old guy, he's been on portable oxygen for the past year and a half. If he only knew what you were thinking."

"I know. I feel guilty thinking about him as the culprit. I decided to get control of my thoughts."

"Good. Again, remember: be cautious and alert at all times."

"I will. I promise," she said, "but I keep thinking about the situation and the fact that everyone who goes to the gym might have done such a terrible thing. In my opinion, they are probably the only people living at the lake who are fit enough to overpower someone."

With a chuckle, Jake asked, "And just who was the next potential murderer?"

"Seriously, I don't appreciate your making fun of me. I'm not just a nosey little lady looking for excitement, despite what your father may say."

"Now, Mom, I didn't mean to hurt your feelings." He put his arm around her shoulder and squeezed. "You know I love you. Forgive me?"

"Well, okay. You're forgiven, but you know how focused I get. I heard someone talking to me and looked over at the treadmills on both sides of me. Rachel was on my right, and Victoria was on the left. They were both laughing at me."

"Why?"

"I was so lost in my thoughts that I had not heard any of their conversation."

"What were they talking about?"

"They had been telling a wild story about a new love affair Rachel was having with a man twenty years her junior."

"I can't believe you'd miss out on some good gossip like that."

Ignoring her son's sarcasm, Lillian continued. "Oh, I know my brain is out of control because I even considered them guilty. . .briefly, mind you. But I do think you or Grant need to talk to Rachel."

"Why?"

"She's the chairman of the hospitality committee and personally welcomes all newcomers to the neighborhood. She may even have welcomed our unfortunate lady."

"That's a good suggestion. When do you ladies meet again to play Mah Jongg? I might drop by or ask Grant to do so. If Rachel didn't meet with her, one of the other ladies might have seen her."

"Excellent idea. It just so happens we meet tomorrow afternoon at my house. Why don't both of you come a little before nine o'clock? We usually break up around that time, and you can talk with them then. Afterward, you can both stay for dinner."

"I'll talk to Grant and get back with you on that. Here we are. This place is packed. I think everyone else in town had the same idea."

Lillian hooked Eli to one of the doggy stations and made sure he could reach the water bowl.

"Stay here, boy. We'll be back in a little while." He obeyed her command and settled down to wait and watch the traffic.

"I hope we can find a table. Don't you think the Corner Bakery is going to be a real plus for downtown?" Lillian asked as she walked into the establishment.

She did not hear the dog's low, menacing growl as a white Lexus stalked its way down the street.

"I'll answer that question after I've sampled their cheeseburger. And, Mom, it'd be a good idea if you don't mention the case in here. We don't want anyone eavesdropping."

"Got it. My lips are sealed."

Mother and son approached the counter and placed their requests with the young teenager who handed them their order number. As they turned to find a table, Lillian nudged Jake, "Look who's here."

Seated in a cozy booth for two were Grant Perryman and Margaret Snyder.

"I didn't know they were an item, did you?"

"I'd advise you to not get too excited about Grant's personal affairs. As you know, he likes to keep his personal life private."

Ignoring her son's advice, she walked over to the booth and greeted the two who had not seen her approach. She overheard Margaret say to Grant, "I know, but how will you keep her safe?"

"Fancy meeting you two here."

Grant gave Lillian a poker-faced look of boredom, but Margaret's face revealed surprise when she looked up and saw Jake and his mother.

She stood, hugged Lillian, gave Jake a nod, and said, "Hi there. So good to see you."

"I see you two had the same idea as Jake and I."

Margaret smiled but did not respond to Lillian's comment. Instead, she nudged Grant who answered, "Yes ma'am, I guess we did." Grant turned his attention to Jake. "See you around one-thirty?"

"Sure thing. I'll be there."

Jake guided his mother to a vacant table by the window overlooking the street. "Let's sit here, Mom, so you can keep an eye on your new pet." He pulled out a chair for her, making sure her back was turned to Grant and Margaret.

Lillian laughed. "Do you think I don't know what you just managed to do? By sitting here, we can give Grant an opportunity to enjoy his lunch and his time with Margaret, especially if all I can see is you, Eli, cars, and pedestrians."

"Of course," her son said with a smile.

Lillian looked out the window to check on Eli. She gazed out the window saying nothing. Jake reached across the table and patted her hand. He said, "I know you aren't that concerned about Eli. I also know when my mom is worried, so tell me what you are thinking."

"I've been thinking about that poor woman your dad and I found. . ."

"Mom, I know it's going to be difficult for you, but you've got to try to. . ."

"Look. Eli suddenly sat up."

"That's what dogs do. They see something interesting and try to investigate. He probably saw another dog or perhaps a cat."

"No, Jake, that's not what he saw."

"How do you know that?"

"Because I saw the same thing."

"Okay," he laughed. "What now? You and the dog share mental telepathy?"

"Let me remind you. I am your mother, and you're not supposed to make fun of me." She laughed and added, "I'm sure it was nothing," *You'd think I'm crazy if I mentioned my suspicions about a white Lexus circling the block and how I know when Eli's upset. Plus, I don't want to hear another lecture about minding my own business.*

* * * * *

GRANT NOTICED JAKE'S gesture and gave him a subtle salute as a thank you. As he turned to resume his conversation with Margaret, she said, "I know you and Jake have been friends all your lives. Has something happened to cause the two of you to not be as close as you were?"

"What makes you ask that question?"

"Nowadays, you two are all business. There's no camaraderie between you."

"Margaret, like you, there are some things in my past I don't discuss, and my relationship with Jake and his family are personal."

"I didn't mean to pry." She put down her fork and stated, "If you're finished, let's walk through the park on our way back to the courthouse. I have a lot of work on my desk needing my attention, but right now, I would love some exercise, rev up my energy level for a long afternoon."

"Good idea. I need to kill some time before my meeting with Jake and Will. And, of course, escorting a lovely lady back to work is always a pleasure." He stood, walked around the end of the booth, reached down, and took her hand in his.

She looked up as she extended her hand, "Why, thank you, sir. Of course, I assume you are describing me."

"Your assumption is correct."

As they walked by Lillian's and Jake's table, Grant stopped long enough to bend down and kiss his surrogate mother on the cheek. "Love you," he whispered. He nodded to Jake and guided Margaret toward the door.

Stepping out onto the sidewalk, he heard Eli growling. "Wait here for a second, Margaret."

"Sure."

"What's the matter, boy? Don't you remember me?" he asked the dog as he squatted down in front of Eli at eye level and scratched the animal beneath his chin. Eli recognized him and licked Grant's nose.

Margaret laughed. "I think you've got a new friend I've not met."

"Come on over and meet Eli."

"Hello. You're a pretty boy," she said while keeping a safe distance from him.

Grant noticed her reticence about approaching the dog but didn't say anything about it. Instead, he took her arm and led her away from the bakery. They walked down the street and entered the park. He put his arm around her as they ambled the winding path that was shaded by the ancient oaks the city's founding fathers saved when they developed the green oasis for future generations to enjoy. He broached the subject he had on his mind.

"I hope you are free next Saturday night."

"Why? What's happening then?"

"The club at the lake is sponsoring a dance, and I would like you to come as my date."

"I would love that. What time will you pick me up?"

"I'll come by around six-thirty. The dinner begins at seven o'clock, and the dance follows right after."

"Great. I'll look forward to it." She stopped in front of the courthouse and said, "You don't have to escort me all the way to my office."

"Hey, I'm going your way, remember?"

"I forgot. You are meeting Jake and Will. Okay, then, walk with me to the elevator, please, sir."

"At your command, milady." He pushed the elevator button with the arrow pointing up. The door opened. Margaret entered and turned toward him. He bowed as the doors closed and whisked her away.

His gallantry disappeared when the doors to the next elevator opened. There stood Jake. Grant stepped inside, and the two men rode in silence down to the county medical examiner's office in the basement. Grant looked at Jake and said, "I appreciate what you did in the café."

"Least I could do."

"I know your mother. I hope she won't drive you nuts about this murder."

"Yep, you do understand her as well as I. Her brain never stops. She's always conniving."

Both men smiled. Jake continued. "She wants both of us to come for dinner tomorrow night to meet with her Mah Jongg ladies. I wouldn't be surprised if she also invites Margaret to stay and join us."

"I don't think she's up to Lillian's scrutiny right now," Grant said.

"What do you mean?" asked Jake.

Any answer Grant would have given was preempted by the elevator bouncing to a stop, The doors slid back. They stepped out and walked down the hall to the medical examiner's office. Will Ogburn greeted them.

"Good afternoon, guys. I want you to know that what I have today is just a preliminary report."

"We understand," said Jake. "Have you had time to read the initial report from the forensics team that worked the scene?"

"Yes, I have, and Grant also gave me a copy of his report that he gave to you."

Jake nodded. "I know you've not had time to complete your examination of the body, but you mentioned some preliminary information?"

"I'm glad you understand procedures. Sometimes, people expect instant results, but it usually takes a month to get toxicology reports. I've put in a rush order for this one, so hopefully, the lab is not too backlogged. We might get lucky and hear from them sooner."

"Any information you have now will be appreciated," said Jake. "Even though the murder occurred at Leisure Lake, I'll take the lead, but I want you to know that Grant and I will be working together as a team."

"That's right," said Grant. "I'll work with you any way I can."

"Great. Now, Will, let's hear what you've got," Jake said.

"Right. This is what we've done thus far. We've taken dental impressions and have faxed them to all of the local dentists in the area to see if we can find a match. I've also taken her fingerprints. If she's ever been arrested, we'll get an identity soon."

"What about her fingernails? I know the paramedics put bags on her hands to preserve any evidence indicating she tried to defend herself. Did you find anything there?" Grant asked.

"We've scraped some skin particles from them. She did put up a fight. Hopefully, we'll get some DNA there."

"DNA would be as good as fingerprints," Jake said. "How long does it take to get DNA results?"

"That depends. We have to rely on the Dallas office for DNA, and they are grossly understaffed right now. Budgets, you know."

"You mentioned dental impressions. Do you usually have a good response from dentists?" Grant asked.

"Actually we do, but they may not be much help to us, especially if she didn't have a dentist here in East Texas."

"Will, from talking with the couple who found the body, who by the way are Jake's parents, I've learned that neither of them recognized her. And, as you know, the lake community out there is so small that everyone knows everybody else."

"Rest assured," said Jake, "my mom will make sure to find out if any of her Mah Jongg ladies knew the deceased, and we will hear about it right away."

The medical examiner asked, "Do you need anything else?"

"I'd like a picture of the deceased to show to people I interview at the lake. I might just find someone who can identify her," answered Grant.

"I'd like a copy, too," said Jake.

Grant turned back to Will.

"What else have you learned?"

"Based upon the temperature of the body and the settlement of the blood, the time of death occurred early Wednesday morning, probably not long before the body was discovered, sometime between seven o'clock and eight-thirty."

"That dovetails with the time Lillian said she saw the dog make the turn up the hill coming directly from the location of the body."

"How did the victim die? Could you tell from her wounds what kind of weapon had been used?" asked Jake.

"Best I could tell, she had been stabbed several times. One stab, however, was not consistent with the others."

"How so?" asked Grant.

"I noticed that it looked different...more round...wider, so I probed around and found a bullet."

"A bullet? Interesting. Makes me ask the question: Why would someone shoot a person and then stab her?" commented Grant.

"That was my question. Only thing I can come up with is that the shot actually killed the victim. The stab wounds were made to throw us off."

"I think you're theory is a good one. Can you tell us the caliber?" Grant asked.

"It looks like a thirty-eight caliber."

"Do you still have the bullet? I'd like to see it," Grant asked.

"No, I sent it over to forensics for further analysis."

"I'll check with them and ask them to give me its particulars," said Jake. "And when I hear from them, I'll let you know, Grant. Anything else you can tell us?"

The medical examiner walked over to the refrigerated section of the lab. Grant and Jake followed him. He opened one of the doors and pulled out the stainless steel tray. Then he lifted the sheet that covered the body of the Jane Doe.

"As you can see for yourself, there are several scars on her torso. Old scars. This woman had been abused, beaten probably more than once."

"What a shame. Can you estimate her age?" Grant asked.

"I'd put her at approximately forty-five. No, perhaps a little older. Mid-fifties, maybe. Despite her wounds, it's obvious she kept her body in good shape. I'll put all of this in my report along with the results of the toxicology report. I'll send it to both of you as soon as I possibly can."

Both Grant and Jake thanked Will, shook hands, and walked outside.

"What's wrong Grant? You're pale. Are you sick?" Jake asked.

"I'm not sick, but I had the strangest feeling when I looked at that body."

"Really? Did you recognize her? Do you think you've seen her at the lake?"

"No, I don't know her. Somehow, though, she vaguely reminds me of someone."

"Interesting. I had the same feeling."

"More strange than interesting, I'd say," responded Grant. "We'll have to think about this some more as we continue our investigation. If both of us had that reaction, there must be something we're overlooking."

"In the meantime, try to come to Mom's around eight forty-five tomorrow evening. Her Mah Jongg group is playing there, and I'd like to show the victim's picture to everyone to see whether or not any of the ladies might have met her. I think it best that you leave Margaret out of the investigation, don't you? Besides, I'll need a backup to keep Mom at bay."

"I will," said Grant. "And, you will definitely need my help to keep her safe."

That's right, Jake. I've always been your backup, but where were you when I was fighting for our country? I needed you to look after my fiancée, keep her safe. How did that work out?

He stopped when he heard Jake continue speaking.

"Maybe we can get a response on the fingerprints and I can locate where she lived, would you like to meet me before we visit the Mah Jongg club? We can take a look around before we call forensics in to investigate the place?"

"Let's plan on that."

Each man walked to his car and drove away, Grant with his own troubling thoughts about the crime and how best to solve it. He wanted to make sure nothing else occurred in his peaceful community.

Chapter 4

ON FRIDAY AFTERNOON, Lillian was ready for her guests. She had prepared two kinds of finger sandwiches -- cucumber and chicken salad -- to be served with chips and, of course, her "famous" toffee/almond cookies. The card table was set up with the Mah Jongg tiles and racks. Coffee, tea, wine, and water were on the sideboard.

She chuckled to herself as she put out the drink options, knowing that Rachel would not partake of the wine in front of the other ladies and would resent every sip that Victoria took. Lillian couldn't help but be thankful she was Presbyterian and Victoria was Catholic. At least, they could drink with a clear conscience. Margaret, with the exception of an occasional glass of wine, drank tea, and as Lillian recalled, Rachel and Margaret usually were the winners.

She looked around the living/dining room to make sure all was in order. She glanced toward the front of the house and smiled at the sight of Eli sprawled on the back of a settee in front of the floor-to-ceiling window.

On guard, eyes focused on the street, he moved his head ever so slightly when he heard, "Well, old boy, today, I'm going to drink tea, too. I have a lot to discuss with the girls and want to keep a clear head."

Bill entered the living room. He carried his golf shoes in one hand and a beer in the other.

"What's that you say?"

Lillian, startled, said, "You scared me. I didn't know you had come in here."

"I'm sorry. I heard you and thought you were talking to me."

She laughed. "Oh, I was just commenting to Eli that I think I'll drink tea today."

"Remember what I told you, and if my guess is correct, so did Jake: don't discuss the murder," he said as he passed her on the way to the garage to gather his golf clubs.

"You don't worry about us," she responded. "You just enjoy your buddies. I don't know why you're packing up those golf clubs when you're really going to play poker."

"Now. . ." he started to object but was interrupted.

"Go on. I'm okay with that." Lillian laughed at the surprised look on his face. "I enjoy my friends, too. We like our games without any male interference."

"Sounds like your first 'victim' is here." Bill laughed, gave her a quick kiss, and hurried out the door.

Rachel parked her black Mercedes convertible in the middle of the Prestridges' circular driveway. As usual, her red, curly hair needed calming down. However, it matched the personality of its owner. Rachel was decked out in all her splendor - diamonds on each hand - black leggings with a long, green tunic top that made her look shorter than her four feet ten inches.

She waltzed in, placed her oversized Louis Vuitton on the floor, and cheerfully greeted Lillian. "Hi, Lillian! I let myself in. Your door wasn't locked."

Rachel did not see Eli until he bounded from his perch on the settee and landed right in front of Rachel and barked. She screamed and froze, afraid to move. He sniffed her hand, turned and resumed his guard post but kept a watchful eye on her.

"I started to say you ought to lock the door until the murderer is found, but if that dog scares everyone like he just scared me, I guess a lock is superfluous."

Lillian ignored the commotion. "I see you've already heard about it."

"What's the dog's name?"

"It's Eli. It was his owner who was killed, so he's more than a little suspicious of strangers."

"Yes, everybody in Leisure Lake has heard the news. Who was the murder victim, do you know? Have you talked to Grant, yet? Does he know?"

"Yes and no. Yes, I've talked to both Grant and Jake. No, I don't know the name of the victim. The last word I had they didn't either, but I thought that we girls could put our heads together and maybe help them find out."

Simultaneously, Victoria and Margaret arrived. Lillian heard them as they stepped up on the deck, so she opened the door for them before Eli could fulfill his watch dog duty. Her quick action prevented another episode of screams.

"Hi, girls, come on in."

Margaret moved around Lillian to avoid the dog, but Victoria paused. Eli jumped off the sofa and greeted Victoria. She reached down and stroked him behind his ears. "What a pretty poodle you are, big boy." She looked up at Lillian. "Who's your friend? Did Bill break down and let you get another dog?"

"The dog is Eli. I plan to keep him no matter what Bill thinks. I've got everything set up. I'll explain everything later."

The two friends put down their purses and hugged both Lillian and Rachel.

Victoria asked, "Okay, Lillian, tell us all that you've heard from Grant. If I know you, you've already pestered him to death about the unfortunate situation. Has he shared anything with you?"

"You know the answer to that question. When has either he or Jake ever trusted me with confidential information?"

"Never is my guess, and they are wise not to do so," piped in Margaret.

"Oh, just because you work for a lawyer and -- as you constantly remind us -- have to be discreet doesn't mean that the rest of us has to be as closed mouth as you," retorted Victoria.

Margaret, standing taller than the rest at five feet eleven inches, straightened her shoulders, pushed her long blond hair behind her ear. "Are we here to play Mah Jongg, or are we here to gossip?"

Rachel, the peacemaker, intervened, "Okay, girls, we are here to play Mah Jongg as usual. Let's eat some of Lillian's sandwiches before they get soggy. I'm starved." She proceeded to the buffet and filled her plate with a pair of finger-sized cucumber sandwiches and two kinds of chips.

"Lillian, I'm glad you also made some chicken salad sandwiches today. I was too busy at work and didn't take a lunch break," stated Margaret.

"Oh, I didn't notice the chicken salad. I'll take some of those, too," Rachel said.

"Victoria, help yourself," said Lillian. She saw the gleam in Victoria's eyes and thought *oh no, here it comes. She's going to tease someone.* Lillian handed her partner a plate.

"No thanks. I'll eat something in a minute. First, I'd like a glass of Ménage à Trois." She winked at Lillian unbeknownst to anyone else. She made a big deal out of pouring the wine and going through the routine of swirling her glass before she took her first sip.

"Oh, just go ahead and show off," exclaimed Rachel. "You know what? Today, I'm going to join you. As I recall, Jesus himself turned water into wine at a wedding reception."

"Glory be! Rachel's coming out of the closet!" said Victoria as she ceremoniously raised her glass and looked heavenward.

"I swear, can't you grow up?" asked Margaret, frowning at Victoria. "I also think Jesus commanded us not to judge our fellow man, or in this case, our fellow woman. Leave Rachel alone."

"Yes, let's move on to more important matters: our game," stated Lillian. "Bring your drinks and food to the table. I've got all of the tiles shuffled and turned upside down and the racks in place."

The ladies took their places. Margaret took a bite of her sandwich. "Yummy. I do believe you make the best chicken salad I've ever eaten."

"As usual, our hostess has prepared a feast for us," said Rachel with her mouth full.

"You know, girls, even though we can be quite sarcastic with each other at times, I'm glad no one is ever offended." Lillian filled her plate and joined her guests at the dining table.

"Just call us Steel Magnolias," said Rachel.

"I like your description of our friendship, Rachel. I agree. It's the kind that allows good-natured teasing." Margaret paused. "I'm sorry, Victoria, if I hurt your feelings for teasing Rachel."

"No need for an apology." Victoria looked at Rachel who shook her head.

"I can't tell you how much I treasure our Friday afternoons." Lillian looked around the table at each of her friends. "But, I've forgotten who's in the rotation for our next meeting."

"I am," came from Victoria.

"It's not like you, Lillian, to be forgetful. I guess that's why I don't see any game chips today," remarked Margaret.

"No, I didn't put them out. I thought we wouldn't bid today. We have too much on our minds," responded Lillian. "I for one won't be able to concentrate on the game."

Laughing, Margaret commented, "Lillian knows when she'll lose her shirt. That brain of hers is too cluttered to pay attention today."

Rachel joined in the camaraderie without her usual smile. "Lillian knows when she and I are at a disadvantage. Today is certainly the day for that."

"Sounds like you're down about something," Victoria said. "The only times I've seen you so solemn was right after Robert died and when your stocks nosedived."

"Exactly, but I'll tell you about it later," said Rachel." Let's toss the dice and see who's East."

"No. The game can wait. I can tell you're worried," said Lillian. "Would you like to share your concerns with us?"

"You know we're good listeners," added Victoria.

Rachel looked from one friend to another, "Well, okay, I will. It's David."

"Who's he?" asked Victoria.

"He worked for our oil company as a land man."

"Okay, humor me," said Victoria. "What does a land man do?"

"I can't believe you've lived in East Texas all your life and don't know what a land man does," said Margaret sarcastically.

"Like I said: humor me and wipe that smug look off your face," said Victoria.

"Girls, girls, be nice," Lillian cautioned.

"He goes to a courthouse and searches deed records to find out who owns a piece of property," Margaret explained.

"Why?" asked Victoria.

"The end result is to obtain a lease agreement between the landowner and an oil company for drilling purposes," Rachel said.

"And that's what David did for your company?"

Rachel nodded. "Unfortunately, Robert left him in charge of the business despite the fact they had worked together for only a couple of years."

She paused and then continued. "Robert thought David was a good employee, but I don't trust the man."

"What kind of shenanigan has he pulled? Nothing illegal, I hope," said Margaret.

"I don't know, but I will soon."

"How so?" asked Lillian.

"He flew in from Houston yesterday, and we met to discuss my share of the profits from the company."

"Doesn't he visit with you monthly now since Robert's death?" Victoria asked as she stood. She retrieved the bottle of wine from the buffet and refilled Rachel's glass.

"Yes, he does, but not because he wants to, but because Robert stipulated in his Last Will that he do so and because I insist on it. He got a little huffy with me yesterday when I raked him over the coals for not following my instructions. I am so mad at him."

"What did he do?" asked Margaret.

Before Rachel could give an explanation, Lillian said, "If I had to guess why she's angry, I'd say he conveniently forgot to bring the company's profit/loss statements," said Lillian.

"And you would be correct."

"I've never thought very highly of him," said Margaret. "He's so arrogant when he's at the courthouse going through land records.

He acts like everyone in the clerk's office should stop what they're doing so they can be at his beck and call."

"He's a good land man. That's why Robert made him a partner. Robert's oil leases grew significantly after David joined him. But now, things are going downhill."

"You think he's short changing you?" asked Victoria. "Let me have some time with him, and he will treat you fair."

Lillian knew Victoria's temper and how it could flare up quickly if one of her friends was being mistreated. "Now, now, calm down."

"Okay," said Victoria. "Finish your story, Rachel "

"He thinks just because he's a CPA, and I'm a retired art teacher, I don't understand basic accounting."

"You've never hinted to him art was your minor in college?" asked Lillian.

Rachel shook her head. "No, the subject never came up."

"Okay, I'm puzzled. What does her major or minor in college have to do with what we're talking about?" asked Margaret.

Rachel explained, "I didn't get my degree in art until after Robert and I married. He insisted I do it. It was something I'd always wanted to do."

"So, what was your major?"

"Business, specializing in accounting. Unbeknownst to David, I'm also a CPA. I continued the renewal of my license all these years just in case. Before Robert hired him, I was the one who stayed in the background and kept the books and calculated all the royalties on the producing wells."

"So, is he returning anytime soon so you can go over the company's books?" Victoria asked.

"Next weekend, with books and balance sheets in hand. He will use the lake's landing strip. Loves to fly his Beechcraft up here."

"His arrogance really kicks in then, I bet," said Margaret with a toss of her head.

"That's enough, girls. I shouldn't have criticized him. He is a sweetheart." With that, she put her finger in her mouth and made a gagging sound and then laughed. "Let's play," said Rachel. "I need to have some fun."

She picked up the dice, shook them, and let them fall on the table. "A three and a two. Here, Victoria. Your turn."

Victoria tossed the dice and passed them to Lillian. Margaret won the toss by having thrown the highest number, a six and a three. She laughed. "Are we sure we're playing by the official rules?"

"Who cares?" asked Victoria.

"I'm with you," said their leader as she pushed aside a wisp of gray hair trying to finagle its freedom from the rubber band encircling her ponytail. She heard a low growl and looked toward the front window to see her new pooch standing on the back of the sofa, one paw raised, nose pointed out. She went to the window, and peered out onto the darkened street. She saw only the usual blackness. "Eli, nothing's out there. Settle down, boy."

Returning to her place at the table, "We can make up our own rules. No one else ever plays with us. Let's begin."

Margaret began to build the wall two tiles high in front of the racks. As East, she threw two dice. The resulting number was seven, so she proceeded to break the wall by starting at the right side of her wall of tiles and counting seven stacks of tiles to the left. She then took the next four tiles, two from the top and two from the bottom. Each of the other players did the same and continued the process three times until they had the appropriate number of tiles on their racks.

Before they began the "fan" process, Victoria spoke up.

"Lillian, when are you going to start your official investigation into the murder of that woman?"

"Who said I was going to do anything?"

"We know you." Rachel stopped in mid sentence as she caught sight of the white standard poodle who had walked over to stand between Lillian and Margaret, who had pushed him away when he put his paw on her knee. She looked at him intently and then exclaimed. "Oh, my!"

"What's wrong, Rachel?" asked Lillian. "Are you okay?"

"I'm just caught off guard. Still not expecting to see -- Eli, did you say?"

"Yes, isn't he beautiful?"

"I think I know that dog. Are you dog sitting for his owner?"

"No, I'm not." Lillian reached down to gently pet Eli on his head.

"Rachel, didn't you hear her say she was keeping him in spite of Bill?" asked Victoria.

"No, I guess I was busy filling my plate and worrying about my finances. But go ahead, Lillian, explain. Margaret, remember, it's your turn to play when the game resumes."

"He is mine, but let me tell you about him," said Lillian. "It was Eli who ran to me and led me and Bill to the scene of the murder."

"Well, I never." Victoria paused. "We all knew that a body had been found, but our grapevine has let us down. No one mentioned that it was you who found the body. I know that must have been a shock."

"Shock it may have been, but how does Eli fit into the scene?" asked Margaret.

"You will never know just how big a shock it was. Grant wanted to take Eli to the shelter and leave him there until a relative could be located," said Lillian.

"Eli. You said his name is Eli?" asked Rachel.

"Yes, you've asked me twice." Lillian pointed to the dog and said, "Look at his collar. You'll see the name engraved on the tag. You said you thought you had seen him before? Where?"

Turning rather pale, Rachel got up, poured herself another glass of wine, her third glass for the evening. She let her friend's rapid-fire questions go unanswered for a few tense moments. Her hands shook as she tried to raise the glass to her lips.

Giving up on the task, she said, "I do know Eli."

"Really? Are you sure?"

"Yes. You see, as chairperson of the hospitality committee, I usually try to personally call on all newcomers to the neighborhood, not only to welcome them but also to give them our welcome packet so they will know about all of our activities here at the lake."

"Yeah, yeah, we know. Go on with your story but leave out your sales pitch," urged Victoria

"Now, Victoria, be nice," cautioned Margaret. "So, you're saying you knew his previous owner, the deceased?"

"That's exactly what I'm saying."

"When did your meeting with her take place?" Lillian wanted to know.

"About two weeks ago, to the best of my memory."

"Amazing. One of us actually knew the woman. What's her name? Do you recall?" said Margaret.

"Let me see. Last name was Dallas, something. I don't remember, but it'll come to me later." Rachel turned to Margaret. "Let's play. It's your turn."

"Whoa, hold on a minute. Don't tease us. We've lost our concentration now. Tell us what you remember about her," commanded Lillian.

"As I recall, she seemed rather shy when she came to the door and I introduced myself. But, as we talked, she seemed to warm up somewhat and wanted to know more about the different organizations we have here. She seemed especially interested in the art guild."

"Is that all? Surely, you learned more than that," chided Victoria.

So engrossed in Rachel's story, the leader of the female amateur sleuths, including her underlings, was startled when Eli barked and then growled. Lights lit up the previously darkened window. A car door slammed, then another. Everything went quiet. Then footsteps. Eli leaped off the sofa and rushed to the door, barking and growling viciously.

"I hear voices. Oh my God. Someone's out there," whispered Rachel.

Victoria went into action. She ran across the room, grabbed her oversized purse, and quickly pulled out her thirty-eight revolver. She stood and aimed the gun at the door.

"Get down!" she ordered. Margaret and Rachel dropped to the floor.

Lillian ran to Victoria and pushed down her friend's arms. "No, Victoria, don't do that. Let me see who's there."

Victoria pushed Lillian away and shouted, "Whoever you are out there, you open that door, you die! I've got a gun." She lowered the gun when loud footsteps made a hasty retreat. Everything went quiet.

Then Lillian's phone rang.

"What else?" Lillian ran, picked up the receiver, and said, "Hello." Pause. "Oh, thank goodness you're safe." Pause. "Yes, I'll tell her. Victoria, put your gun back in your purse. Right now." She waited until Victoria followed her directions. "It's safe now." She put the phone down in its cradle.

In walked Jake and Grant. Relieved that her two sons had not been murdered by her best friend, Lillian walked over and welcomed each of them with a big hug and a kiss on the cheek.

"Come in, guys. Refreshments are on the buffet. Help yourself."

"No thanks, Mom. I lost my appetite when I thought you were going to shoot us."

"Did you forget we were coming?" asked Grant.

"No, I remembered, but. . ."

"She forgot to tell us," said Victoria. "I'm glad you heard me and made haste. I'd never forgive myself if I had killed or even maimed you."

Her face had turned ashen.

"You'd better sit down. You look faint," said Grant, who led her to an empty chair.

"Margaret, bring her a glass of water," Lillian ordered.

"Forget the water. Bring me my glass of wine," Victoria said, her voice weak and hoarse.

"Mom, was your door locked?"

"I know it wasn't locked when Rachel came – she was the first one to arrive and reminded me – so I thought I had locked it after Margaret and Victoria arrived."

"Jake asked you a rhetorical question, Lillian," said Grant. "FYI: the door was not locked.

"I want you and Dad to keep it locked at all times. Even here at the lake, you should practice safety precautions." He looked at the other ladies. "You, too. I want all of you to be safe."

"You bet we will," said Rachel. "This was too scary for me, especially with Eli carrying on the way he did."

"He is a good guard dog," said Grant. "I'm glad you have him here with you, Lillian."

"Yes, me also. I know you two must be hungry after all you've been through just trying to come in the door." She motioned to the buffet still ladened with food.

"Like Jake, I'm not hungry, but I would like a glass of iced tea."

Jake poured for both of them. Lillian pulled out extra chairs so that they could sit down, and Grant began the conversation.

"Ladies, as you all know, we have experienced a first in our community. A murder has occurred. Jake and I would like to talk to you if you don't mind."

"We will be glad to help if we can," said Lillian. "In fact, you two need to hear what Rachel was just telling us. She visited with Eli's owner recently."

"Please tell us." Grant took his notebook out of his front pocket and flipped to an empty page. He looked at Rachel and nodded for her to begin.

"Well, as I was saying before you guys scared the wits out of us, I told the girls I recognized Eli. I saw him in the home of the murdered lady."

"When was that?" asked Grant.

"Two weeks ago, thereabouts."

"What name did she give you?" asked Jake.

"That was the most unusual thing about her. I thought the name was rather strange. I've never known anyone whose name was that of a city."

"For crying out loud, Rachel, quit musing and just answer Jake's questions," exclaimed Victoria.

"Excuse me! I'm doing my best." Rachel raised her voice. Everyone waited while she struggled to remember. "Okay, it was Dallas, uh, Stella Dallas to be exact."

Eli whimpered and then barked. Lillian reached out, took hold of his collar, and pulled him close to her. He calmed down as she stroked his back.

"Oh my," said Lillian, "no wonder you thought it was strange. It sounds like an alias to me."

"Mom, keep your opinions to yourself. We just want the facts as Rachel can give them to us." Jake continued with his questioning as Grant took notes. "So, did you talk about the amenities of the lake and the various clubs ladies enjoy here?"

"Yes, quite thoroughly. As a matter of fact, she was interested in only one group."

"Which one was that?"

"The art guild."

"Interesting. Do you remember where she lived?" asked Grant.

"Not too far from here."

"Where, exactly is that?" asked Jake.

His mother rested her hands on his shoulders. She could feel them growing tense, equal to her own.

"Hold on. Let me get my list of newcomers from my purse, and I can tell you exactly where it is." From her large purse, Rachel retrieved a file folder. She scanned a few pages and looked up.

"It was at 408 N. Pecan Street. Two streets over from here."

"Which house is that? Do you recall?" Jake said.

"The A-frame in the middle of the block. It has a lovely swimming pool in back."

"Did you go inside or just visit with her at the door?" asked Grant.

"I was inside." Rachel continued. "She offered me a cup of tea, and we reviewed the lake's welcome packet. That's how I know about the pool. I could see it through the French doors and the windows that line the whole back side of the house."

"Since you say she was interested in the art guild, did you notice whether or not she had any artwork in her house?" Grant asked.

"No, I didn't pay that much attention at the time. You know, some artists don't display their own work."

"Describe her appearance to us," said Jake.

"She was taller than I, had brown hair, not too fat, not too skinny, average looks, but there was something about her, about the way she talked."

"How did she talk?" Jake asked.

"Oh, I don't know. I guess I would describe her as being average all around."

"Did you notice anything of significance?"

Rachel interrupted Jake. "What do you mean?"

Grant supplied the explanation. "You know, like a ring or any other piece of jewelry she may have been wearing?"

Rachel pressed her lips together, closed her eyes, and rubbed her forehead, obviously trying to recreate the event in her mind's eye.

"Take your time," Jake looked at his mom and held up his empty glass.

Lillian, who had been taking her own notes, missed his signal, so Victoria refreshed the tea in both his and Grant's glasses. Margaret poured herself and Victoria another glass of wine. Lillian looked up and nodded when Margaret whispered, "Do you want more wine?" Lillian grabbed her pen when Rachel continued her story.

"I did notice that she was wearing a most unusual pendant."

"Can you describe it?" asked Grant.

"I'm not sure. Don't hold me to this, but it looked like a basket of some sort. Very intricately designed."

Good work, Rachel. Lillian silently cheered on her friend.

"Rachel, is there anything else you can tell us about your visit?"

"Right now, I can't say that I can, but I got the impression she was a very sad person, maybe lonely would be a better word. I can usually tell by a person's eyes, you know, but I do know one thing."

"What's that?"

"She loved her dog. She kept Eli beside her, patting him the whole time we visited."

Jake continued. "Rachel, do you mind looking at this photo? It is a picture the medical examiner took. You don't have to look if you don't want to. I don't want to upset you."

"I'll look at it," said Rachel. "I want you and Grant to catch whoever did this awful thing."

Jake handed the photograph to Rachel. She took the picture and walked over to the buffet where two tall lamps stood on each end. For several seconds, she held the picture close to the light of one and analyzed it from every angle. *That's so like Rachel* Lillian thought. *The flamboyant, care-free Rachel is a perfectionist at heart. She doesn't want to make a mistake.*

"Yes, it's Stella Dallas," said Rachel.

Eli whimpered again. His new owner hugged him close. "You recognize the name, don't you?"

"Thank you, Rachel. You've been a big help," Grant said.

He turned to face the other women. "I'd like for each of you to also take a look at the photo. You may have seen her around the lake, at the clubhouse, perhaps with someone else."

He then handed the photo to Victoria. Lillian observed Victoria's reaction. Victoria barely glanced at the picture, handed it to Jake. "If she had carried a defensive weapon, she might still be alive. I don't go anywhere without my revolver. I have no patience for helpless women." Lillian made a mental note: *Interesting. Until tonight, I didn't know that she always had her weapon with her. Guess that's why she guards her purse.*

"So, have you ever seen her around the lake?"

"No," Victoria said.

Jake then looked at Margaret, who shook her head. "No, I don't want to look at it. I don't know that many people who live here. I'm sure I won't know her."

Most interesting, thought Lillian, especially since Margaret often frequented the parties at the clubhouse and had met a number of the lake residents. She noticed that Margaret, usually very calm and reserved, seemed more than a little shook up.

I will have to follow up on this most curious attitude concluded Lillian.

"Ladies, I must tell you that this conversation cannot be discussed outside of this room. Do you hear me?" Jake warned.

All of the women shook their heads in unison, all except one. Margaret gave Jake a knowing smile. *Those two have shared many secrets in their work, and I know Jake can count on her for discretion.*

Grant scanned each face. "If any of you can think of anything you may have seen or heard that morning, whether you think it significant or not, please call me."

"And remember. Lock your doors." Jake nodded to his mom. "That goes for you, too." The women assured him that they would do so.

"Well, girls, since our game has been interrupted and all focus on it gone, I suggest we call it a day."

Their hostess needed time with Grant and Jake. Taking her hint as a command, the three collected their belongings.

After seeing all of the ladies out the door, Lillian poured three cups of coffee and joined Grant and Jake at the game table.

"We may as well drink some caffeine. You two are going to need as much brain power as you can gather before this case is solved. I need to put our dinner in the oven." Both men followed her into the kitchen.

"Where's Dad?"

"Down at the clubhouse. It's Friday, remember?"

"Playing poker, as usual?"

"Yes, he left with his golf clubs, but I let him know that his playing poker on Fridays is no longer a secret."

"How did he take that revelation, Mom?"

"He laughed, but kept up the ruse, put the clubs in the trunk."

Grant laughed. "Seriously, though, he needs to join us."

"You're right," Jake agreed. "Mom, will you call him and tell him we need to talk with him?"

"He doesn't like it if I interrupt their game. Knowing those men, it could last all night. He won't mind if you call him. He'll listen if you tell him to fold and come home."

"Oh, Mom, I don't know. . ."

"Tell him we're dining al fresco on the patio tonight. He loves to eat outside. He'll come if he knows you are here." She opened the oven to check the food's progress. "You two were wise not to snack earlier."

Grant smiled and said, "I hope that's my favorite Mexican casserole I smell."

"I remember well what your favorites are. I'm so glad you could join us. It's been too long since you put your feet under my table." Lillian gave Grant a hug. Looking over his shoulder, she noticed the scowl on Jake's face before he stood and walked over to the telephone and dialed the number of the club house.

When the manager answered, Jake asked for Bill Prestridge. The manager put him on hold. While he waited for his father to come to the phone, he walked to the buffet and poured himself another cup of coffee.

"Hello. Dad, Grant and I are here with mom. We'd like for you to come home as soon as you can easily get out of your game. It's imperative you hear what we've learned during our investigation." Pause. "That's right. See you in a few minutes."

Ten minutes later, Bill arrived. "Now, boys, whatever you have to say ought to be good if I had to leave a winning hand."

"It is," said Jake, "we know where the victim lived."

"Where?" asked Bill.

"On Pecan Street, not too far from here," said Grant, "but we're not releasing her name until we have a definite ID."

"Is that all you know?" asked Lillian, "I could have told you where she lived."

"Why didn't you?" asked Grant.

"You didn't ask."

"Who told you?" Jake asked.

"Would you believe me if I said Eli told me?"

Grant laughed. "No, can't say I would. Never known a dog who can talk."

"Mom, I told you," Jake began but was interrupted by Lillian.

"I know what you said, but right now, let's eat." She sat down at the table and waited for the men to join her.

Jake and Grant looked at Bill for support. He merely shrugged. "Your mother's right. I'm hungry." He pulled out a chair and sat down. "And let's don't ruin our meal by talking about the victim."

The four enjoyed a delightful evening. No one mentioned the murder. Even Eli lapped up the bowl of food Lillian poured for him.

"Good dinner, Mom." The other two men nodded in agreement.

All too soon for Lillian, her boys bade her farewell and promised to keep in touch with her. She stood in the doorway and watched them walk to their cars. There was a cool, gentle breeze blowing from the east. It carried Jake's comment to Grant, "I'll contact Judge Kinsey early tomorrow and get a search warrant for the house. As soon as I have the judge's permission, I'll get forensics to go out as well."

"You'd better do that early, early. If I know your mom, she'll be busting at the seams to be there, too," said Grant.

"Yeah, you're right. In fact, I'll call the judge tonight and ask him to have it ready for me first thing tomorrow morning. Let's try to meet there at eight o'clock if that's okay with you."

"I'll be there."

Lillian smiled. *That's okay, boys. You meet with the judge. I'll be at 408 North Pecan Street long before you.*

Chapter 5

THE NEXT MORNING, HUSBAND and wife lounged on the front deck of their house. Eli had been dozing in the early rays of the sun. He stood, stretched his legs, and walked over and licked Lillian's hand.

"Would you like to take a walk?" Lillian asked the dog.

He barked and pranced around excitedly.

Lillian laughed at the dog's antics. She placed her empty coffee cup on the table between their Adirondack chairs and stood. As she passed by him on her way to the front door, she grabbed Bill's hat, leaned over, kissed him on the top of his forehead, and plopped his hat back on his head at an awkward angle.

"I think he understands you," remarked Bill jokingly. He positioned his hat to shield his eyes.

"Of course he does."

She had her hand on the doorknob but stopped, turned to face the poodle, and addressed him as if he were human.

"I'll get your leash and my sunglasses, Eli, and we'll walk down to the dam and back." The dog stopped prancing and sat down. "See, I told you he understands everything."

"Well, he certainly acts intelligently. I'll give him that."

Bill leaned back in his chair, lowered his Panama hat over his eyes. "You two have fun on your trek. I'm going to sit here awhile longer. May even take a nap."

As soon as Lillian and Eli were down the hill and out of Bill's eyesight, Lillian bent over and patted the dog on the head. "Okay, Eli, be a good boy and take me back to your house."

The dog sat down and looked at Lillian. He turned his head from side to side as if trying to process her command. He didn't move.

Using a sterner voice, Lillian commanded, "Eli, go home."

Immediately, the dog jumped up trotted away, repeating the same route the two had taken the day before. Again, Lillian followed as closely as she could without breaking into a run. She didn't want to be seen chasing the dog by anyone who happened to pass by.

Eli turned onto Pecan Street and headed straight for the A-frame numbered 408. He slowed down at the front sidewalk and waited for Lillian. When she caught up with him, he led her around to the back of the house and through the opened gate.

"Let's go back up the stairs, Eli, and have another look through the patio doors," Lillian said as she patted him on the head. They climbed the stairs slowly. Lillian was careful not to touch the handrail. She did not want to leave her fingerprints on it.

"Hmm. . .interesting," mused Lillian. Peering through the French doors, she saw an opened book that looked like a photo album or scrapbook of some kind as well as a cup and saucer on the coffee table. "Hmm. . ."

Eli wagged his tail in a greeting. He recognized the two men sneaking up behind her

"Hmm is right," a deep voice said right behind Lillian.

Startled, she turned around. Staring back at her were the two boys she loved most: Jake and Grant.

"Oh my gosh! You scared me to death," Lillian sputtered.

"I don't suppose you're scared enough to go home, are you? Mom, this is exactly why Grant and I decided to come on out here early. We knew you would be snooping around," Jake said.

"Have you touched anything?" Grant asked.

"No, I was very careful when I came up the stairs."

"Good. I had a feeling we'd catch you in the act of breaking and entering." Jake took his handcuffs off his belt and stepped closer.

"Now, son, you can't be serious."

"Grant, do you think I ought to take her in?"

"No, just lock her up in your patrol car. That ought to do."

"And I thought you would defend me. Guess I don't know my two boys as well as I thought I did."

Jake and Grant laughed. She did not join in their mirth.

"Mom, you know we were just teasing."

"In that case, can I go in the house with you? I might see something you would overlook."

"I guess, since you are already here, you may as well, but leave the dog outside," commanded Grant.

"Okay," said Lillian. "Stay, Eli." The dog sat down. Guard duty again.

Grant retrieved his black bag from his car and pulled out surgical slippers and nitrile gloves. He handed both Jake and Lillian a set of each. "Here, put these on," he said. "I'm glad you brought this kit, Jake. Never needed them at the lake until now."

"Let's pray you don't ever need them again," Lillian said.

"Mom, what was all that 'hmming' for just before we startled you?" asked Jake as Grant opened the door.

The three entered and put on the slippers. They scanned the room. Lillian pulled her cell phone from the pocket of her jeans and began snapping pictures.

"Well, I noticed the cup and saucer on the coffee table and what appeared to be a scrapbook of some kind. Then, by the stairs, I saw an overturned table and a broken vase with its contents scattered on the floor."

Grant walked across the room and picked up the book. He thumbed through the pages.

"This isn't a scrapbook. It's a photo album, full of baby pictures. Looks like they cover the baby's life from birth through about age one. From the words beneath the pictures, this baby's named Michael. There are also some photos of our victim, obviously a much younger version of her, and a man. Presumably, he's the father, based upon the comments beneath the pictures. Looks like a happy family. I guess she was looking at it before she left the house."

"Well, there's nothing unusual about that. Every once in awhile, I like to peruse yours and Jake's baby pictures. A mother always likes to reminisce about her baby," said Lillian.

She noticed the pleased look on Grant's face when she included him as her baby and smiled inwardly. Jake turned his back to them and moved toward the overturned table. Lillian walked over to Jake and put her arm around him. "Are you going to try to find Michael Dallas to let him know about his mother?"

Her son looked down at her. His eyes expressed the nonverbal communication of love between child and parent.

"Mom, we didn't say anything in front of the ladies last night, but the woman's name is not Stella Dallas. You were right. That was an alias. We just don't know why she didn't use her real name when she moved to the lake."

"Oh, dear, what is her real name?" asked Lillian.

"It's Sheila Davis, and you don't know that in case anyone asks," stated Grant.

Lillian nodded an okay.

The three then began a search of the house being careful not to disturb anything. Eli had grown restless with his guard duty and scratched at the door.

Jake walked to the door and opened it. "I think it's okay if he comes in. Apparently, he has lived here, and there will be evidence to that fact."

Grant agreed. "You're right. He can't hurt anything. Just from my first look around in this room, there's not much he can disturb." He turned to the dog. "Sit. Stay."

As soon as Grant walked away from the dog, Eli ignored the "sit and stay" commands. Whimpering, he ran from one room to the other downstairs. Not finding his master, he returned to the living room and let out a loud howl.

Grant stopped inspecting the TV console and patted the dog on his head. "Poor little guy, I saw you searching. You didn't find her, did you?"

Lillian went up the stairs that led to a loft and a master bedroom. Soon, she yelled down, "Come up here, boys. I want to show you something."

Eli had heard her yell and bounded up the stairs ahead of the two men. He ran and jumped on the bed and lay down. Lillian pointed to a picture on the dresser. It portrayed a young couple with their baby.

"Do you see anything especially interesting in this picture?" asked Lillian.

"I sure do," responded Grant as he pointed to the pendant the young woman was wearing. "What kind of basket is this?" he asked.

Lillian responded. "Don't you recognize it? It's a Moses basket. I haven't seen one of these in a long time. In fact, the last one I saw was in an antique store. If it's like that one, it would have held a small photo. Sometimes, these kinds of lockets had room for a picture on each side, but also, it could have held a lock of hair as well."

"Interesting," said Grant.

"Why so?" asked Jake.

Grant pulled out his notebook, referred to his notes, tapped the end of his pen on a page, and then explained. "When I first saw the body, I made note of the lady wearing a gold chain and wrote the word 'pendant' with a question mark. I don't remember the medical examiner mentioning a pendant anywhere on the body, do you?"

"No, but I did notice that one earlobe appeared to be torn," said Jake.

"Yeah, I noticed that, too," responded Grant. "I guess if we find the missing jewelry, we will also find the murderer."

"But I wonder about the significance of it all," stated Lillian.

Jake prompted his mother to leave right away. "The forensics team should be arriving any minute now, and I want you well gone by then, Mom."

She nodded and picked up Eli's leash. He jumped off the bed and walked with her out onto the deck. She paused and looked around the yard thinking about a young family that had looked so happy once upon a time. She looked down at the dog and wished he could tell her about his owner.

Tomorrow is Sunday. I will say an extra prayer for Michael. My boys and I will find him, wherever he may be.

Chapter 6

ALL THROUGH THE Sunday morning sermon, Lillian did not pay any attention to the minister's message. Instead, she jotted her thoughts down in a little notebook she always carried in her purse.

She deliberately procrastinated after the service, greeting fellow church members, all the while maneuvering to be the last one out the door, waiting for Reverend Don Hammon to be alone. As he finished shaking hands with the couple in front of them, Bill and Lillian stepped outside the chapel. Don shook Bill's hand and turned to Lillian. She took his hand, hesitated, and then asked, "Don, do you have a few minutes?"

"I sure do, Lillian," responded Don, and then asked, "What do you have on your mind?"

"Could we meet in your office? What I have to say is private."

"Of course." Don looked at Bill, who shrugged his shoulders and shook his head. He did, however, accompany Lillian to the pastor's office. The three settled themselves in the comfortable brown leather chairs in the pastor's study.

Don asked, "Can I get you something to drink? Coffee? Water?"

"No thanks. We had coffee in our classroom." Bill said. "I don't know about Lillian, but I'm coffee'd out."

The minister looked at Lillian expectantly.

"Lillian, I can tell you are troubled about something. In all the years I've known you, I don't ever remember seeing you take notes during one of my sermons, no matter how interesting they are," Don said jokingly. Then, more seriously, asked, "What can I do to help you?"

Lillian cleared her throat and began, "I know you've seen the newspaper article about the murder we had at the lake."

Don nodded. "Yes, I read the article. Most unfortunate for the young lady."

"I know it will be awhile before the medical examiner releases the body. Jake and Grant have begun a search for next of kin."

"Hopefully, that process can be completed soon. But I have a feeling you don't want to discuss her family. Am I correct?"

"Yes, you are. I have a heavy heart about the lady and have an important question to ask you."

"Okay. Let me hear it."

"Would you be willing to deliver the eulogy at her memorial?"

The reverend spoke slowly when he answered, "Lillian, I think it would be best if we don't jump the gun. Let's give the authorities time to locate any next of kin. Don't you agree that if there are any relatives, we ought to let them make decisions about how they would like to have the lady remembered?" asked Don.

"Yes, of course, I agree with you on that. The problem is my gut tells me there may not be any next of kin. But if there are some and if the authorities can find them. . . well, I'm not sure they will come forward to claim her."

"Why does 'your gut' feel they wouldn't want to honor their loved one?"

"I can't explain that now without divulging confidential information about the investigation. You'll just have to trust me."

"I understand," Don said sympathetically, "and if in fact that turns out to be the case, please understand it would be difficult to present a eulogy for someone I don't know anything about. Usually, a minister relies on the person's family to give him some insight as to the best way to proceed with his remarks. For example, which scriptures may have been her favorite as well as favorite hymns. All of those things are important for a family to gain closure."

"Just in case no one can be found, would you be willing to do it if I could provide some information about her life?"

"Of course, I would, but let's give the authorities time to do their job. When they have made the decision that no relatives exist, then we will proceed. And, Lillian, if no one is found and you don't discover anything about her, we can, at least, say a prayer, read some appropriate scriptures, and sing a couple of hymns to honor her life. Would that be okay with you?"

"Oh, yes, it would. Thank you so much. I appreciate all that you do for God's children."

* * * * *

Bill, who usually always knew what his wife would do next, had been surprised by her request to Don. Relieved there was nothing seriously wrong with her and that she was being her usual motherly self to everyone, he spoke up.

"Now, I know why you have seemed so preoccupied these last few days, my dear. Your silence had begun to worry me."

He turned to their minister. "Don, you don't know it, but you have given Lillian a challenge. I should say an additional challenge because she is already committed to helping Jake and Grant solve the crime."

"Why does that not surprise me?" The minister smiled as he spoke. Then he grew serious and shook his head. "You two take care of yourselves," cautioned Don. "And tell Jake and Grant I'll be praying for them."

"We will," Bill promised. "Now, we'll let you enjoy your Sunday afternoon, and I pray it will be a good one."

"Goodbye, you two, and don't worry about this. If and when the medical examiner gives us the go sign, I'll take care of the eulogy for you." Don walked outside with them and shook hands with both of the Prestridges. As they got in their car, he gave his usual blessing: "God be with you."

As they sat in their car before driving away, Bill looked over at Lillian and stated, "You know, you are the sweetest person I have ever known. I'm so lucky to have you for my wife."

Lillian smiled and said, "No, I'm the lucky one. You will never know just how much I love you."

Then she laughed heartily, the first time in several days, and commanded, "Home, James, and make it quick. I'm starving."

Bill laughed and said, "Let's stop by the club and see what's on the Sunday buffet."

"Sounds good to me."

* * * * *

AS THEY ATE their Sunday lunch of prime rib, mashed potatoes smothered in brown gravy, and green beans sautéed with pinion nuts, Lillian couldn't help but watch her neighbors and wonder if any of them murdered Sheila. Then, feeling guilty about suspecting the innocent, she concentrated on the lemon meringue pie Bill had brought to the table for dessert. They lingered at their table, drinking their favorite coffee, hazelnut cream.

"I think I'll have a Sunday afternoon nap today when you have yours instead of reading all afternoon," announced Lillian.

"Are you sure about that? Doesn't caffeine keep you awake?"

"Most of the time, but today I think I can overcome it."

"Well, if that's the case, let's go." Bill pulled out her chair, offered her his arm, and escorted her to their car. He led her to the passenger side and opened the door for her. He walked around the front of the car to the driver's side. Seated, he turned on the engine and opened the sunroof. "Let's enjoy this warm weather while we have a chance."

"Yes, let's do." Lillian pushed the automatic button, and the window on her side eased down. "Autumn will soon be approaching. Have you noticed that the leaves are starting to turn golden?"

"They are pretty. Would you like to drive around the lake before we go home?"

* * * * *

THIRTY MINUTES LATER, the phone was ringing when Bill and Lillian walked into the kitchen. Bill hurriedly picked up the receiver and answered, "Hello," and after listening for a moment, said, "Yes, son, have you called the pro shop for a tee time? Great! I'll change clothes and be there in about fifteen minutes."

He hung up the phone and turned to Lillian, "Jake wants to play golf this afternoon. I guess I'll forgo my usual Sunday afternoon nap."

"Tell that sweet son of mine that I'll call him tomorrow. Maybe we can meet at the new bakery during his coffee break first thing in the morning." After Bill hung up the phone, she added, "Right now, Eli and I will take our afternoon walk around the lake. Maybe, some exercise will help wake me up after eating all that food."

"Be careful," cautioned Bill.

"Will do," Lillian responded.

Lillian changed into a navy blue sweat shirt, a pair of jeans, and donned her straw hat. After slipping on her athletic shoes, she attached Eli's leash to his collar. The two of them took off for a leisurely stroll around the lake via Pecan Street. Lillian wanted to see if any of Stella's neighbors were out in their yards. She planned to visit with them at some point, but on this particular day, no one appeared to be out and about. *Oh, well,* she thought. *I don't have any authority to question them, but if I continue to walk by here every day, I will eventually see someone and will strike up a conversation.*

Eli whimpered as they passed house numbered 408.

"You poor dog, I didn't mean to make you sad. I won't bring you by this house again. After all, you have a new home now."

Chapter 7

AS CHIEF SECURITY officer for the lake area, Grant was on duty even though it was Sunday. He decided that, until the murder was solved, he would be more than his usual diligent self. He had parked his cruiser on the main entry street, not too far from the club house. He could see the eighteenth fairway and green to his left.

The afternoon grew longer as the sun's rays danced across the fairway, bounce off the hood of his cruiser, and prance into his car. He began to daydream and several times had to remind himself to stay alert.

It's a good thing I brought a thermos of coffee. Man, it's hard to stay awake on stakeouts this boring. He poured himself another cup. *Got to stay awake.*

He took a sip of the thick, brown brew.

Late in the day after carefully observing all passing vehicles, he had not noticed anything unusual. All of the cars sported the required resident windshield sticker. *I haven't seen one visitor pass on any car. This stakeout has been a wash* he thought as he poured yet another drink. Around six-thirty, he noticed the silhouettes of two men walking down the fairway.

Now, he was wide awake. "You sorry so and so," Grant uttered under his breath. He well recognized the silhouettes as those of Jake and Bill.

Bill walked slightly stooped, probably from having sat at his desk writing first one story and then another for some forty odd years. He knew Jake by his swagger. Grant felt that he had always been at Jake's beck and call, even when they played college football together at Sam Houston State University. Jake was the quarterback and everyone's hero. Grant was merely the fullback who delivered the bone-crushing blocks to protect Jake so he could pile up the passing yardage.

Grant resented the fact that Jake, in his opinion, was spoiled. Jake's parents paid his college tuition, but Grant worked during high school to save money for a higher education and held down a job all during college to pay expenses over and above his Pell Grant. He always appreciated Lillian who helped him complete the application for the grant. After graduation, he joined the Army reserves to supplement his meager starting salary as a police officer for the Dallas PD.

If it weren't for Lillian, Grant thought, *I would have had it out with Jake when I first returned from the Gulf War.* Feeling the bile rise in his throat, Grant remembered the day before his unit shipped out.

Jake, buddy, you know how much I love Alice. Would you keep an eye on her for me while I'm away? Make sure that she's all right?

Grant, you know I will. Don't worry about Alice. I know that when you return, she will cease to be Alice Schooner and will become Mrs. Grant Perryman. Rest assured. You just take care and promise me that I won't lose a good friend. . .you come back whole. . .you hear? Jake had responded.

Grant was saving for an engagement ring and planned to ask Alice to marry him when he returned from the war. However, Jake ruined all of his plans.

Grant's cell phone rang and brought him out of his bitter reverie. It was Lillian.

"I need to talk to you about something important. If you are nearby, could you stop by the house for a couple of minutes?"

"Sure, Lillian, I'm not too far away. Have some cold iced tea ready, and I'll meet you on the front deck."

"Good. The deck is in the shade now, and we can see the sunset on the lake. It's so beautiful this time of year."

* * * * *

GRANT PARKED ON the street and walked up the drive. Eli barked a friendly greeting. Stepping onto the deck, Grant squatted down and gave the dog a hug. "Good boy."

Lillian appeared with a tray in hand. She not only had made iced tea but also had prepared a ham and cheese sandwich for him and cut a slice of her German chocolate cake. "I thought you might need a little 'pick me up' right about now, so I made you a snack."

"Great. I could use a 'pick me up' after my boring afternoon."

"Well, have a seat and dig in." Lillian sat the tray on the table between the two deck chairs. "I'll join you. I made myself a glass of tea." She took the other chair, and Eli lay down beside her feet.

So, you didn't take the bait about my boring afternoon remark. I guess I'll find out soon enough what you want me to do.

Grant took a bite of the sandwich. After washing it down with a big gulp of tea, he asked, "What's on your mind, Lillian?"

"Well, Grant, I was thinking. . ."

"That's always dangerous," laughed Grant. "But go on, finish your sentence."

"I'll wait until you finish eating to tell you what I'm thinking."

"No, go ahead and talk. I can listen and chew at the same time." He looked up and waited for her next statement.

She continued. "I was wondering whether or not the forensics team was finished at Stella's house."

"Yeah, they are. Why?" asked Grant.

"Can you share with me what they found?"

"No, but I can tell you what we didn't find."

"Okay. I'll take any information you can give me."

After Grant chewed and swallowed the next bite of his sandwich, he resumed, "We did not find any fingerprints but those belonging to the deceased. . . I was surprised about that."

"Why?" asked Lillian.

"Well, because, according to Rachel, she visited with Stella recently and left some welcome material on behalf of the hospitality committee."

"I guess Stella could have polished her furniture. From what I remember, her house was immaculate and orderly except for the broken flower vase."

"That's true," said Grant. "But don't you think it strange that there was none of the welcome packet left? I would think that a newcomer would want to hold onto that type of information for future reference." He paused.

Go ahead. Think about it.

"Oh my, yes, I would think so," Lillian retorted. "Would you give me permission to go back inside her house? I'd like to see more."

"So, sweet lady, what do you think you could find that we didn't?"

"I'm a woman. I know other women. You guys were looking for the obvious. Maybe, just maybe, I could see something that would tell us a little about her personal life, other people she might know, places she's been. . .things like that."

You know what I'm saying is true. How many times have I heard you say I have a different perspective than you?

"Okay, Lillian, you're free to look just as long as you do it discreetly. But I have a feeling that there is more to your wanting in that house than just trying to help me," he said.

"As a matter of fact, there is. This morning after church, I met with Reverend Hammon."

"And what did you talk to him about? Not the case, I hope."

"Oh, no. He already knew about the incident from the article in the newspaper."

"Yeah, everyone in the county knows about it by now. So, what did you discuss with the Reverend?"

"I asked if he would give Stella's eulogy whenever the medical examiner released her body so we could have a memorial for her."

"What was his response?"

"He said he would." Grant looked surprised.

"He also urged me to wait until you find some next of kin, but just in case none can be located, he agreed to conduct the service if I can give him some information about her."

"So, you want to look through her house to find out some facts about her life?" said Grant.

"Yes, I do. And, of course, I would share any information I find with you first. I may learn something that will give us some more leads."

She waited silently, knowing that he was mulling over her request, weighing whether or not he should agree to it. She was relieved when he spoke.

"That's not a bad idea, but promise me, one thing."

"Anything. What is it?"

"Swear to me that you won't go off on your own trying to solve the murder."

"I think that's your job, Grant, so rest assured, anything I figure out will be information I give to you. You can share it with Jake or anyone else of your choosing."

"Okay, then. I'll meet you at the house on Pecan first thing in the morning and open it up for you. You have to promise me that you will lock the door and let no one in but me and tell no one except Jake about our arrangement."

"I promise." Then she remembered. "There's one other thing I wanted to talk about, get your opinion."

"Yes?"

"Did you happen to pay attention to the response of the Mah Jongg ladies to the photo when you and Jake showed it to them on Friday?"

"No, with the exception of Rachel, I didn't expect them to recognize her. Why?"

"Oh, no reason. Just wanted to get your thoughts. I worry about Rachel, though. I know her and know that she will feel bad about not introducing Stella around."

"If she says anything about that to you, reassure her, let her know she's not at fault."

"Of course. I'll try to allay any doubts she may have."

"Good."

Grant, finished with his food and drink, stood up. "I need to get back on the job. I appreciate the snack. I think I'll be able to make it through my shift now."

Lillian stood as well. He hugged her. "I have a question for you before I leave."

"Ask away."

"This conversation stays between us, no one else. Okay?"

Lillian nodded.

Grant continued. "I've noticed that Eli stays close to you when I'm around. Do you take him everywhere you go?"

"I do."

"Good. Keep him close."

"I will. Of course, I will. He's a good dog." Eli heard the 'good dog' remark and raised his head.

"Watch his behavior around strangers."

"I will, but tell me what you have on your mind."

"He's a smart dog."

"You're right about that. Even Bill commented to me that he thinks Eli understands everything I say to him."

"I agree with Bill."

"Aren't all dogs on guard around strangers?"

"One way or another they are. Dogs sense who's friendly and who isn't. They greet them accordingly – either with a growl, a bark, or a wagging tail."

"I understand. What you're saying is that he may react negatively to whoever murdered Stella. Right?"

"All I'm saying is that his reaction to strangers may be of help to us."

"I agree and will report his behavior to you."

"Thanks."

Grant was almost down the stairs to the deck when Lillian exclaimed, "Oh, wait. I can't meet you in the morning. I just remembered I have an appointment in the city first thing tomorrow. Can we meet shortly after lunch instead? Say, around one-thirty?"

"Sure. No problem. I'll meet you then."

Grant left Lillian's deck and climbed into his car. As he drove away, he glanced at his rear-view mirror and saw Jake and Bill coming around the corner.

I'm glad Lillian and I had finished our talk before they arrived.

* * * * *

JAKE AND BILL had indeed seen Grant's car as he drove away. Bill glanced at Jake and saw the frown on his son's face.

"Jake, I've noticed that you and Grant just don't seem to enjoy being around each other the way you did before he left for the Gulf. Would you like to talk to me about it?"

Jake shook his head. "No, Dad, it's something he and I need to deal with. Frankly, I'm not sure how to do it, but I will talk to Grant at some point and clear up whatever burr he has in his backside."

"Well, that's good. I won't bring up the matter again. I'm confident you can handle it."

"Thanks, Dad. Don't mention any of this to Mom, please. You know how she is."

"Mum's the word. Let's find out what Grant was doing here, though."

"I am curious about that," said Jake.

The two men walked up onto the deck. Eli greeted them, wagging his tail. Jake reached down to pat him on his way into the house. Before he or his dad could enter, Lillian opened the door and carried out a large tray.

"I've just fed Grant a snack, and I bet you two guys would love one also," she announced cheerily.

"Thanks, Mom. By the way, Dad and I did notice Grant's car leaving just as we turned the corner. Did he just come by to make a social call?"

"Not exactly. I called him."

"Why, is something wrong?" asked Bill.

"No and yes. I told him about our visit with Reverend Hammon."

"I don't understand," said Jake. Lillian noticed the look of concern on her son's face. "It must be serious if you two had to talk to Don."

"Yes, it is serious."

"Don't tell me you and Dad are having marital problems." Jake sounded concerned.

Lillian looked at her son. "Oh, dear me, no. Your dad and I are fine. No problems there."

"Whew. What a relief." Jake visibly relaxed, "Okay. Do you want to tell me anything? Is that why you called Grant?"

"Yes. And yes. After church, I asked Reverend Hammon if he would be willing to give the eulogy for Stella whenever the medical examiner releases the body."

"What did he say?"

"He said he would if no kin could be located. I assume that you, like Grant, have been unable to find anyone. Am I correct?"

"Yes, you are, but why was it necessary to call Grant over just to tell him that?"

"I asked him to give me permission to go back into the house on Pecan Street."

"Why?"

"I want to try to find some information about Stella's personal life. I think it would be good if the reverend could have something relevant—you know, something personal about her – you know -- to mention in her eulogy."

"What was Grant's response?" asked Bill.

"I know what it was," responded Jake. "Grant can't say 'no' to Mom. When are you going over?"

"Tomorrow afternoon. Would you like to join me?"

"No, I think you will be able to snoop without me. I'm sure that Grant gave you instructions about not disturbing anything."

"Don't worry. He did, and I intend to do exactly what he told me to do," Lillian stated.

"Okay, but do be careful. Remember, there is someone around who has already committed one murder and may not hesitate to commit another one."

Jake hugged his mother and prepared to leave for home. "I don't think we have a serial killer on the loose. Stella's death was, no doubt, a personal thing, and whoever killed her is long gone."

"Don't be too sure about that," said Lillian.

She then changed the subject, "Tell Jessica 'hello' for me and ask her to drive out and visit when she can."

"Will do, but you know the kids keep her pretty busy. Angela is taking swimming lessons. She wants to try out for the school's swim team. And Jack wants to play soccer this fall, so she is involved in the YMCA league."

"I remember those days," Bill said.

"So do I," said Lillian. "And I would do them over again if I had the chance."

Jake laughed and said, "You just may get your wish. I've teased him, saying his mom may have to be his coach. In his nightly prayers, Jack petitions the Lord, asking that his mom doesn't end up being his coach."

"Shame on you."

"I know, Mom, but he understands I can't with my job and all. He mentioned to us that he plans to ask his grandfather to coach his team."

"If you can't, remember Grant played with you. He'd be a pretty good coach."

Jake shook his head. "Absolutely not. He wouldn't know how to begin to coach."

Lillian shivered at the harsh tone of Jake's voice.

"Next time Jack says that, tell him I'd be honored," said Bill. "But I bet one of the other dads will step up to the plate."

"Sounds like that's what you might be praying for tonight," Lillian teased.

"Be sure and give us his schedule. Your mom and I will enjoy watching his games."

"Okay. Bye now."

As he drove away, Lillian turned to Bill and stated, "I'm worried about our son. Something is bothering him, but I can't put my finger on it. Did you see how quickly he put down my suggestion that Grant could coach?"

"Lillian, when will you learn that he is all grown up and you don't have to worry -- or should I say 'hover' -- over him anymore?"

Smiling, Lillian responded with "Never" and turned back into the house. "Let's turn on PBS and see what's on Masterpiece tonight."

She picked up the tray, Bill opened the door, and Eli growled as a white Lexus inched its way worm-like down the street.

"Come on in, pretty boy," Lillian ordered. Eli turned and followed them inside.

* * * * *

THE NEXT AFTERNOON, Lillian met Grant at the 408 Pecan location.

"Where's Eli?" Grant asked.

"I didn't bring him with me."

"Why not? Do you not remember our conversation yesterday? I remember you told me that he goes everywhere with you."

"Last time I walked him this way, it was obvious he was in distress. I promised him I wouldn't bring him by his old home again."

"Somehow, I'd feel better if he were with you. Just be careful. Okay?"

"I promise I won't do anything foolish."

As he unlocked and opened the door for her, Grant handed Lillian a pair of nitrile gloves and surgical slippers.

"Oh, boy, this makes me feel quite official," Lillian said light heartedly.

Grant gave her a serious look and spoke with a stern voice. "Lillian, listen to me. I don't want you to leave any fingerprints here. Forensics may have to return based upon anything you might find, and I don't want the evidence contaminated."

"I understand."

"And," Grant continued, "Do not–I repeat–do not open that door for anyone. Remember, a murderer may be lurking out there. Lock the door when you leave today. Call me if you find anything you think I might need to see."

Grant left and Lillian locked the door behind him. She proceeded to walk through the house. *Glad, I charged up my cell phone today. Wouldn't be able to go home for it. My, it is so quiet, it's almost eerie.* Lillian put on the gloves and slippers. She walked around the living room and looked closely at everything in it. She reached into her shoulder bag for the notebook and pen she had brought so she could write a description of what she saw as well as her thoughts about it.

Initial Observations

Notation #1: House is clean -- almost too clean even though only one person resided here.

Notation #2: Nothing out of order except for flowers on the floor -- spilled from the vase on the floor? Why an upturned table? An innocent accident or the result of a struggle?

Notation #3: No blood found – unusual if an attack actually occurred here.

Notation #4: Teacup and saucer on coffee table – cup is empty – didn't forensics take fingerprints? Check kitchen area to find teabag and teapot.

Before leaving the living room, Lillian looked at the paintings on the wall.

Notation #5: Victim interested in art guild (per Rachel). Artwork on walls – minimal and inexpensive (the kind found at the local dollar or thrift store).

Notation #6: No family photos visible – only those in the album. Where is it now?

Lillian proceeded through the small dining area and into the kitchen. She opened the cabinet door beneath the sink and found a small trash can.

Notation #7:   Welcome packet left by Rachel tossed. Did forensics check this item for fingerprints? Note: Grant said they didn't find it. Why didn't they? – I plan to tell Jake and Grant I don't think they did a thorough job.

Lillian retrieved one of the plastic bags she brought and placed the welcome packet inside of it. *I'll take this to Grant* she thought and then felt guilty because, for some unexplained reason, she had doubted Rachel's version of her having met Stella. *Okay, Lillian, old girl, get a grip. Leave emotions out of this setting. You had no reason to doubt Rachel even though Grant questioned her statement.*

Lillian turned around and looked for a used teabag. None in sight. She picked up the teapot. Empty. *Looks as though someone tried to stage this.*

Lillian picked up her cell phone and dialed Grant's number.

He picked it up after the first ring.

"What's wrong? I know you haven't gone through everything in that house in such a short amount of time."

"Nothing's wrong, Grant. I called to ask if you knew whether or not forensics would have poured water from the teapot or would have taken a used tea bag."

"No, I don't recall their report mentioning anything about a teapot."

"Could you check on that for me?" asked Lillian.

"I will as soon as I can get them on the phone. I'll call you back ASAP."

"You don't need to call me. We can share notes when we get together later."

"If there's anything else you need before we meet, buzz me."

"Thanks. I will."

Hanging up, she continued her exploration of the kitchen. She found several dog-eared cookbooks on a shelf, some very specialized utensils in the drawers, and specialty baking pans in the cabinet. She looked through the cookbooks, specifically those with turned down corners.

Notation #8: Stella liked to cook -- Recipes on dog-eared pages indicate a preference for baking decorated cakes.

Lillian opened the refrigerator. It was virtually empty, and there was nothing in the freezer section. She went to the pantry. Empty.

Notation #9: How long had victim been here? There ought to be some food in the house—at least some baking goods.

She went back into the living room and noticed a bookcase in the foyer. *So, this lady liked to read. Guess I didn't see that first time through.* She scanned the titles of the books. *There are quite a few books in a bookcase. I wonder if forensics went through each individual book.*

Not wanting to bother Grant with another interruption, Lillian began to remove each book from the bookcase and fan through the pages.

She found nothing unusual until she flipped the pages of Bernard Malamud's novel, *The Fixer.*

As she examined its pages, a newspaper clipping fell out. *If Stella hid this clipping, then it must be important.* Lillian read the story. She put the book and the clipping in one of her plastic bags.

Notation #10: Make sure Grant and Jake read the news story.

Notation #11: Check photo album again. Connection with news clipping?

Lillian diligently checked all of the other books. Most of them were classics. *Stella was quite an intellect.* She found nothing of interest in any of them, so she then proceeded upstairs to the bedrooms.

Notation #12: Guest bedroom sparse: one twin bed, night stand, nothing in closet.

She opened the door to the master suite and headed first to the bathroom to check the medicine cabinet.

Notation #13: Nothing in medicine cabinet other than aspirin and a bottle of antacids.

Lillian opened drawers in the dresser and the wardrobe. She felt discouraged. She saw nothing other than what could be expected. Then, in the closet, she glanced up at the shoe boxes on the shelf. Each one was labeled with the type of shoe it contained. *It might be worth a try. I sometimes put something other than shoes in a box.* She methodically removed the boxes and made notes in her book regarding the position of each one. *If forensics took pictures, I need to replace them in their exact order.* Then she began the tedious process of opening each box. The first two contained shoes, but looking into the third box, Lillian made an important discovery. She removed the contents and placed them in a plastic bag.

Notation #14: Letters/documents hidden in shoe box -- Read letters when I get home. Share their contents with the boys.

Lillian placed the collection of plastic bags and their contents in the large oversized shoulder bag she had brought with her.

Suddenly, in a house that was too quiet, there was the sound of someone trying to open a locked door. Lillian held her breath. Just then her cell phone began to ring. It was Grant.

"Hello," Lillian whispered. "I'm upstairs. I think I heard a noise at the door, like someone trying to enter."

"Did you lock the door after I left?"

"Yes. I'm sure it's just my imagination. It's pretty creepy in here."

"Don't hang up. Go out on the landing and peek downstairs and tell me what you see."

Lillian tiptoed to the rail overlooking the living room and peered over it. She took a deep breath.

"Everything looks okay, so I'm going home. I won't hang up until I am out on the street, so stay on the line, will you?"

"Yes, tell me when you are out the door and on your way home."

Lillian slowly crept down the stairs, wincing each time one of them creaked. *I don't remember all this creaking when I climbed these steps just a few minutes ago.* When she reached the bottom step, Lillian hurried to the door leading out to the deck. She could feel her heart pounding as though it would jump out of her chest.

"I'm out," she told Grant.

"Good. Now, go home. I'll check with you later about what you've found and what I hear from forensics about the teapot."

"Thanks, Grant. I'm going straight home."

Lillian did not slow down until she reached the sanctuary of her home. She quickly stowed away the items she brought from Stella's house and then made a hot cup of tea. She walked out on the back deck and whistled for Eli, who was rolling in the backyard grass, basking in the warm sunshine of a beautiful sunny day. He bounded over to her for some attention. He sniffed her clothing and whimpered.

"I know. You can smell your old home on me. I'm so sorry your owner can't come and get you, but don't worry. Bill and I will take good care of you." Eli licked her hand as if to say he understood. Lillian sat for another thirty minutes drinking her tea. She picked up a tennis ball and played fetch with Eli. She laughed and said, "You could retrieve this old tennis ball all day, I do believe." She glanced at her watch and groaned.

"Oh, Eli, I've got to end our game and get ready. Mah Jongg is at Victoria's tonight. I've lost all track of time. Can't believe I spent so much of the day at Stella's."

* * * * *

LILLIAN PARKED HER car behind Rachel's, and together, along with Eli, they walked through Victoria's front door. "We're ready to play," Rachel announced. Eli jumped up on the sofa and settled down for the night, keeping a watchful eye on his new master.

"Is it all right for Eli to be on your sofa?" Lillian wanted to know.

"He can't hurt it. Don't worry about that old thing."

"By the way, your door was not locked. Don't you remember what the boys told us last Friday when they visited us at my house?"

"All I remember is that I nearly shot both of them."

"Let's don't make that mistake again," said Rachel

I think I'll put a sign on the front door that says: Beware. Women playing Mah Jongg. If you value your life, go away. I'm warning you."

Rachel looked serious, so Lillian laughed. "I'd say that would surely get an intruder's attention."

"Why are you so grumpy, Victoria?" asked Rachel. "I've never seen you like this."

"If you remember, we didn't really get to play last week." She grinned. "I just may shoot anyone who dares to interrupt us today. I would love to finish our game tonight."

Lillian laughed. "Well, now that I know you're always packing, I'll be sure and not make you angry. By the way, when did you start carrying a gun all the time? I was surprised to hear you confess that to the boys the other night."

"I've carried a concealed weapon for the past five or six years ever since I passed the course and received my license."

"So, you must be a good shot."

"You ought to see my targets when I go to the gun range. I can definitely change the lifestyle of any perpetrator."

"I just can't believe you've never mentioned that. When do you have time to practice?"

"I make time for it. Since we've had a major crime here at the lake, I suggest you, Rachel, and Margaret buy a gun and get a license to carry."

"You may be correct. I think I'll talk to Bill about that. We have an anniversary coming up. He might just buy a new handgun for me."

"Good. Then we can go to the range together and target practice."

"Sounds like fun. We can pretend we're shooting the bad guys." Lillian said and gave Victoria a high five.

"Oh, you two, don't joke about shooting anyone. It's bad enough we still have a murderer on the loose without my best friends making smart remarks about it," said Rachel, who was obviously stressed as she sat down at the game table.

"We were just teasing. We didn't mean to upset you." Victoria walked over to her friend. "Here, let me pour you a drink. It might help you to relax," she said soothingly.

"Thanks. I'll take you up on that."

Lillian looked at her Rolex. "It's time for us to start. Where's Margaret? It's not like her to be late."

"I forgot to mention it. She called earlier today and said she wasn't feeling well and that Sally Jane will sub for her," said Victoria.

"What time today did she call you?" asked Lillian.

"Early this morning," said Victoria.

"Sure hope she's better by Sunday. I planned to call her before I left the house and invite her and Grant over for dinner, but I ran out of time," responded Lillian.

"It's about time that boy fell in love again. How long has it been since–" Victoria's question dangled, incomplete. Eli began a low, menacing growl and soared off the sofa.

"Stop, Eli. Sit," commanded Lillian. *Grant surely knows dogs. He was right about mine. I do need to be more alert. Eli might attack someone. Don't want a lawsuit.*

"Knock, knock," said Sally Jane, peering through the door. "Is it safe to enter?"

"Come on in. Lillian has her dog under control," Victoria said.

As Sally entered, she flung her belongings down on the floor and kept plenty of distance between her and the white poodle, still on guard and growling softly.

"I'm sorry I'm late, but as usual, when I have something planned, a mother walks into my classroom and wants to talk about her child's grades. It's not like my students are vying for valedictorian or honor roll. I've decided parents of kindergarteners are the worst. They never call in advance for a meeting. Instead, they just waltz in."

"Never mind rude parents, failing grades, or anything else that goes on at your school, we're here to play Mah Jongg. Let's get to it," responded Victoria obviously antsy to play with no interruptions from the outside world.

"You're right, of course." Sally grabbed a glass of wine from the buffet. "I need this." She sat down at the table.

Victoria said, "Let's get on with it." She proceeded to shuffle the tiles.

"Wait a minute."

Lillian put her hands on top of Victoria's and stopped the shuffle. She motioned toward the buffet. "What about food? I, for one, am starved."

"I knew there was a reason I liked you so much," Sally said as she saluted Lillian.

"I remember being in the classroom." Lillian smiled when she looked at Victoria who feigned boredom by a fake yawn. Ignoring the antics of their hostess, she plowed on. "I never had time to eat, and I taught secondary. Teaching kindergarten students has to be more time intensive."

"Okay. Okay." Victoria laughed. "You educators are not as subtle as you think you are, but I admit you do know how to remind someone of her duties to her guests. I guess I'll have to feed you before you'll play with me. Besides, I like being known as the hostess with the mostess."

"Oh, good grief. You are perhaps the hostess *avec sans humilité*," said Lillian.

"Impressive," Victoria gave her a mock bow.

"We are steel magnolias, remember?" Rachel, finally relaxed, roared with laughter. "I've enjoyed your performance, ladies. But, right now, I say: Let's eat."

Thirty minutes later, fully sated, the ladies grew serious about their Friday rendezvous. Victoria asked Sally Jane to shuffle the tiles. They then rolled the dice to determine who would begin. Rachel won the toss with a nine, and as East, she counted off nine tiles. The room had gone quiet as each of the ladies took their tiles.

Lillian stated, "This is just about where we were last week when Grant and Jake walked in and disturbed us."

"If they get past my locked door and interrupt our game tonight, Lillian may not be able to keep me from shooting," announced Victoria as she concentrated on her copy of the 2006 Mah Jongg card and the tiles on her rack.

Everyone laughed.

Lillian noticed that the women never took their eyes off their tiles, but it was clear by the way they played that their minds were not on the game. Rachel bid, and the women played several rounds, pausing only long enough to refill empty wine glasses.

Suddenly, Rachel yelled "Mah Jongg!" and giggling stated, "When was the last time you heard me say that?"

Victoria laughed. "It must be the wine. You're not nearly as uptight as you are when you drink that gosh awful tea. Tell us what you have."

"Okay. Here it is. See for yourself. Winds – Dragons: FFFF N EE WWW SSSS [four flowers, north wind, two east winds, three west winds, four south winds]."

Each of the ladies congratulated Rachel as she counted her chips. She suddenly quit counting and looked at Lillian.

"Four flowers. That reminds me. What kind of flowers did you say that you saw in the vase at Stella's?" asked Rachel.

"I'm not sure," responded Lillian and then to herself. *Did I? I don't remember saying anything about flowers and the vase to anyone other than Grant and Jake.*

"Maybe you didn't mention them. Maybe I remember seeing them when I called on her," said Rachel.

"Flowers, smowers," declared Victoria. "Let's shuffle. We have time for someone else to win a round."

"As I said, I haven't eaten today." Sally Jane stood and walked to the buffet. "So, if you don't mind, I still need my nourishment. You two go ahead and discuss flora and fauna while I fill my plate. I'll bring my food to the table. I don't mind playing and eating at the same time."

"No, don't do that. Let's all take a break and partake some more of this agape feast that our hostess has prepared," said Lillian.

"Fine with me." Victoria stood. "Let me freshen everyone's drinks."

Rachel and Sally Jane refilled their plates with pimento cheese sandwiches, vegetable dip, and chips. They sat down to munch their way through the food. Lillian noticed the puzzled look on Rachel's face.

"What's wrong, Rachel?" she asked.

"Flowers. My hand. It made me think here's something I ought to remember about those flowers at Stella's house, but for the life of me, I can't," said Rachel.

"Don't worry about it, Rachel. It'll come to you, whatever it is," consoled Lillian. *Here I am, doubting Rachel. I've already doubted*

Margaret and Victoria. What am I doing? These ladies are my best friends. Lord, help me to be wise.

"I hope so," said Rachel.

"It will. When it does, call me."

"Sure."

The women put their empty plates on the sideboard. Each of the ladies took her seat. The tiles were shuffled, the wall broken, and play began.

"Let's play!" Victoria said with gusto.

Sally Jane reached for her glass of wine.

"Before we begin the Charleston [fan], I have something important to say."She did not have time to say anything. The door bell rang.

"When will we ever have an uninterrupted evening?" moaned Rachel.

"Ignore it," ordered Victoria.

Someone began banging loudly on the door.

"For crying out loud!" yelled Victoria.

"Well I never!" exclaimed Sally Jane when Victoria grabbed her gun and yanked the door open.

Brandishing her weapon, she said, "You'd better have a damned good reason. . ." Victoria stopped her tirade.

There stood Grant. Obviously, more enraged than she.

"Put that gun away, Victoria, before you hurt someone," he ordered and then asked, "Is Lillian here?

"Why, yes, she is."

"Ask her to step outside, please."

Victoria turned to relay the message, but Lillian was already half-way across the room on her way to meet Grant.

Eli, every hair standing on end, began to bark and growl and head for the door.

"No, Eli. Stand down." Lillian ordered.

He ceased growling and sat down but still watched her as she approached Grant who stood clinching his fists.

Chapter 8

BEFORE LILLIAN COULD step outside, Grant began. "Did you lock the door as I told you to when you left the 408 location?" he asked as calmly as he could through clenched teeth.

"I thought I did."

"Well, think about it. I received a call from Mr. Peters."

Lillian stood on the front porch and mentally reviewed her actions and the end of the search. She shrugged her shoulders. "I'm beginning to doubt that I did. Why? Is it important? And by the way, who is Mr. Peters?"

"He was Stella's neighbor. He lives across the street from her at 407 N. Pecan."

"Why did he call you?" asked Lillian.

"He saw a woman running away from 408. Guess what else he saw?"

"I can imagine that the woman he saw was none other than myself. Do you think he saw someone enter after I left the house?"

"That's exactly what he saw: a man, less than five minutes after you left."

"I am so sorry, Grant. I was so spooked by the noise I heard that I just ran. Now, I'm sure I didn't lock the door," Lillian said.

"Lillian, I'm not mad at you. I'm angry that I didn't get the word as soon as the incident happened."

"Why not?"

"Mr. Peters didn't think it was necessary to call until after his afternoon nap. Whether or not you locked the door, the intruder would have gotten into the house one way or another."

Grant hugged her to him.

"I couldn't live with myself if something had happened to you. When I received Mr. Peters' call, I was scared for your safety. I had to find you."

"Bill could have told you I was safe. Did you call him?"

"I tried. There was no answer."

"My goodness. No wonder you're so upset."

"If the intruder saw you leave, he could have followed you to find out where you live. You could be in danger."

Victoria, who had been standing in the doorway and listening to the exchange, commanded, "You two, get in here off the porch. Grant, tell the rest of us what is going on."

"Well, you heard it. Stella's house at 408 N. Pecan was burglarized. I've called Jake, and he is waiting for me there now. Lillian, would you ride over with me, please?"

Grant turned to the other three women. "Ladies, please accept my apology for ruining your game again."

Determined to have the last word, Victoria responded, "I guess eventually we will not have you pestering us. Just take care of Lillian." And, to Lillian, "I'll check with you tomorrow."

Before he and Lillian left, Grant turned to the other women. "Ladies, I want you to know that you also may be in danger. If the culprit followed Lillian home, he might also have followed her here tonight."

"Why would he be stalking her?" Sally Jane asked.

"If, during his search of Stella's house, he did not find what he wanted, he may think that Lillian took it. The culprit must have known he spooked her."

"That he did, indeed. I didn't think I could run that fast anymore." Lillian laughed, trying to bring some levity to the situation for her friends whose facial expressions revealed their concern. "My shoulder bag slowed me down, though."

"That's a good point," Grant said. "I'm sure he's wise enough to know that most women don't carry an oversized bag when they are out for a walk. He may have followed her here thinking she may have given the bag to one of you."

"I didn't think about that." Lillian turned and spoke. "Girls, I am sorry if my actions cause you any problems."

"We're not worried," said Victoria. "I have my gun." She looked at Rachel and Sally Jane. "If you would feel safer with me, you can certainly spend the night."

"No." Sally Jane spoke up. "I'm not afraid. Remember, I teach five-year-olds." Her comment brought some smiles to the other women.

"I think I'd sleep better in my own bed," Rachel said.

Grant nodded. "You have to decide what makes you feel better, but let me emphasize I want all of you to be extra careful. If you think someone is following you home, keep driving. Go to the main security office."

"We will," Rachel said. "Victoria, thanks for being such a good hostess. And, Grant, I appreciate the good job you do for all of us. Think I'll go home now."

"I will, too," said Sally Jane. "I'll feel safer walking out to my car while you're still here, Grant."

"I understand. Let me walk you to your vehicles." He made sure that both women were safely ensconced in their cars. "See you girls later." Grant watched as the other ladies started their vehicles and drove away before he returned to the house to escort Lillian to her auto.

"Do you mind if I leave my car here? I'd like to ride home with Grant."

"Sure, no problem," Victoria added, "If you'll leave me your keys, I'll put it in my garage out of sight."

"Good idea. I'd hate for someone to break into it. Thanks so much." Grant said. "Why don't you go ahead and do that now, Victoria. We'll leave after you've gone back inside and locked up."

"Okay."

Before they drove away, Lillian watched to make sure Victoria locked her doors and closed the drapes on all of her windows.

Toting her shoulder bag, Lillian followed Grant to his car. She opened the back door for Eli before sitting in the passenger seat herself. As she fastened her seatbelt, Lillian asked, "Did you tell Jake that I left the door open?"

No longer angry and no longer needing a stern voice for warnings, Grant spoke gently. "I'm not sure it would have mattered. Don't beat yourself up over this. I promise you, we will get to the bottom of it."

"I know you will. It's just that I'm always so careful. I just can't believe I let a little noise scare me so much that I ran away so quickly."

"I'm glad you didn't hang around any longer." Grant parked behind Jake's squad car in the driveway of the house on Pecan. He walked around to the passenger door and opened it. "Let's leave Eli in the car for now."

"I don't understand. Why is that necessary? You said yourself that he should be with me at all times."

"You said he was upset the last time you brought him here, so I think it best he stay put right now. I promise I'll let him out as soon as possible."

Lillian nodded and walked beside Grant until they reached the gate leading into the back yard. When they reached the bottom of the steps to the deck, Grant stopped and put his hand on her shoulder. "Brace yourself. It's not pretty."

"Now, you're scaring me." She led the way up the steps. *I think every light in the house is on right now. I can't imagine why Grant is so solicitous.*

They walked into the house. Lillian stopped so quickly that Grant bumped into her. She scanned the room. Within seconds, numbness and speechlessness vanished. Anger consumed her.

What was once an extremely neat and orderly house was now a shambles. Bookcases had been stripped of their treasures. The books, some with their covers ripped, exposed naked spines. All of them had been thrown into a pile in the middle of the living room floor along with torn cushions from the sofa and chairs.

Lillian walked into the kitchen.

Cabinet drawers were spilled out onto the floor, and utensils lay scattered. Broken dishes made it impossible to walk past the small breakfast table.

Upstairs, mattresses were thrown off the beds. Someone had viciously made long cuts in them. Torn pillows, along with their stuffing, were tossed randomly throughout the room.

Lillian, red-faced, stomped her foot and almost growled. "Damn that sorry so-and-so. How dare he do this to Stella's house. If I could get my hands on him right now, I'd turn him wrong side out." She shook her fist. "I'd make him regret being born. I'd –"

Both Grant and Jake attempted to calm her down.

"Mom, I knew that sooner or later Grant would give you the okay to come into this house and explore, and I concurred with his decision."

"And – she waved her hand out, pointing to the cluttered bedroom – I'm glad I did before this."

"Neither Grant nor I hold you at fault for any of this mayhem."

"We don't know who or why, but we will get to the bottom of it." Jake promised. "Grant told me the culprit tried to get in while you were here. I'm glad you got out when you did."

"So am I."

"Mom, understand. If there were something here that contained incriminating evidence, whoever broke into this house would have done so whether or not the doors and windows were locked."

"I told her pretty much the same thing. Lillian, you know that no one in this neighborhood has a burglar alarm system. They all depend on the lake's security force to protect them. If anyone is at fault, I am for not having a twenty-four/seven watch on this place," said Grant.

"No matter what you two say, I feel so responsible for all of this," Lillian said.

"Don't. It's obvious that someone was searching for something," said Grant.

"Yeah, you're right," agreed Jake, "and maybe that something would have implicated him or her as the murderer."

Since walking into the house, Lillian smiled for the first time. "Well, boys, I have a confession."

"Mom, you don't have to confess anything. Like I said before, you're not responsible for any of this."

She looked from son to son. "That's not what I was going to say." She couldn't help laughing at their puzzled expressions. "I'll quote Grant: Brace yourselves, boys. You'll like this confession."

"Okay. Tell us," Grant said. "I don't think anything you do could surprise us."

"You'll be glad to hear this. Before I left in such a hurry, I packed up some items and took them with me. They are locked up in my bedroom's closet safe."

Instead of chastising her, both men grinned.

"For once, Mom, I'm glad that you tampered with evidence." She, too, was feeling better now that she realized she may have removed documents, some which might, perhaps, help identify Stella's murderer.

"Let's go over to the house, and I will show you what I discovered," offered Lillian. "Maybe we can find something of importance."

When the three stepped outside, they heard Eli barking and growling, trying to get through the window of Grant's cruiser.

"What's got him so riled up, I wonder," said Jake.

"I don't know, but I hope he hasn't torn up my car seats."

"Come on, Grant. Let's check around the house, make sure no one's lurking, just waiting for us to leave."

"I'll take the south side of the house and will meet you back in front." Both men left Lillian standing in the driveway.

Lillian headed toward Grant's car. "Hold on, I'm coming." The dog stopped barking when he saw her approach the car. *I've never seen him so upset.* She opened the door to the back seat. "Good dog, you need to..." Before she could grab his leash, the dog took off. Lillian yelled, "Come back here, Eli." He ignored her command. "Well, that's a first." She ran after him.

Both men heard her calling the dog. They ran around the house. Both Lillian and Eli were gone. "Do you see them?" asked Grant.

"No, but I hear Eli barking." Jake pointed. "They went that way."

"They're headed for the dam. Let's go." Grant ran toward the barking. Jake followed yelling his mother's name.

Lillian heard the boys calling her, so she stopped in front of the fifth house down the street. She motioned to them as they approached her. "Look," she said. "Eli is chasing that car. Go get him, Grant." Jake stopped and put his hand on his mother's back as she bent over, hands on her knees, taking deep breaths, in an effort to recoup from her sprint. She stood and with shaky hands tried to repair her gray pony tail which was totally askew. Its mooring had somehow fallen during the run. Unable to do anything with her hair, she let her hands fall to her side. "To hell with it."

"Mom, are you all right?"

"Yes. I'm so mad at myself. I can't move as fast as I did when I was your age."

"Hey, I'm proud of the way you get around." He put his arm around her and then asked. "Were you able to get a good look at that car?"

"No, not at first, but when Eli jumped up on the driver's side of the car, its headlights came on, and it sped away. I'm pretty sure it was a white car."

Unable to keep up with the speeding car, Eli stopped and sat down in the middle of the street. Lillian whistled for him. Grant picked up the dangling leash and slowly walked with the dog back to Lillian. She patted Eli on the head when he reached her. "Good boy. You knew that person, didn't you?"

He sat down and growled softly.

"Yes ma'am, Eli knew him," Grant said. "and if I see a car with scratches on its driver's side door panel, I'll know him, too."

"And when you do, I want to know. It'll be a pleasure interrogating the SOB who tried to harm my mother."

Grant took his cell phone out of his pocket and dialed security. When the dispatcher answered, he said, "There's a car speeding away from 408 N. Pecan. Who is on patrol right now?" Pause. "Good. Get on the horn. Find out if he's close to Pecan." Pause. "Okay. Ask him to intercept the car before it reaches the gate." He waited a moment, listening. Then, "Yes, alert the gate, too." Pause. "I want you to hold the person until one of the sheriff's constables arrives to take possession." Pause. "Ten-four."

He ended the call and said to Jake. "Hopefully, we can nab him. Dispatcher is alerting your office. If they catch him, he's all yours." Jake nodded.

"The excitement's over, boys. Let's go home."

Chapter 9

BILL WATCHED THE two squad cars park in the circular drive. The three people whom he loved most climbed out. "Uh oh," he whispered when he saw Lillian's hair. She had a grip on Eli's leash. The group climbed the steps to the deck. He saw how utterly drained they all appeared and became concerned. He knew that whatever was wrong, Lillian was right in the middle of it and could have caused it.

"I saw flashing lights and heard the sirens," Bill said. "What's going on?" He didn't wait for an answer. "Lillian, you look frazzled. Are you okay?"

"She's okay, Dad." Jake spoke before she could answer her husband. "She's just had a scare and needs to sit down, rest awhile."

"We all need to sit down." Grant spoke hoarsely. "It's going to be a long night."

Bill hugged Lillian and helped her sit down in his recliner, propped her feet up. "Are you sure you're okay, sweetheart?"

"I'm fine, really."

"Dad, do you have any wine? I think it might help her relax."

"Of course, I'll get it right now." As he proceeded the kitchen, he looked over his shoulder and asked, "Jake, Grant, could I get you two anything to drink?"

"Just a glass of water for me, thanks," said Grant.

"Me, too, Dad, water is fine."

While Bill was filling drink orders, Lillian looked up from the recliner.

"Jake, why did you make your dad feel that I need all of this pampering? You, too, Grant. You've frightened him."

"Well, mom, when he finds out how close you came to having a potentially dangerous encounter with the intruder – possibly the murderer -- he will be livid. You know he did not want you involved in this, and if he finds out what happened, he won't let you out of his sight for the next several days."

"So, I take it you're doing this for effect -- to get what you want -- to get me sequestered."

"I'm not sure that's such a bad idea," Grant said. "I don't want you hurt, Lillian. You know how much we all love you, especially me."

"Thanks, but Jake is right. Here comes Bill. I'm not going to be tied down. Follow my line of thought here. Okay?"

Both boys nodded as Bill arrived and placed a tray containing their drinks and a plate of chocolates on the coffee table.

"Here, now, this ought to perk you up," he said gently.

"Bill, I have something to tell you," Lillian said softly to get his attention.

Bill knelt down in front of her, took her hand, and urged her on. "Tell me," he said.

Lillian sipped her wine, "I'll try to describe things without scaring you any more than you already are."

"I'm listening. I'll try to understand, whatever it is. I just pray you've not gotten yourself in trouble."

"No, I'm not in trouble, though I could have been," she replied. "Grant and Jake gave me permission to go inside Stella's house and go through it."

Bill glared at both men. "I wish you boys had not encouraged her," he said.

"Don't blame them. I am to blame for this. I convinced them they needed a woman's point of view, so I explored the house earlier today. However, later, after I left to go over to Victoria's for our regular Mah Jongg evening, the house was burglarized."

"Good lord, Lillian! I'm glad you were gone before that happened," said Bill.

"Oh, yes, that was good," she said. "However, the boys think there must have been some incriminating evidence in the house and, perhaps, that is why it was broken into." She paused and took a sip of wine, then looked up at her husband.

Bill recognized the smug look on her face.

Yep, I think my wife may have gone way beyond just being in the middle of something. I'm almost positive she's the one who caused the ruckus.

"But, they didn't find anything."

"How can you be so sure of that?" *I'm sure I know the answer to that question.*

"Because -- the good thing is this: I brought some items home with me today when I ran out of time."

"What do you mean by 'run out of time'?"

"It's Friday, remember. Mah Jongg was at Victoria's. I had to come home and get dressed and rest a little. Digging through someone else's personal possessions is really hard work."

"I'm sure it is. But promise me you won't go down that street again. I do not want you going back into that house."

She shook her head but made no promises.

Bill noticed the exchange of glances between Jake and Grant. "I know you two are amazed at your mother's performance tonight."

They opened their mouths to speak, but Bill raised his hand and stopped them. "I don't want to hear any denials from either of you. I'm sure there's more to her story, but it can wait for another day." Bill rose from in front of Lillian and sat on the armrest of the recliner.

"I'm definitely not going to walk that way with Eli," Lillian said. At the mention of his name, Eli rose from the floor and put his paw on her knee.

"Yes, I mentioned your name, you sweet boy," she said as she took his paw in her hand and gave it a shake. "Now, sit. We have business to tend to." The dog sat down beside the recliner. "Guard duty again, huh?"

"So, Lillian, let's see what you've got," said Grant.

When she sprang up from her resting place and hurried out of the room, Eli also rose from his spot on the floor, trotted over and jumped up on the back of the sofa where he began his usual nightly vigil, watching cars and pedestrians who traveled the street below.

Lillian brought an armload of items from her bedroom and spread them out on the dining room table. She sat down, and the three men pulled out chairs and joined her. "One of the things I want you guys to read is a newspaper clipping."

"What's it about?" asked Leisure Lake's security chief.

"We'll get to that, Grant, but first, I want Mom to explain how she found the article our county forensics team missed. I plan on addressing their ineptness come Monday."

"Good point," Bill said. "They need to be reprimanded."

Grant nodded in agreement.

Ever the school teacher, she began to explain, speaking slowly and precisely. Bill smiled and nodded

"After examining the items in the kitchen – you know, Grant – those I called you about, I walked back through the house and saw a bookcase in the foyer, so I –"

"Don't tell us." Jake laughed and said to his dad and Grant. "If I know my mom, and I'm pretty sure we all do." He looked at his mother before continuing. "You went through all of the books in the case, page-by-page."

"You know me well. I did, and in the process, the clipping fell out of one of the books. Right now, I don't remember the title of the book, but I brought it with me."

"That's not important. Are you going to tell us what the article was about or, at least, summarize its contents?" Grant asked.

"In due time, but the next most important clue I found was a rubber-band bound stack of letters."

"And just how did our forensics team fail regarding the letters?" asked Jake. "Where were they?"

"In a shoe box, on the top shelf of the master bedroom closet."

"Total incompetence," said Bill. "I suggest, son, that you make a recommendation to the county officials to budget for and provide some much-needed training for its investigative teams."

"I'd say you're right on, and you can consider that a done deal."

* * * * *

WHILE ALL THREE men sat around the dining table, waiting to hear more about her discoveries, Lillian picked up her oversized handbag which she had also brought to the table. She reached into it and pulled out her notebook.

She reviewed the observations she had written and then, for emphasis, made eye contact with each of the men for a moment.

"Before we begin, let me give you my thoughts," said Lillian.

The men nodded agreement, and she continued.

"First of all, remember the teacup and saucer on the coffee table?"

Both Grant and Jake nodded.

"Well, I checked the kitchen. I'm sure forensics made note of this: There was no used teabag anywhere, not even in the trash can, and no water left in the tea kettle. Of course, the water could have evaporated, but I don't think so."

"Their report did not include that information," said Grant.

"Well, don't you think if she had been drinking tea just before leaving the house there would have been a bag at least in the trash and water left in the kettle?"

"That is puzzling," said Bill.

Lillian knew she had aroused his investigative instincts.

"Yes, I agree. Go on," instructed Jake.

"Also, according to Rachel, Stella asked about the art guild, but I found absolutely nothing on the walls to indicate she had an interest in art. Nothing, not even a sketch pad, colored pencils, etc."

Eli began a low growl. Lillian stopped talking and looked his way. "It's okay, Eli. Sorry I mentioned her name." He turned his head upon hearing his name and then renewed his guard duty. Ever so softly, he continued his grumbling.

"She might not have been able to afford fine arts or the supplies she'd need to draw," said Grant. "Perhaps, her interest in the guild stemmed from the fact that she planned to decorate her home with her own masterpieces after she settled in."

"True. But don't you think that if she were an art lover, she would have hung a print of some kind, even a colorful poster, on the wall?" asked Lillian.

"Good point, Mom."

"Surely, if she could afford to buy a house here, she could have afforded some inexpensive prints to liven up the house." Bill piped in to support his wife's opinion.

She continued her thoughts, confessing, "I'll be honest with you, I had begun to doubt Rachel's account of having visited with her. But, upon searching the trash can, I found the welcome packet Rachel had given her. It had her business card inside."

"I'm glad you've exonerated Rachel, who just happens to be one of your good friends. Maybe, we ought to exonerate Stella, too. She might not have been here long enough to hang any pictures," Bill suggested.

Keeping the conversation moving, Jake added, "Okay, Mom, continue. What else did you note?"

"What's more important than the lack of paintings, I think, was the lack of family pictures. There was only one photo of what appeared to be family, the photo on the dresser in the master bedroom."

"I remember it, a portrait of a young family. Did you find any other items that would indicate she had family connections anywhere? I know you were specifically looking for information that would help Reverend Hammon with respect to her funeral," said Jake.

"I did, but probably not anything suitable for her eulogy."

"Double check your notes. Do you have any other thoughts about Stella before we begin examining the documents?" Grant asked.

Lillian read over the next few notations she had made in her notebook and looked up at Grant. "Yes, as a matter of fact I do."

"Let's hear them," said Jake.

"Well, as I looked through the kitchen, I found Stella's cookbooks. She had dog-eared numerous pages of recipes for specialty cakes." Lillian thought for a moment and then continued. "Either she was an amateur who liked to cook or she was a professional baker who specialized in making cakes for special events."

"A professional caterer, maybe?" asked Bill.

Lillian paused, trying to get a handle on what was wrong with that assumption. Then she continued. "But, there was almost no food in the pantry or refrigerator, and the freezer was empty. Don't you think that's strange?"

"Definitely. I think it's time we looked at the documents you have," said Grant.

"Let's divide them up. Each of us needs to make notes, and then we'll compare what we've learned," suggested Jake.

Lillian dumped all of the documents on the dining room table. "It's sad, but here is all that remains intact of her life. I guess the old saying 'you can't take it with you' rings true."

The four solemnly sat down to examine the items.

"Wait a minute," cautioned Grant. "Don't touch anything yet. I'll go to my car and get some nitrile gloves."

"Thanks, I'm so eager to see these items, I didn't think about leaving our fingerprints on them." Jake stood and stretched.

"Would anyone like a sandwich? I'll make some. We may be here a while, and I predict we'll need nourishment before we finish," Bill said.

Jake and Lillian nodded yes, and Grant gave him a thumbs up.

Lillian heard Eli begin a menacing growl. Surprised, she watched her gentle poodle jump from the sofa and run to Grant as he approached the door. The dog reared and stood on his back legs. He pushed Grant, almost knocking him down.

"Stop it, Eli. What's wrong with you?" he said as he pushed the dog away. He opened the door, but quickly closed it.

"Good dog," he said . And to the others, "Someone is out there," he warned as he walked over to close the drapes. Then he yelled, "Get down," as he, too, followed his own instructions.

Just then, the front windows exploded.

Chapter 10

NONE OF THEM hesitated or asked any questions. Even Eli followed Grant's order and immediately dropped to the floor as bullets zinged overhead. Glass lay all over the floor. No one moved. They clutched the carpet and held their breaths.

Lillian reached out to Bill who extended his hand to her. "Are you okay?"

"I think so," he said. "Are you hurt?"

"No. I'm fine. Jake?"

"I'm good, Mom. What about you, Grant?"

"Good, thanks to Eli." When he heard Grant say his name, Eli very carefully low crawled over the shards of glass and went to check on Grant, who ruffled the dog's hair as the pooch licked him in the face.

"Do you hear that?" Lillian raised her head.

"It's a car's engine," Grant said as he jumped up. He opened the door and ran outside onto the deck. Eli was right behind him.

Lillian sprang up, followed by Jake. She ran through the front door in time to see a white Lexus race around the corner but not in time to get a good look at the license plate.

Grant ran to his squad car. Eli jumped in the front seat when Grant opened the door. Man and dog took off in pursuit of the automobile. Lillian watched them as Grant backed out of the driveway and sped away. *I know someone with a car just like that white Lexus. But who? Too rattled right now. It will come to me later.*

* * * * *

JAKE THOUGHT GRANT and his team would surely intercept the car this time, so he went back inside to make sure that Bill was okay. The older man still sat on the floor, too stunned to get up.

"Whoever that was is gone for now. Are you okay, Dad?"

"Yes, I am," responded Bill. Struggling to stand, he reached up and took his son's hand. Lillian entered the living room.

"Twice in one day I've seen two houses wrecked. I hope Grant nabs the culprit this time. I really want to give him a piece of my mind."

"Where's Eli? Is he hurt?" Bill wanted to know.

"He's fine. With Grant right now." Lillian reassured him. "Thank goodness. We're lucky he jumped off the couch when he did."

Jake ignored her concern for the dog. "Mom, I hope you have what that person thinks you have. I'd sure like to tie up this case as soon as possible."

"I'm with you on that," said Bill. "The sooner we get this case solved, the sooner I won't have to worry about your mother."

* * * * *

"WHAT IN THE?" The car had disappeared. "That's impossible," Grant said to Eli, who sat in the front passenger seat, staring out the window. "You look as puzzled as I feel, old boy. Wish you could talk. You may have seen where it went." Grant slowed the car. He eased down the main road leading to the front gate. "This beats all. It's as if the car disappeared into thin air."

He pulled over to the side of the road and stopped the car. He reached out, picked up the receiver to his car radio, pushed the transmission button, and said, "Chief calling front gate security. Come in."

His radio crackled. "Front gate here. What can I do for you, boss?"

"If a white Lexus tries to exit, stop it, and notify me."

"Ten-four."

* * * * *

GRANT RETURNED TO the Prestridges. Accompanied by Eli, he climbed the steps to the front deck. He carried a box of nitrile gloves.

Lillian greeted him first. "Did you catch the slime who shot out our windows?"

"Lost him."

"I don't understand," she said. "You were right behind him."

"I was at first, but my ten-year-old cruiser couldn't keep up with that brand-new, Lexus sports car."

"Well, did you check with your men to find out if he drove through the front gate?" asked Bill.

"I put out an APB. They will call me if he tries to leave the lake."

"Grant, I know you did your best, but I don't see how he could have lost you on these narrow roads here at the lake," Jake said. "What happened?"

"By the time I got up to the top of the hill and around the corner, it was gone. It's as though the car disappeared into thin air, but don't worry," he said confidently, "I'll check our records tomorrow. Everyone who lives here or visits here has a sticker on his or her car. We'll find the culprit."

"I hope so," Bill said.

"Like I said: We'll find him." His voice sounded a warning similar to Eli's growl.

"In the meantime, boys, help me cover up the window with some of the plywood I have in the garage. Can't get the glass replaced until tomorrow morning," ordered Bill.

The security chief didn't move. Like Eli, he now stood vigil by the window making sure the others were safe in case the car's driver decided to return.

Jake helped Bill carry the plywood into the house. He held the board in place as Bill nailed it up to secure the gaping hole, once a window offering a view of the lake and the peaceful community surrounding it.

"I'll take care of the glass." Lillian swept the room and then ran the vacuum. "Grant, would you take Eli to the kitchen so he won't cut his paws on the shards?"

"Sure. Come with me, Eli." The dog followed Grant. He went to his water bowl and drank half of the liquid. Then he paced back and forth across the room, making sounds, somewhere between a whimper and a soft growl.

"Settle down, Eli. The show's over." Grant knelt down and gave the dog a hug and received a wet kiss in return. "You, big boy, tried to warn me."

"Next time, listen to him sooner," added Bill as he finished hammering the last nail into the plywood.

"Ten-four."

"Okay, guys, now that all is quiet, let's get back to the letters," suggested Lillian.

"Let's do. Bill, weren't you going to make sandwiches?" asked Grant. "All this excitement has made me hungry."

Lillian went back to the table, "You'll need something to help you come down off your adrenaline high."

"Dad, put on a pot of coffee. I think we will be here for awhile," Jake said.

"You boys are always hungry, no matter what. No food for me," said Lillian as she gave each person a yellow legal pad and a pen, "but I would love a glass of wine, no caffeine."

"Just call me a short-order cook." Bill exited to fill all of their requests.

Everyone laughed when Eli picked up his empty bowl and dropped it in front of Bill.

"Guess you're hungry, too, huh?" He received a sharp bark as an answer.

The other three sorted out the envelopes. Some contained letters and some contained legal documents. As they read, they jotted down a description of each item.

Lillian opened the thickest envelope from the shoe box. She extracted two documents and began reading. After a thorough perusal, she made the following notes and said, "Listen to this."

Jake and Grant stopped reading to listen.

Lillian read, *Marriage license issued to Sheila Davis and Jonathan Davis on March 30, 1962. Divorce petition filed by Sheila Davis against Jonathan C. Davis on September 27, 1974.*

"Interesting," Grant said. "After reading the contents of this envelope, I wrote the following: *Adoption papers for infant boy dated June 14, 1971.*"

Jake said, "I found a birth certificate for an infant – first name Michael – born in October of 1970."

He jotted down his find: *Birth certificate for infant with date of birth on October 30, 1970. Per birth certificate, no other children had been born to the parents.*

Bill came back into the room. All three were busy reading and making notes, so he stood holding the tray of ham and Swiss cheese sandwiches. He spoke to announce his presence. "Here, guys. I made plenty so don't hesitate to take more than one."

As each one finished writing and looked up, he placed their order of food and drink on the table beside them. "From the looks on your faces, I'd say you guys have found something important."

"Perhaps," said Grant.

"I'd like to hear what you've found," said Bill.

"Okay," Lillian said. "Let's do recap the major facts we've discovered for your dad. I'd like to have a fresh opinion regarding these documents."

Bill joined them, sitting down in the vacant chair. "Jake, what've you got?"

"My envelope contained a birth certificate for one Michael Charles Davis, born October 30, 1970."

"Was that the only birth certificate in the box?"

"Yes, sir."

"Did it mention other siblings who could have been born before the baby – you said his name was Michael, didn't you?"

"Yes, that's the name on the birth document, and it does not mention any other children."

"Okay."

"Interesting," said Grant, "because my envelope held a Certificate of Adoption for an infant boy named Michael Charles Davis."

"To me, it sounds like this couple adopted the child," said Bill.

"I bet they are the family in the photo we found in the master bedroom."

Lillian reached into her big bag and retrieved the frame that held the picture.

"Here look at it." She passed it around. Each of the men examined the faces of the three people in the photo.

Bill looked at it last and returned it to Lillian. "I'd estimate Michael would be about the age of you two boys right now."

"I agree," said Lillian. "And, my envelope held a marriage license filed on March 30, 1962, to Sheila Davis and Jonathan Charles Davis. The stamp indicates it was filed in Dallas County."

"I'll get on those names first thing tomorrow," volunteered Jake. "Maybe we can find Jonathan and hopefully the child, Michael. Guess he's grown by now."

"That would be great. Perhaps they can enlighten us on who would want to kill Sheila a/k/a Stella or. . ." began Grant before he was interrupted by Lillian.

"Maybe, one of them is the killer," she offered. "I'll get on the internet and see if I can find any information about a Michael Davis while you three eat your sandwiches."

"No, Lillian, this can wait until tomorrow. I want you to sit down and drink your wine," Bill said. He picked up the glass and placed it in front of her.

"You're right. She's done enough sleuthing for today," said Jake as he looked fondly at his mother.

"Enough to get our windows shot out," agreed Bill. "I'll call the glass folks first thing tomorrow to come out and repair the window." He turned to the one whose command had guided them to safety. "Thanks for being on the ball tonight. You saved our lives."

"Thanks, Grant, for being alert. I shudder to think what could have happened," said Jake.

"No thanks needed. Actually, it was Eli who was on the alert. He's the real hero tonight." He rose and started for the door but stopped and turned to say, "I think I'll make one more drive around the lake and see if that Lexus pops up anywhere."

"I need to leave as well. Jessica is beginning to complain that I spend more time with my parents than I do with her and the kids," said Jake. He stood and looked at Grant. "Would you like for me to take these envelopes down to my office and lock them up in my safe until we can complete examining them?"

"That makes more sense than keeping them in my office here at the lake," agreed Grant. "I think there's someone in this neighborhood who doesn't want us to learn the truths those papers hold."

"Would it be okay if I come downtown tomorrow and look over them some more?" asked Lillian. "If we can't find Jonathan or Michael, I need to work with the Reverend to prepare for Sheila's funeral."

"Yes, Mom, but only when I am in the office." Jake added, "I'll let you know as soon as I have any luck finding any next of kin."

Before he left, Grant cautioned, "Lock all your doors and windows. Leave on all of your outside floodlights. I'll have one of my security officers keep an eye on the house. I don't want a repeat of what just happened here tonight."

Both men left and walked down the drive. "Grant, I appreciate your keeping a close watch on them." Jake shook the hand of his friend.

"Talk to you tomorrow. Be safe." Grant opened the door and climbed into his car.

* * * * *

LILLIAN STOOD IN the open doorway for a moment and watched both of the boys she dearly loved. *It's good to see them shake hands.* Closing and locking the door, she sighed, knowing they, not she, would have to repair their relationship. *Perhaps, their working together on this case will be good for them.*

Feeling momentarily useless, Lillian sat down on the sofa and slowly sipped her wine. Eli climbed onto the sofa and rolled over exposing his tummy and holding one leg straight up in the air. Lillian laughed at his antics.

"Oh, you sweet boy," she said as she began to rub his tummy.

She sat there for a long time patting Eli and thinking about a young couple who obviously had adopted a child and then -- for some reason known only to them -- had sought a divorce.

How sad, she thought, *that baby's second set of parents let him down. I wonder where he is now and what became of his life.*

Chapter 11

WITH THE EXCEPTION of the sofa where Lillian sat, Bill moved all of the furniture in the living room. "I'm going to vacuum again in case any glass shards could have ended up in the carpet."

His wife nodded but made no comment.

He turned off the vacuum, parked it in the dining room, and picked up the dirty plates from the table. He carried them to the kitchen and deposited them in the kitchen sink. He turned on the faucet, covered the soiled utensils with hot, sudsy water, rinsed their soapy film, and put them in the dishwasher. Then he returned to the dining room where he vacuumed around and under the table. Bill moved at a snail's pace, deliberately postponing completion of the simple house cleaning tasks.

Need to keep an eye on you, my beloved, Bill thought as he moved about the room. *I know you too well. You have that baby on your mind and won't stop thinking about him until you know where he is now.*

Unable to prolong his tasks any longer, Bill put away the vacuum and sat down beside his wife. He put his arm around her shoulder, pulled her next to him and cuddled her in the crook of his arm. "A penny for your thoughts."

"I was just thinking about that family in the photo, particularly about the baby. I wonder where he lives and whether he has kept in touch with his mother."

"Well, my dear, I'm sure that Jake will do everything he can to find him, but think about something else."

"What?"

"Our victim may not actually be his mother."

"That's a thought. I wish it could be the case, but –"

"Here's what I think --" Bill paused long enough to kiss her and hold her close. "I think you've had enough excitement for today. You need some rest."

"I agree, but I need to finish my wine and gear down a bit before I go to bed. Why don't you go on, and I'll join you shortly."

"Are you sure you're okay to be alone right now?"

"I'm fine. Really. You've done enough work tonight, covering the window, vacuuming, washing dishes, watching me." She paused, hugged her husband, and continued. "You didn't think about my watching you while you were watching me, did you?"

He laughed. "You amaze me."

"Thank you for straightening up. Now, get some rest. I'll be right behind you just as soon as my glass is empty."

"Goodnight, dear." Bill, with one last glance at her, left Lillian alone in her thoughts.

* * * * *

THE HOUSE WAS quiet after Bill went to bed. Lillian lounged on the sofa, slowly sipping her wine. She glanced down at Eli who snored contentedly at the opposite end of the couch. She finally rose and walked over to her desk. Hesitating only for a brief prayer of thanksgiving that the four of them had not been shot during the attack on her house, she turned on her laptop computer and waited for the "Welcome" screen.

I wonder if I could find out anything about Michael, or for that matter, Jonathan.

Lillian went to Google and typed in Jonathan Charles Davis. There were several Jonathan Davis listings on the Web, but it was the article in the *Dallas Morning News* that caught Lillian's attention. As she read the article, she slapped the counter with her hand. It hurt, so she made a fist and continued beating the top of the desk.

Her anger and frustration boiled over and she exclaimed, "You sorry so-and-so. How dare you? I'm so mad at you I could tear you from limb to limb."

Awakened by her tirade, Eli jumped off the sofa and ran to stand beside her. He howled encouragement to her rage.

Hearing the commotion, Bill rushed into the living room. Lillian did not hear him enter as she continued to threaten the screen of her laptop. Bill knelt down beside her.

He put one arm around her and one around Eli, patting both. "What's wrong?" He glanced at the computer. "Tell me what upset you two."

Both woman and dog grew quiet at the sound of Bill's voice. Lillian took a deep breath and began. "I've just read a newspaper article about Jonathan and Michael."

"And, what did it say that angered you so much?"

"Evidently, Jonathan was abusive, and Michael suffered his wrath. I'm so angry." She wiggled out of Bill's embrace and continued. "The article stated Jonathan had been served with a restraining order after Sheila was hospitalized more than once because of his abuse."

"What about Michael? Was Jonathan also abusive to the child?"

"Michael is dead. He lived to be only about two years old. Actually, Bill, I'm surprised their names meant nothing to you. You would have been a reporter back then."

"I'm sure I don't remember the story. But then, I've written about many situations and don't remember all of them."

"I'm sure you don't." Lillian suddenly felt completely drained. "I'm going to call it a day and try to get some rest."

"Good idea." He held her hand as he guided her to the bedroom.

Eli followed. He waited until he heard Bill's snore and then ever so gently snuggled down between them. Lillian, still awake, smiled when Bill rolled over, wrapped his arms around the dog, and continued to snore.

* * * * *

AT DAYBREAK, LILLIAN felt her husband ease out of bed and tiptoe out of the house. She chuckled out loud when she heard the sound of his golf clubs clinking against each other as he carried them to the trunk of the car. Next, she heard the slam of the car's door. *The more you try to be quiet, the clumsier you are, my dear.*

When Lillian heard him drive away, she decided it was time to get going. There was much to do before her meeting with Reverend Hammon. First thing on her list was to call Grant and let him know what she had found out about the Davis family.

"Then, I'm going to call on Jake and look through the rest of the documents," she said to Eli. Before getting dressed, she called Margaret at the courthouse. She knew Margaret always went to work early in order to have some time to line up her tasks for the day. When Margaret answered her phone, Lillian wasted no time in making her request.

"Margaret, I need your help with something," said Lillian.

"Sure. What can I do for you?" said Margaret.

"I wonder if you could work with the Clerk of Dallas County and get copies of some documents I need to see."

"What kinds of documents?" asked Margaret.

"I need a copy of the divorce decree of a Sheila and Jonathan Davis."

"Why do you need that document?"

"It's relevant to the murder out here at the lake," explained Lillian.

"You know you're supposed to stay out of that matter, or have you forgotten what Grant and Jake, not to mention your husband, asked of you?"

"I'm not interfering with their work. I can't explain everything now over the phone. I wish you would help me out."

"No, Lillian, I won't do that. Perhaps, Jake or Grant as investigating officers would request copies of the document if you asked them," responded Margaret.

"Okay, I will," said Lillian. She hung up the phone puzzled. *And, Miss Margaret, why were you so curt? You'd think I asked you to do something illegal. And why did you suddenly turn cold and ultra professional at the mention of the name Davis?*

* * * * *

AS SOON AS Margaret heard the dial tone, she immediately punched in the number of Bill's cell phone. She heard it ring three times.

"Hello."

"Hi, Bill. We need to talk," said Margaret. "Can you come into town and meet me at the bakery around ten o'clock this morning?"

"Well, I was just teeing off on the back nine, but if it's important, I guess I can."

"It's important, or I wouldn't ask you to leave the golf course," said Margaret.

"Okay, tell me. What's so important?" asked Bill.

"Lillian just called me. She wanted me to get copies of the court documents relating to Sheila," Margaret said, "and, Bill, you do know Donna has moved to the lake, don't you?"

"No, I did not know that. Under no circumstances do I want Lillian to meet her," said Bill. "She might say something."

"You know she would."

"I'm on my way," he said as he ended the call.

* * * * *

BILL RUSHED DOWNTOWN to meet with Margaret. He was concerned about the news she had shared with him, both the news about Donna as well as the fact that Lillian was getting too close to the case. Bill understood his wife's persistent nature, and he knew she would keep digging until she learned too much about the past. After parking his car off the street in a crowded parking lot, he walked two blocks to the Corner Bakery. He opened the door and saw Margaret in a back booth.

"Bill, I'm really worried about Lillian and what she will do with the information she's bound to learn," said Margaret.

"Me, too. But I'm also worried about others at the lake." Bill sat down in the booth.

"Yes, I know. There is, after all, a murderer on the loose," Margaret added.

"And guess who the murderer's last target was," said Bill.

"Who?" asked Margaret.

"You're looking at one of them," responded Bill.

Margaret looked shocked.

"My goodness. What in the world happened?"

"Let me bring you up to date. Grant and Jake gave Lillian permission to go through the house on Pecan day before yesterday," said Bill.

"Did she find anything of importance?" asked Margaret.

"She found a bunch of letters and other documents and brought them home. And, it was a good thing she did."

"Why is that?" Margaret said.

"Later, after she left, neighbors saw a suspicious person break into the house. Whoever it was ransacked the place, apparently looking for something," explained Bill.

"And I'm guessing Lillian has already read through the documents," said Margaret.

"Some of them, but not all. Jake has them in his safe to make sure they remain intact," Bill said.

"I can't stand the suspense. What did Lillian learn?" asked Margaret.

"Enough. She googled their names and learned all about Sheila's divorcing Jonathan as well as Michael's death."

"Who's Michael?"

"The child they adopted."

"I can just imagine how she responded to that," said Margaret.

"I had already gone to bed, and her screaming at the computer, threatening to beat someone, woke me up," said Bill, shaking his head.

"That's not good for her blood pressure," said Margaret. "I feel guilty because I cut her off rather bluntly this morning when she called."

"Don't worry about that. Let me finish my story. Whoever broke into the Pecan Street house also shot out our front windows last night. At least, I'm guessing it was the same person," said Bill.

"I'm hoping that only the windows were hit." Margaret's eyes grew wide with concern. "Were you two alone?"

"No, Jake and Grant were there going over the documents with Lillian."

Margaret turned ashen. "And Grant, is he okay?"

"Both boys are in good shape," said Bill with a knowing smile. "But you might want to call Grant."

"I will, just as soon as I get back to my office."

"You know, Margaret, it is becoming more and more difficult for you and Grant to hide your relationship. My wife is picking up your vibes."

"I know, but Grant is not ready to commit, and I am not going to rush him."

"He has a lot of healing to do. I hope you understand and don't lose your patience."

"I'm not." She paused and then, "Okay, back to Donna."

"What about her?"

"She has just recently moved to the lake and has been employed by the club manager as the bookkeeper."

"I hope she doesn't like to play Mah Jongg," said Bill.

"I wouldn't know. We haven't communicated at all for the past twenty years."

"Oh?" said Bill. "Then how do you know she's working for the club."

"Duh. In case you've forgotten, I'm dating the chief of security out there. He and I do talk, you know."

"Sorry. Go on."

"The last time I saw her was at Mom's and Dad's funeral. I'll always blame her for their deaths."

Bill interrupted. "You've got to move on and leave the past behind. You can't change it. She is what she is."

"I know, and I've tried," admitted Margaret. "But enough about me. I would really hate for Lillian to learn Donna and I are related. I just hope that Donna and Sheila never met."

"I can understand your concern about that."

"If they had met, then I'd have to wonder if my sister could be the murderer."

"Don't worry. Your secret is safe with me," assured Bill. "After all, you and I arranged the adoption."

"If Donna found out about Sheila and the baby -- well, I've got to get back to work," said Margaret.

"And, I still have a round of golf waiting for me."

Bill paid for their coffee, and they left the Corner Bakery. He walked with Margaret to the end of the block. As they reached the corner across from the courthouse, he leaned over and gave her a reassuring hug. "I repeat, don't worry." Margaret nodded.

He watched his confidante enter the courthouse and then strolled to the parking lot and retrieved his car and drove away. Entering the right lane, he looked in his rearview mirror. Lillian stood in front of the courthouse.

I hope she didn't see us.

Chapter 12

LILLIAN HAD SEEN Bill and Margaret as they finished their tête à tête on the street corner. *I wonder what that's all about? I know I heard Bill gathering up his golf stuff this morning,* she thought.

Not wanting them to see her, Lillian waited across the street until Margaret entered the courthouse. She then tugged on Eli's leash and hurriedly walked to Jake's office. *Don't have time to worry about them now. Hope those two didn't see me.*

"Hi, Mom," said Jake as Lillian entered the room.

"Hi, darling, are you busy right now?"

"I'm never too busy for you."

"You know that's always the right answer when your mother wants some of your time. I guess I taught you well." Lillian laughed.

"You're here to see the documents, aren't you?" Jake stood up and walked across his office to the safe and retrieved the shoe box. He handed it to Lillian along with a pair of gloves.

"Where should I examine them?"

Jake motioned to a door on the west wall of his office which opened up into an adjacent room. "Just use the conference table in the next room. I'll make sure the door going into the hallway is locked."

"Thanks. Hopefully, this won't take too long."

Lillian donned the gloves and began to sort through the envelopes. She arranged them by postmarked dates and then began reading the four communications on top. None contained any pertinent information.

The next letter, however, was important. It was written by Lana Perrault, Sheila's attorney informing her that Jonathan had been released from prison. In her letter, the attorney stated she feared Jonathan would try to reconnect with his former wife. Ms. Perrault advised Sheila to move away from the Dallas area. In fact, she suggested a move to the East Texas area and described Leisure Lake and its security.

Lillian opened her handbag and extricated her trusty notebook. She wrote:

Jonathan released from prison – six months ago.
Sheila's attorney suggested she move to Leisure Lake.
Sheila moved into house on Pecan Street.
Sheila and Perrault were afraid of Jonathan?
Did he find Sheila?

Lillian read through the remaining letters, most of which were between Sheila and Lana Perrault. The lawyer had referred the name of a Realtor, and he was the one who helped Sheila make the decision to move into the house on Pecan. In one of the more recent letters, Sheila had invited her attorney for a visit as soon as she had gotten settled.

"Jake, come in here, please," said Lillian.

Jake stopped at the doorway. "Okay, Mom, what is it?"

"It's this letter. I just read something that might be related to the case."

"Right now, Grant and I are ready to listen to any suggestions."

"I don't know if it will help you solve the murder, but I think I've found someone who may be able to tell you a little bit about Sheila and whether or not she has any next of kin." Lillian handed the communications to him. "Here are some letters written to her by Lana Perrault, her attorney. Read these. You should be able to locate the lawyer at the return address."

"Excellent work. I'll get right on it," he said.

"Wait a minute." Lillian took a deep breath and continued. "You might want to read these letters first."

"I will, but what's in them?"

"It appears to me that Sheila and her attorney had a close friendship. I predict that she may be devastated when she hears about Sheila's death. How do you plan to handle it?"

"I thought I would call a friend of mine who works in the Dallas PD and ask him to meet with her and break the news to her."

"Good plan." Then Lillian had another thought. "Will it be necessary for her to identify the body?"

"I think that is the usual procedure if there is no family member to do it."

"I can't begin to imagine how sad she is going to be, especially since she recommended this move," said Lillian softly. And then, "You know she will need a place to stay while she is here. Have your friend tell her that she is welcome to stay with us when she comes down," offered Lillian.

"Are you sure you can handle this, Mom?" asked Jake.

"I can if she can," responded Lillian more bravely than she felt. "Oh, and I guess we need to call Grant right away and share this information with him."

"Consider it done," said Jake. "You go home and get some rest." He picked up the phone and called Grant.

Lillian had started for the door and then stopped when she heard Jake say, "Grant, Mom has been here reading through the letters and documents she took from Sheila's house. Could you come downtown and meet me for lunch? We'll go over them." He listened and then, "What? Oh, no. Yes, yes, sure, I'll tell her."

"Tell me what?" said Lillian.

"You'd better sit down," said Jake softly. He stood there for a moment, hands in his pockets, shaking his head.

"Tell me."

"I'm not sure I know just how to say it," he said as he removed his hands from his pockets and reached out to take his mother's hands.

"Is something wrong with your dad?" asked Lillian.

Jake sensed Lillian's rising panic, so he knelt down in front of her.

"Dad's okay, just shook up. He got home a few minutes ago. Called Grant right away. Mom, someone's broken into your house."

Lillian blinked and said, "Let's go." She hurried from the conference room. Eli and Jake sprinted to catch up.

Jake yelled, "Let's go in my car." Without slowing down, his mother turned into the courthouse parking lot. "Over here." He pointed to his cruiser.

Jake opened the passenger door of his squad car, ran around to the driver's side, jumped in, turned on his siren and blinking lights, and sped out of town toward the lake. When they arrived at the house, the paramedics were parked in the drive.

"I thought you told me your dad was okay," snapped Lillian. She opened her door and raced up the drive.

"He is," said Jake to an empty seat.

Lillian, panting from the run up the driveway, threw open the door. "Bill, Bill, darling. Are you hurt?" she said.

"I'm fine, sweetheart," said Bill. "Just a bump on the head."

"What happened?" Jake looked to Grant for an answer.

Grant walked over, hugged Lillian, and then turned to Jake. "Evidently, Bill walked in on the culprit who had hidden behind the screen between the living room and the computer area."

"When I turned to pick up the phone, he/she/whoever smacked me on the head," said Bill. It was obvious to his wife that he was trying to hide how badly he hurt at the moment.

They heard a car door slam and someone stomping up the steps of the deck. The door opened, and there stood Victoria, gun in hand.

"I heard the sirens but didn't pay any attention to them. Should have," said Victoria as she stormed into the room. She stopped short when she saw the bandage on Bill's head.

"Who in the. . .?" She caught herself just in time. Victoria's language had been known to rival that of a sailor. In the past, Lillian had chastised her more than once about her choice of words.

"Just go ahead and say it," said Lillian. "If I could get my hands on who did this, I may not even need your gun, Victoria."

"Grant, you and Jake have got to do something. It's just not safe here in our quiet little community anymore," ordered Victoria.

"We're doing the best we can." It was Grant who responded.

"Just make sure you are." She stomped back down the deck's steps.

"Don't mind her," Bill said. "She means well. I know how hard you two are working."

"Yes, we have been, but from now on, to be on the safe side, I'm staying here with you," said Jake. "I'll get Jessica to call her parents to come down and stay with her and the kids for awhile."

"Oh, Jake, that's not necessary," said Lillian.

"Leave him alone, Lillian," Grant ordered. "Jake, I sure do appreciate your help. I'm staying here, too. With both of us, I know we can protect them."

"Sounds good, partner," said Jake. "We may be able to solve another problem while we're here."

"One problem at a time," Grant said. He turned and motioned to one of his security officers who was waiting on the deck. "Wait for me. I'll be with you in a sec."

"Thanks, boys, I appreciate that," said Bill.

Now, maybe I'll learn about their disagreement. Strange, thought Lillian, as she looked from one to the other, *how it takes a near tragedy to straighten things out.*

"Come on, Bill. You need to lie down."

Chapter 13

EARLY THE NEXT morning, Jake contacted the law office of Lana Perrault, the Dallas attorney whose letters Lillian had wisely taken from Sheila's house. The secretary answered the phone.

"Law office. May I help you?"

"Ms. Lana Perrault, please."

"May I tell her who's calling?"

"Let her know that Sheriff Jake Prestridge needs to speak to her about one of her clients. It's very important."

"Yes, sir. Please hold."

Ms. Perrault picked up the phone and said, "Sheriff Prestridge, what can I do for you today?"

"I need to discuss one of your clients, ma'am."

"I can tell from your accent that you're from deep East Texas."

Jake smiled. He knew the cheerful lilt of her voice would soon grow serious. "Yes, ma'am, thank you for noticing I'm not from the city." He paused.

"Why do I have the feeling you haven't called with any good news?"

Jake cleared his throat. *This is the part of my job I hate.* "I'm afraid I have some bad news for you."

"I hope you're not going to tell me that one of Dallas's finest—especially one of mine--has gone and gotten in trouble in your jurisdiction."

"That depends on what you call 'trouble'; I'm calling you about a Ms. Sheila Davis."

"Sheila? Is she in trouble?"

"Not in trouble, *per se*. I'm calling to inform you that she's been murdered."

Lana's response was not unexpected. "Oh my God, I can't believe it."

"Yes, ma'am, it's true, I'm sorry to say."

"What happened?"

Jake brought her up to date regarding Sheila's death and the progress of his and Grant's investigation into her murder.

He heard soft, muffled sobs, indicating that the attorney was indeed saddened to hear about her client's death. He waited a few minutes to give her time to compose herself. When the seconds dragged on, he asked, "Ms. Perrault, are you there?"

"Excuse me for a moment, Sheriff." Jake heard the phone's receiver being placed on the desk, a drawer opened and closed, and the sound of the lady blowing her nose. He was not surprised by her next reaction.

"Are you sure the victim is Sheila?"

"To the best of our knowledge, yes, but we need confirmation from someone who knew her."

"How did you discover my connection to Sheila?"

"Good question. Going through her house, we found several legal documents including letters, which you and she had exchanged, some quite recent in fact."

"Sheila is—was—my client for years, but we had become more. We were friends. I don't mind telling you she was a pitiful woman whose life was filled with many disappointments. I had hoped -- oh, well, there's no use in saying anything more."

Jake sympathized with the attorney. He could almost feel the sorrow as she spoke. "Ms.Perrault, I hate to ask, but would it be possible for you to drive down to --"

"Of course, I'll be glad to make a formal identification for you," said Lana, "it's the least I can do for Sheila."

Jake exhaled. *Glad you are being so cooperative.*

"I just hope that you can find the person responsible for this."

"Rest assured, Ms.Perrault, we plan on doing everything in our power to –"

"Please call me Lana," she interrupted.

"Sure, and it's Jake here," he responded. "I noticed that in one of your letters you suggested that Sheila move away from the Metroplex."

"I did and for good cause." Lana went on to explain, "You see, Jonathan was being released from prison, and I feared he might try to harm Sheila."

"And what made you think he would?" asked Jake.

"Why don't we continue this conversation when I come down," she suggested.

"That's probably a good idea. I want you to meet Grant Perryman."

"Who?"

"The Chief of Security at the lake. He's working with me on this case."

"Good. I'll drive down after work today. If you will hold on a minute, I would like for you to give my secretary directions to your office. Also, recommend a good hotel so she can make a reservation for me."

"That reminds me. My mother and father live at the lake, and for the time being, my mom said to invite you to stay with them."

"That is so nice, but I will decline the offer," said Lana.

"You are a wise woman. You'll understand what I mean when you meet my mom. She's the ultimate helicopter mom to everyone she meets." Jake laughed.

"I look forward to meeting her."

"I recommend the Holiday Inn situated on the highway leading through the center of our fine city. Call me when you arrive, and I'll pick you up. We can drive out to the lake, and I'll show you where Sheila lived. Then you can meet Mom and Dad," said Jake. "I'm staying with them as an added security measure."

"Do you think they are in danger?" asked Lana.

"I do. I'll explain why when you get here. Drive safely," cautioned Jake as he ended their conversation. He immediately called Grant and told him about his conversation with Lana. Then he called Lillian.

"Hi, mom. I just called to let you know that I contacted Lana Perrault, Sheila's attorney. She is driving down today after work," said Jake.

"Be sure to bring her on over to the house. I hope you asked her to stay with us while she's here."

"I plan to introduce her to both of you. I extended your invitation, but she declined."

"That's too bad. I had hoped to learn more about Sheila from her."

Jake nodded. *That's my mom.* Then to Lillian, "She plans to stay at the Holiday Inn."

"I understand," Lillian said. "I would probably want to do the same if I were she. Of course, I'll be glad to prepare dinner so you two can visit here. It would be more conducive to the type of discussion you'll want to have, don't you think?"

"Perfect, Mom," he said, but he thought: *A conversation you'll hear is what you really mean.*

Lillian paused and then continued. "And since it will be late, we'll just plan on a light dinner. Perhaps a large Greek salad, grilled chicken, and chocolate pie. How's that?" asked Lillian.

"Works for me. I'm going to call Grant and ask him to join us. We can fill her in on everything that has happened with the case."

"And, you may learn something other than what we read in her letters," added Lillian.

"That would be good. I'm ready to wind this up so our lives can get back to normal."

Lillian sighed. "Exactly, but what is normal, Jake?"

He thought for a minute.

"You tell me as soon as you figure it out."

Lillian thoughtfully said, "Let's see, John Ortberg wrote about that in his book, *Everybody's Normal Til You Get to Know Them.*"

Jake laughed, "I think he hit the nail on the head. Goodbye, Mom, see you later tonight."

"Goodbye. Love you," said Lillian.

* * * * *

LATER THAT EVENING, after the meal, Grant, Jake, Lana, and Lillian were seated comfortably in front of a warm fire discussing the case. Bill volunteered to clear the table and serve coffee and dessert while the others talked. Eli obviously remembered Lana and had not left her side since she had arrived.

Lillian began the conversation.

"How, exactly did you and Sheila get to know one another?"

"Sheila came to me for advice after having been treated in the hospital. It was one of the times Jonathan had beaten her up," said Lana.

"I see."

"Was that before or after they adopted Michael?" asked Grant.

"It was after although she told me he had caused her to be hospitalized more than once before they adopted the baby."

"I don't understand how they managed to adopt a child if she had been hospitalized because of her husband's abusive nature," stated Jake.

"Since both of them wanted a baby, they became quite good at covering up what was going on at home," said Lana.

"Do you think she thought that, perhaps, Jonathan would change if they had a baby?" asked Grant.

"She told me that during one of our meetings," said Lana, "and it did during the adoption process. After the adoption, however, the abuse returned and kept getting worse and more frequent."

"I'm sure she had to worry about the baby, too," said Lillian.

"The baby was her whole life," said Lana. "I don't think I've ever seen a mother treasure a child as much as she."

"Did she have any family who could help her?" asked Jake.

"No, and that made it worse. She thought she had the baby's future covered, though," said Lana.

"How so?" asked Grant.

"She named me his custodian in her will," said Lana. "She feared for her life and wanted to know the child would be safe if anything happened to her."

"Did Jonathan know about her will?" asked Grant.

"I don't think so, but I can't say that for sure," said Lana.

"It sounds as though you two became very close, closer than normal for an attorney/client relationship," said Lillian.

"We became quite good friends even though we didn't see each other often after Michael's death," said Lana. "Now, I wish I had been more diligent than I was."

"You can't blame yourself for any of this," said Jake. "Under normal conditions, the lake is a safe place to live. Grant and his team do an excellent job of screening out those who shouldn't be here." He nodded toward Grant.

Grant smiled and then said, "Thanks, Jake. I appreciate your faith in what we do here at the lake, but even though the men and women in my department do their jobs well, I'm inclined to think that whoever the murderer is, he or she is probably someone we all know and trust right here in this neighborhood."

Even though he was in the kitchen, acting like a waiter, Bill listened to the question and answer session occurring around the dining room table.

"I tend to agree with you, Grant," he said as he entered with a tray of cookies and drinks." He set the tray on the table and sat down to join the others.

"I'm beginning to think that also," said Lillian. "I'm so glad you boys are staying here with us."

"Well, it's getting late, so Jake, would you mind driving me back to my hotel?" asked Lana. "I'll meet with the M. E. tomorrow morning and get back with you before I leave town."

She turned to Lillian and Bill. "I want to thank you two for everything you're doing. Let me know if you need me to take Eli off your hands."

"Don't even think about it," said Lillian. "Eli and I are good friends now. Can't think of losing him."

As if Eli understood the conversation, he stood up and walked over to stand by Lillian.

Lana laughed, "I guess Eli doesn't want to move back to the city."

"No, he's happy here," said Bill. "Country life's good for him."

Lana and Jake departed. As they rounded the curve in the street, Jake picked up his phone and called Grant.

"Hello," said Grant.

"It's me," said Jake. "Why don't you do a perimeter walk around the house. "I would swear I saw someone in my rear view mirror standing beneath the deck."

"Will do."

* * * * *

GRANT PUNCHED OFF his cell phone and announced to Lillian and Bill. "I'm going to walk around the house, make sure all is quiet before we lock up for the evening."

"Thanks, Grant. I think I'll go to bed," said Lillian, "I'm tired."

"Me, too," said Bill and then added, "Are you going to wait up for Jake?"

"That's probably a good idea. Goodnight, you two." Grant stepped outside and into the dark of night.

Chapter 14

JAKE RETURNED FROM taking Lana back to her hotel. He parked his car and was climbing the stairs to the deck when he heard someone groan. He hurriedly retraced his steps, turned on his flashlight. Following the sounds of distress, he found Grant beneath the deck. Grant was trying to sit up but falling back after each attempt.

"Damn, what happened to you?" asked Jake.

"You were right. Someone was out here." Grant rubbed the back of his neck.

"Let's get you in the house and see what kind of damage you've suffered." Jake helped Grant stand and climb the steps to the deck.

"Quietly. I don't want to awaken your parents. Let's keep this between us."

"Good idea."

Jake quietly opened the front door, led his friend to Bill's recliner, and helped him sit down. "I guess it's a good thing we decided to stay here."

Grant tried to nod in agreement. "I do believe someone has it in for them."

"You might have a concussion," said Jake, obviously concerned at Grant's discomfort.

"I don't think I was knocked completely out."

"Yeah, yeah, like there's a difference between being sorta knocked out and completely knocked out. You don't have to lose consciousness to have a concussion. How long do you think you were out there?"

"I had walked around the house, checked the garage and the storage building, and was just coming back around to the front deck when everything went black," said Grant. "It couldn't have been more than a minute or two before you showed up."

"Well, I don't know about that," said Jake. "It took me longer than two minutes to drive Lana to her hotel and then back here."

"Did you see anyone leave?"

"No," said Jake. "If you were attacked right after I left, you've been unconscious at least twenty to thirty minutes. That's why I think it might be a good idea to get you checked out."

"That will have to wait until tomorrow." Grant squared his shoulders. He made eye contact with Jake, "Right now, let's you and I talk about something. . ."

He paused to breathe in and out. Jake took advantage of Grant's hesitation.

"That we probably should have talked about a long time ago, I think," said Jake.

"You're right. I've never let you explain your side of the story about Alice." He rolled his shoulders. "And I blamed you for everything."

"We need to talk, but right now, I think you need to take care of yourself and get some rest. Will you trust me when I promise to tell you everything?"

"I know you, Jake. I may get mad at you, and I do tend to hold grudges, but maybe you're right. This isn't the time. I'll be waiting to hear your side of the story."

"And tell you I will, but, Grant, afterward, I want us to still be friends like we've always been," Jake said as the two shook hands.

"Agreed," said Grant who managed to stand. He headed for the guest bedroom, the room that felt more like home than the one in his own house.

As Jake watched him walk away, he said a silent prayer that when he told Grant what had happened to Alice, Grant would be able to handle the truth. He also hoped the truth would not cause the bridge to crumble between Grant's relationship with Lillian and Bill. *I know how much you love my parents. I love them more and don't want them hurt, not by us anyway.*

* * * * *

AS THEY SAT around the breakfast table early the next morning, Lillian stated, "Okay, Grant, what happened to you last night after we went to bed?"

"What do you mean?" he asked as innocently as he could.

"I see that pump knot on the back of your head. Just how did you get that?"

"It's nothing. I just bumped into something in the dark before I went to bed," he lied.

Jake looked at him, laughed, and said, "I told him he was drinking too much."

Grant ducked his head but didn't respond to Jake's remark.

"You two have been covering for each other all your lives, so I won't ask you to lie anymore today." Lillian laughed.

"Mom, on a serious note, after Lana identifies the body, and we've talked to her about what kind of memorial service would be appropriate for Sheila, I'll give you a call. Please stay close to the house."

"I should be here all morning. I can't think of any reason I need to leave the house today. Don't worry about me." She kissed both her boys on their scruffy cheeks and sent them on their way. "Have a good day, you two."

"I think I'll grab my golf clubs, play a round," Bill announced.

"Why doesn't that surprise me?" She laughed. "Don't lose too many golf balls."

He pecked her on the forehead and headed out the door.

She looked down at Eli who sat by the pantry door. "I guess it's just you and me now, buddy. I know what you want."

She opened the cookie jar and pulled out a milk bone. "Shake." The dog, eager for his goodie, offered his paw. He took it gingerly from her hand, ran into the living room, found his favorite spot on the back of the sofa, and began to gnaw the treat.

Lillian hummed to herself as she straightened up the house. It dawned on her that she had not checked her emails for the last couple of days, so she sat down at her laptop and booted it up. She scanned her emails.

I'm glad I checked, or I would have forgotten about Mah Jongg. Don't want to miss that. Rachel is such a good hostess. She quickly deleted all of the junk mail and answered the three emails that needed a response.

For the first time in over a week, she felt that the rest of the day would be good. She looked forward to being with her friends later in the day. She decided to complete one of the daily crossword puzzles that were free on the internet and finished it quickly. She closed that game and clicked on computer solitaire. Playing computer games provided a challenge and helped her relax and think at the same time.

Okay, she thought, *I really need to quiz Rachel a little more. Maybe, she has thought of something else, something she didn't know she knew.*

The thought was cut short by the insistent ringing of her phone. The ring tone told Lillian the identity of the caller. She picked up the phone and said, "Hello, son."

"Mom, go ahead and call Reverend Hammon. Lana said he could contact her. She would be glad to give him everything he needs to know about Sheila."

"Oh, good. Thanks. I'll do that right now."

"Let him know he can reach her at the funeral home in about thirty minutes or so. She will be there making arrangements. The M.E. is releasing the body to her as I speak," said Jake.

"Wonderful. I'm so thankful you were able to contact Lana and that she is as concerned about a proper burial as you and I."

"I'm glad she came down. Her cooperation takes a burden off you."

"Jake, have I told you how proud I am of you?"

"Many times, Mom, many times."

"Remember it." Lillian ended the call.

Before contacting Don Hammon, Lillian paused to give thanks to the Lord for the life and resurrection of Sheila Davis. "And, Lord, be sure that Sheila sees her baby boy first. Amen."

* * * * *

LILLIAN HAD JUST finished relaying Jake's message to the reverend when she heard the ambulance siren.

"Sounds too close for comfort," she said to Eli who had finished his milk bone and had gone to the kitchen for water. He ran to the newly repaired front window and began his too familiar growl.

"I'm learning, Eli. When you make that sound, evil is close by."

He responded with a loud bark. "Yes, I know you do understand every word."

The phone rang. Again, she recognized the number.

"Hello, son. Again."

Dispensing with formalities, he began giving instructions. "Good. You're home. Make sure all the doors are locked. Where's dad?"

"Where do you think?"

"Playing golf, of course. Call the Pro Shop. He needs to get home now."

"What's so urgent, Jake?"

"There's been another murder, and it's too close to you."

"Who was it this time?"

"Can't explain. I'm in my car on my way to the lake now." In the background, Lillian heard the siren coming through the phone as Jake turned it on.

"Be careful."

"Will do. Now, do what I've told you."

"Okay."

"Talk to you later."

Lillian hung up the phone and immediately dialed the number of the club's grill. She spoke out loud to the dog. "If Bill and the guys are finished with the eighteenth, they sometimes stop by the bar for a drink." Eli tilted his head sideways and listened to her logic.

The person on duty answered on the second ring.

"Hello, this is Lillian Prestridge. Would you please look around the grill and let me know if my husband Bill is there?"

"Yes, ma'am. Do you need to talk to him?"

"Yes, I do."

"Hold on a minute."

"Sure. Thank you."

A minute later, the voice she wanted to hear said, "Hello?"

"Bill, darling, Jake just called. He said you need to come home now, right now."

"Why?"

"There's been another murder."

"Who?"

"He didn't say."

"I'm on my way."

"Hurry."

Five minutes later, Lillian heard Bill's car pull into the garage. She ran to the back door and opened it. As he walked into the kitchen, the two soul mates grabbed each other, hugging until they felt the comfortable security of being in each other's embrace. Lillian broke away from Bill and said, "I can't imagine who it is, but Jake said it was too close to us."

"You'd better prepare yourself, dear."

"I know. I just hope it's not one of my Mah Jongg girls."

"Me, too."

More sirens could be heard. One, in particular had a familiar shrill.

"That may be Jake now. It sounds like the siren on his car. I heard it when we were on the phone."

"If it would make you feel better, why don't we call the girls, see if they're all right?"

"Good idea. I'll call Rachel and have her call Victoria. You call Margaret and ask her to call Sally Jane."

Lillian dialed Rachel's number and was relieved when she heard her friend answer.

"Listen, Rachel, I have only a minute. I'm calling to make sure you're okay."

"Why wouldn't I be?"

"There's been another murder."

"Oh no, not again. Who?"

"Don't know, but I'm calling all the girls to check on them."

"Do you need some help?"

"Yes. Would you call Victoria and check on her?"

"Glad to. I'll call you back after I talk to her."

"Great. Thanks."

Lillian hung up the phone and listened as Bill's conversation with Margaret mirrored hers with Rachel. Within minutes, her cell rang. Before she could answer, Bill's cell phone was vibrating on the table where he had placed it. Both Victoria and Rachel reported that Margaret and Sally Jane were okay.

"I suggest we pour ourselves a drink and wait to hear from our son."

"Maybe a drink will help calm me down. I'll get the glasses. You get the wine." Bill walked across the kitchen and opened the fridge. He retrieved a bottle of Clois du Bois.

Chapter 15

LILLIAN AND BILL sat side by side on the sofa watching the news on the television in their living room. They heard their back door open and close. Bill jumped up, grabbed the shotgun he had placed on the coffee table, ready to confront the intruder.

Both were relieved to hear Jake call out, "It's just me. I have my key."

Jake glared at the TV as he walked by and plopped down in the closest easy chair.

"Don't tell me. It's already on the local news, isn't it?"

"Afraid so. Is Grant with you?" Bill asked.

"No, if you stay tuned, you should be able to see his interview in a minute. When I left him, Jan Tomlin from the local television station was questioning him about the latest victim out here."

"There he is now." Lillian pointed to the screen. The three watched the interview, and during a commercial break, she asked, "How did you manage to escape the scene?"

"I kept a low profile, watched every gawker who walked down Pecan Street."

"When you said close, you meant it. I'm afraid to ask the identity of the victim."

"I hate to tell you."

"Might as well get it over with," Bill said.

Lillian heard Grant as he spoke to the reporter.

Even though Grant did not reveal the identity of the victim to the reporter, Lillian knew. "Oh no, not Mr. Peters. Surely, not." Pause. "This is my fault. He saw me run away from Stella's house."

"Think about what you're saying, Mom."

"She doesn't have to. I get it."

"Now you know why your house was burglarized."

Bill nodded. "Yes. Whoever killed Mr. Peters knew he was watching you."

"And, if he saw me," her voice trembled, "then he also saw the person who frightened me. How was he killed?"

Jake ignored her question. "I'd say whoever committed this crime, got ahead of himself. When Grant interviewed Mr. Peters, the old guy couldn't identify the culprit who watched you. He gave only a sketchy description." Jake looked at his mother to make sure she understood the seriousness of the situation.

"I had already removed the papers he was probably looking for, so he followed me home and came here to get them."

"When I interrupted his search, he bonked me on the head," Bill stated.

"Bingo."

Lillian picked up the remote and turned off the television. "How soon do you think Grant can get away?"

"Don't know, but I'd say he'll be there for at least another hour or so. Crime scene has been secured, and the body has been removed." Jake stood to leave.

"Where are you going?"

"Have to meet the victim's son at the morgue. I notified the family right after I arrived on the scene."

"Grant didn't mention any names during the interview," Lillian said.

"Word will filter out. His son lives in Dallas. We didn't want him to hear about it on the news or be bombarded by reporters. I sent a deputy to the office where he works. The deputy said he's taking it pretty hard." Jake paused to listen to a message coming through the radio clipped to the collar of his uniform.

He snapped off the receiver and stood to leave.

"How can I help? I feel so guilty." Lillian said.

"By staying inside, Mom."

He made eye contact with his father. "Don't let her beat herself up over this. And don't wait up for us. Grant and I will be coming home late tonight."

Bill followed him to the back door. "Be alert, son. Don't let anything happen to you." He locked the door and went back to Lillian, but she was not in the living room. He turned as she walked out of the bedroom. "Now, Lillian."

"Don't 'now, Lillian' me," she said as she buckled her belt. She attached the holster holding her new thirty-eight revolver. "No one is coming through that door tonight except our sons."

Bill turned and walked away.

"Where do you think you're going?" Lillian said.

"To get my nine millimeter."

Eli began his low, menacing growl. As if on cue, the doorbell rang. "It's me, Lillian," yelled Victoria. "Let us in. We're here to help." The dog barked at the sound of the familiar voice.

Lillian opened the door. There stood Victoria and Rachel, shotguns in hand. "Hurry, come in." She locked the door as soon as her friends were inside. Bill walked in carrying a shotgun in one hand and his handgun in the other.

"Glory be. Will wonders never cease?" said Victoria as she laughed. "I'd say we're locked and loaded. Didn't know you had a gun, Lillian."

"Yep, let'em come. I'm mad."

"Well, since we're all here, and it will be a long night, let's try to relax," Bill said. "We're going to have to gear down. If Grant and Jake come home sooner than they thought, we don't need to over react. It would be tragic if one of us accidentally shot one of them."

"True, but how do you propose we calm down when there's a murderer running loose in our neighborhood?" asked Rachel.

Bill did not respond, but Lillian did.

"Let's all take a deep breath and have a seat."

"I'm staying close to the door so I can hear anything that goes on outside," said Victoria. She looked at Rachel. "You sit over there." She motioned to indicate a dining room chair that was aligned with the back door. "Keep watch. Make sure no one tries to get in the back."

Lillian realized her friends were ready to wage war and knew she had to get them to relax. "I'm going to make a pot of tea. A good cup of calming tea ought to do the trick."

Bill sat down in his recliner and watched the women take their assigned positions. No one said a word as they waited for the promised tea. When Lillian returned with a tray holding a pot of the hot brew, cups and saucers, and a plate of cookies, Bill cleared his throat to speak.

"Ladies, I've been thinking," he began.

"What about?" asked Victoria.

"I think you girls need to postpone any future Mah Jongg meetings until Jake and Grant get to the bottom of what's going on here at the lake."

"Surely, you jest," said Victoria. "It may take weeks to discover who's committing these crimes."

"Of course, we're going to continue our weekly Mah Jongg," said Lillian. "No one is going to scare us away from our routine."

"Right," Rachel said. "Remember, we meet at my house on Friday."

The self-appointed Leisure Lake posse laid their guns on the floor beside their chairs while their hostess served each of them. By midnight, tired from analyzing the meager facts they had about the murders and getting nowhere, the four were sound asleep.

Eli's bark woke Lillian and her friends.

Someone was coming through the back door.

Jake and Grant walked into the living room. They faced two ladies holding shotguns, their mother pointing her thirty-eight, a dignified gentleman aiming his nine millimeter, and a white poodle yelping, wagging his tail, and bolting across the room. He reached Jake and dispensed several slurpy doggy kisses.

"Stand down, everyone. We're too tired to die tonight," said Grant with a big grin on his face. "Glad to see you all, too."

Chapter 16

LANA PERRAULT AND Reverend Don Hammon had planned a graveside memorial service for Sheila Davis in the prestigious, historic cemetery near Leisure Lake. The sacred land in which Sheila's body would rest for eternity had, for the last century, allowed only the descendants of the town's founding families to repose among a stand of ancient oaks. The staid power brokers of the town consigned all others, especially those unknown to them, who needed a final home, to the hot sunny meadow on the other side of town. According to them, it was a more "contemporary environment," completely appropriate for the deceased. Therefore, Lillian knew it was quite a coup for Lana to negotiate the plot's acquisition with officials of the proud, antebellum community, as well as a testament to her legal expertise.

Victoria, Margaret, Rachel, and Bill were all seated on the back row of folding chairs set up by the funeral home. Lillian, next to Bill, sat on the aisle seat. Eli, fresh from the groomer, regally sat next to his new owner, on guard, watching, nose twitching.

Large, ancient, gnarled oak trees provided a rich shade for the attendees. A short distance from the seating area, the funeral director had set up a tall tripod on which a small jam box perched. Its melodies, unlike those of Chanticleer, wafted soft, solemn, dirges through the towering foliage.

Over and above the sound of the hymns, all other noises seemed to be muffled by the greatness of the outdoors. The sighing waves of the wind slinking through the tree branches, the humming of passing cars on the highway parallel to the wrought iron fence and its prisoners identified only by the markers above their heads, and even the roaring of a jet plane overhead seemed far, far away to Lillian. Subconsciously, she absorbed them all. On guard, ever watchful, both she and the poodle beside her took note of everyone who showed up for the memorial.

Rachel leaned forward so she could whisper to Lillian, "I'm watching everyone, too. I'll let you know if I see someone who seems out of place."

Lillian nodded an acknowledgment but said nothing in response to Rachel's comment, but thought *after today everyone will know that Stella was only an alias. But at least one person won't show any surprise at her name. I need to observe all reactions to this news.*

She nudged Bill and whispered, "I need to walk Eli around for awhile." As an afterthought, she added, "Save my seat." Rachel and Bill both nodded an assent while continuing their vigilant surveillance of the crowd.

Lillian smiled and greeted several of the lake's residents she recognized and merely nodded to those she didn't know as she led the dog around the area and stopped beneath a large oak tree adjacent to the seating area. *To have been relatively new at the lake, Sheila either made quite a few friends, or we have some really nosey people who live out at the lake.*

She noticed that Jake and Grant had positioned themselves on the other side of the grave site, a spot where they could watch without being conspicuous. *Smart, she thought, they are in plain clothes today. I'll stand where I can see them as well as the audience.*

The funeral director turned off the canned music. Silence. *Need to pay close attention now. Watch everyone.* Lillian tightened her hold on Eli's leash. The dog strained against the lead. She heard his familiar low growl, a sure sign of danger. "Shh, shh. Heel, Eli," she bent and whispered to the dog. "Everything's okay. I've got you." He obeyed her command, but she noticed a ridge of hair down his back. Each tendril stood on end.

Reverend Hammon rose and walked slowly to the podium to deliver the eulogy. He began with a recitation of Sheila's full name, her birthdate, and date of her untimely death. He paused and looked at the audience, There was a slightly audible collective buzz when he read her name. Obviously, most of those present had not anticipated that the name Stella Dallas would be an alias for Sheila Davis. The Reverend waited until he saw Lillian's nod. Then he regained the audience's attention and continued.

There were only two faces in the crowd – those of a dark-haired woman and a tall gentleman -- who did not seem to be surprised. She knew neither of them but memorized their features. The woman, back stiff, face dour, looked bored. The man's shoulders sagged, and the lines etched in his face revealed a deep, painful sadness.

After the service, Lillian listened to the hushed hum of voices as people began to greet one another. She could tell that to most of the lake residents, Sheila was indeed a puzzle. Questions like

Who was she?
Did you know her?
Had you met her?
Did you ever see her at the club?
How long had she been living at the lake?

were being passed back and forth. Having already asked herself those same questions, Lillian was far more interested in any answers to them that she might overhear. But none came, only more questions, so she turned her attention elsewhere.

* * * * *

RACHEL HAD KEPT her eyes on the tall dark-haired woman who sat all by herself and spoke to no one. *I remember you,* Rachel thought as the woman stood and made eye contact with her, *but you* *had blond hair the last time I saw you.* The woman quickly glanced away and turned to walk toward the drive lined with parked cars.

Rachel waved a greeting and caught Lillian's attention. She titled her head to the side and discreetly pointed to the woman to let her cohort know that she would follow the lady.

Lillian nodded and mouthed the words, "Be careful."

* * * * *

DETERMINED TO MEET the tall gentleman, Lillian positioned herself so he would have to come by her as he exited the area. The man's gait was slow, and he walked as if he had the weight of the whole world on his shoulders. Lillian noticed that the gray pinstriped suit he wore had lapels and sleeves that indicated it had seen better days. The unbuttoned coat hung loosely, and the trousers, held up by a tightly cinched belt, were clearly too large for him.

As he approached, Eli bellowed a warning and lunged. Lillian struggled to hold him back. "Down, Eli. Sit," she commanded and kept the leash taut as she stuck out her hand and said, "Good afternoon, I'm Lillian Prestridge. You'll have to forgive my dog."

"Quite a guard dog, you have there." The man kept his distance. *Eli doesn't like you. I wonder why.*

"Yes, he is, but as you see, he follows commands quite well." Eli had sat down when commanded to do so, but the ridge down his back still stood at attention. She continued. "I didn't know Sheila very well, but I live around the corner from where she lived. Are you a friend of hers?"

Eli had stopped his low growl, so the man risked reaching out to take her hand. He gave it a brief shake and said, "Good afternoon, ma'am. I'm Jonathan Davis."

Lillian froze. *So you're the husband I read about in the news clipping.* Recovering quickly, she posed, "Oh, you must be a relative."

"No and yes, ma'am," he said politely. "Sheila and I were once married," he explained.

"I'm so sorry about Sheila," said Lillian. "Please accept my condolences."

"I had not seen her in years but was saddened by her death just the same. Thank you," he said as he turned to leave with shoulders slumped. The minute he walked away, Eli ceased his soft growl, and the furry ridge on his back relaxed.

Lillian looked around and saw that Jake had watched the exchange between her and Jonathan. She motioned for him and started walking toward him. When Jake reached her, she said, "That man's Jonathan Davis, Sheila's ex-husband."

"Thanks, I'll follow him," said Jake. He hurried away so he could catch up with the man.

* * * * *

JONATHAN HAD NOT heard the exchange between Lillian and the young man, but when he looked over his shoulder, he saw the stranger pursuing him. He quickened his pace and then began to run. Jake, too, broke into a trot.

* * * * *

FROM ACROSS THE street, Grant saw the incident and raced to his squad car. He revved the cruiser's engine to life, beeped his warning signal to stop other drivers, and scooted across the thoroughfare. He slammed on the brakes and skidded to a stop blocking the exit of the narrow ornate cemetery gate leading to the sidewalk. He jumped out of the car as Jonathan reached it.

"Stop," he commanded. Like Eli, the man obeyed instructions. "There's no need for you to run away."

"I haven't done anything. Why'd you stop me?"

His pursuer arrived, bent over, hands on knees, and took several deep breaths.

"You okay?" Grant placed his hand on Jake's right shoulder.

"Yeah. Let me catch my breath."

After a few more gulps of air, he began. "There was no need for you to run from me."

"Hey, man, my ex-wife's been murdered, and when I see a stranger tailing me, I don't wait around to meet him."

"I just want to talk to you."

"Why? What'd you want from me?"

"To begin with, I couldn't help but overhear your conversation with my mother. Please accept my condolences for your loss."

"Thank you, and you are?"

"My name is Jake Prestridge. I'm the county sheriff." He extended his right hand.

Jonathan shook it. "I see." He paused and then glared at Grant. "Who's your sidekick here? He nearly ran over me."

"I'd like you also to meet Grant Perryman. He's the security chief at Leisure Lake."

"That's where Sheila lived, isn't it?"

"Yes, it is."

Jonathan looked from one man to the other and finally announced to Grant, "I'm glad you stopped me." He reached out to shake hands.

Grant didn't respond but retained his official pose, arms folded across his chest, a permanent scowl on his face.

Jake continued his introduction. "I'm the leading investigator in the murder of Sheila Davis. Officer Perryman is working with me."

"I would like to know more about what happened to Sheila," Jonathan said turning back to Jake.

"Good to hear that, Mr. Davis," said Jake. "Would you mind coming over to my office so we can talk in private? That is, if it's okay with you?" The sheriff looked at Grant for confirmation.

"Sure, that's fine with me. I'd like to get to know more about Sheila and you as well, Mr. Davis. I'm eager to wind up this case."

"Where is your office, Sheriff? I'll catch a taxi and meet you there."

"That won't be necessary, Mr. Davis. I have my car right here. You can ride with me."

"Okay," said Jonathan.

Grant opened the back door to the cruiser, and he and Jake crawled in and settled down in the front seat.

* * * * *

GRANT DECIDED TO drive slowly through town to give him and Jake time for casual conversation with Jonathan about Sheila. If Jonathan didn't feel like he was being interrogated, he might reveal more about their lives.

At first, the ex-husband was not receptive, but as they drove along together, Grant pointed out landmarks in the town, and Jonathan began to relax somewhat. When Grant parked in front of the courthouse, Jonathan looked as though he wanted to cut and run again.

"Take it easy, buddy," said Grant. "You're not in trouble."

"Courthouses and I just don't seem to get along." He sighed. "Nothing good ever happened to me in one."

"Well, consider this a new start, Mr. Davis."

"Is that possible, you think?"

Grant looked in his rearview mirror and made eye contact with the pitiable creature in the back seat for a moment before answering.

"I know it is. I've done it myself." Then, after a quick glance at his fellow front seat passenger, he continued. "Jake and I have been working hard on this case and have run into a dead end. Hopefully, you have some information that might help us."

"I don't think I can be of much help. . .you see, I've been away for a number of years."

Jake opened the car door and stepped out. He walked to the back door and opened it. "Come on into my office. I think it's best if we talk in private, and I'll explain why when we get there."

He unlocked his office and stepped inside with the two men following him. "Would either of you like some coffee?" he asked.

"Don't mind if I do," responded Grant. "Do you have any hazelnut blend?"

Jake laughed and looked over his shoulder at the man whose whole countenance oozed grief. "You'd think a big hulk like Grant wouldn't want any of the frou-frou stuff, wouldn't you."

Jonathan smiled. "Well, to tell you the truth, I kind of like flavored coffee, too, though I've not had the privilege of enjoying it these last few years."

"Well, I just happened to have some, so hazelnut it is."

The sheriff opened the louvered doors on the wall opposite his desk and revealed a small kitchenette. He began preparing the coffee while the other two men settled down in the leather arm chairs around the small table in front of Jake's desk.

Grant looked at Jonathan, sized him up, decided to test his honesty. "Mr. Davis," he began, "you were about to tell me where you've been just before we got out of the car. Do you mind continuing?"

"Not at all. You see, I made a horrible mistake when I was much younger," Jonathan's eyes began to tear up.

"Go on," urged Grant gruffly, not feeling any sympathy for a man who beat his wife and killed an innocent child.

"First, let me say that Sheila and I had a wonderful marriage for many years."

"What happened?"

Jonathan opened his mouth to answer the question, but Jake, tray in hand, interrupted the conversation. He set the tray containing a carafe, sugar bowl, creamer, and three cups on the table. After pouring coffee into each of the cups, he passed them around.

"If you need sugar or cream, here's a community spoon." He laughed. "Don't worry. It's clean. Washed it myself."

Grant watched as Jonathan dosed his coffee with three spoons of sugar and stirred slowly. He picked up the cup, and after the first swallow of the brew, closed his eyes, obviously savoring the flavor of hazelnut and rich half-and-half creamer.

Jonathan opened his eyes, blushed for a moment, and asked, "You guys treat all your prisoners like this?"

Jake laughed. "What do you think?"

Jonathan let that question go.

Looking back at Grant, he said, "To answer your previous question: I ruined our marriage and any chance of happiness for Sheila. I started drinking heavily after I lost my job. Bills started piling up. We argued and then began fighting. It wasn't pretty."

"Mr. Davis, we know about the baby's death," said Grant. "Can you tell us what happened?"

Tears rolled down his cheeks. Jonathan wiped them away with the back of his hand, took a deep breath. "Sheila left him with me while she went to buy groceries. I rocked Michael to sleep while I watched a football game on TV. Instead of placing him in his crib in his room, I laid him on the sofa, opened a six pack, and sat down beside him." Jonathan paused.

"I can tell this is hard for you to relive," said Jake softly, "but if you can, it might help to get some of it off your chest."

Grant thought, *Oh yeah, you are your mother's son. You sound just like her. And that's a good thing right now. I'll let you take it from here. You'll get more out of him than I can. I'd just as soon beat him to a pulp. So far as I'm concerned, he's scum. His crocodile tears are worthless. Just ask Michael.*

Jonathan continued.

"I woke up when I heard Sheila screaming. Michael was on the floor. I was so drunk I didn't know when he rolled off the sofa. Poor little thing never regained consciousness. I'll never forgive myself for that."

"But surely that was an accident, not worthy of a prison sentence," said Jake.

"You have to understand," said Jonathan, "Sheila blamed me for Michael's death, and because of my past treatment of her, it didn't take the jury long to find me guilty, especially when the prosecutor provided evidence of the times I caused her visits to the hospital. I tend to agree with the jury. I deserved my sentence."

Jake sat silent for a moment and then asked, "So, do you feel you've changed as a result of your prison sentence?"

Jonathan nodded. "I don't know what I would have done had the prison chaplain not been there for me. You see, he headed up an AA meeting in the prison."

"That must have been Father Kelly," said Jake. "I've read about his prison ministry and how effective it is."

"He ministers to those who are down and out," added Grant. "Unlike some of us, he thinks everyone can be reformed."

"Well, all I know is that he helped me."

"How so?"

"He told me God is more forgiving of our sins than we are. It took me a long time to believe him and then even longer to believe in myself. I go for weeks at a time when I really hate myself for the things I've done."

Grant looked at Jake and said, "Sometimes, we humans hold grudges far too long."

The three men sat silently and sipped their coffee. Grant asked the next rhetorical question, another test for honesty.

"When were you released from prison?"

"Two months ago."

Jake nodded. "Jonathan, tell me this. Did you know that Sheila had moved to the lake before or after your release?"

Jonathan thought for a moment. "After."

"Who told you about her?"

"I contacted an old friend of mine at our church. He didn't want to talk to me, but I convinced him I meant her no harm. He finally told me she had moved. I believe she moved out there about eight or nine months ago, but I'm not sure about the date."

"You have any contact with her at all?" asked Grant.

"As a matter of fact I did," admitted Jonathan. "As soon as I could, I tried to telephone her to see if I could meet her someplace, but she didn't want to talk to me."

"Did that make you angry?" asked Jake.

"No. As a matter of fact, I told her I understood why she felt the way she did."

"Why did you contact her?" asked Grant. "The divorce took place years ago. I would think you would want to forget the past and start over."

"I don't expect you to understand."

"We'll try," said Jake.

"Help us out here," Grant said.

"Well, I guess I wanted further absolution. I wanted her to know how sorry I am for everything. . . for all the pain I caused her. . .and especially about the baby."

Silence. Jake and Grant waited for him to continue.

"But I guess that won't happen now," said Jonathan sadly.

"One other question," said Grant, "how did you know about the memorial service?"

"Lana Perrault. She called me."

"Wasn't she Sheila's attorney?" asked Jake.

"Yes, but she works with Father Kelly in the prison ministry program," said Jonathan. "She's a good woman."

Jake and Grant glanced at each other when Jonathan stated that Lana Perrault was a "good woman." Jake stood up and poured Jonathan another cup of coffee.

"Would you excuse us for a moment?"

"Sure."

Grant followed the sheriff out into the hallway. "Good woman, my..."

"Don't even say it, Grant. I feel the same way, too. It seems as though our little attorney wasn't quite as open as she wanted us to think she was," said Jake. "We need to talk to her before she leaves town."

"We'll get back to that, but in the. . ."

"But in the meantime, we have no evidence that links Jonathan to Sheila's murder," added Jake.

"Furthermore, he doesn't match the description of the person who broke into Sheila's house either," Grant said.

"Let's find out where he's living now and tell him we may have to talk to him again."

Both men walked back into the office. As they stepped through the door, Jake held up his hand to halt Grant. Jonathan was still seated at the table with his head bowed. The man's lips moved as if in prayer. They waited respectfully until he raised his head.

"Jonathan, you may go now. Just let us know where you are living and how to get in touch with you," said Grant.

Jake handed him a legal pad. "Write down your address and phone number if you have one. Also, write down where we can reach you at work in case we need to."

"I can't talk on the phone at work, but they will take a message and give it to me, and I can call you later. Is that all right with you?"

"That'll be okay," said Grant. "By the way, if you don't have a car, how did you get here from Dallas?"

"I rode the bus." Jonathan glanced at his watch. "And I think one leaves in about thirty minutes, so I do need to get to the bus station."

"I'll drop you off on my way out of town," offered Grant.

"Thanks, I'd appreciate that."

Chapter 17

JAKE STOOD AT the window and watched Grant and Jonathan climb into the car. He also glanced across the street and saw Eli parked at the doggy station in front of the Corner Bakery. His mom sat at a table facing the street. It looked as though she stared straight at him. *I see you, Mom, watching the courthouse.* Grant's car pulled away from the curb and eased on down the street. Jake began counting and chuckled when he saw her rummage through her purse and pull out her cell phone.

* * * * *

"**WHOM ARE YOU** calling?" asked Bill.

"Our son."

Bill heard their order number called. He walked to the counter to pick up their food. Returning to their table, he set down their tray.

"I got you a Diet Coke. Is that okay?"

"Of course." She picked up the Styrofoam container and took a sip. She held the phone to her ear, listening to its ring.

"Why are you calling him?" he mumbled while chewing on the first big bite of his cheeseburger.

"Don't talk with food in your mouth."

"Don't try to change the subject by attacking my eating habits. Answer my question, please."

"I just saw Grant with Sheila's ex-husband in tow leave the courthouse."

"I do wish you'd mind your own business and let the boys do their jobs."

"I can't. They need my help. This case has them totally baffled."

"I'm afraid you might get hurt. Listen to me. Haven't you learned anything?"

Listening to the ringing of Jake's phone, she grumbled, "Pick up, son, pick up." And then it dawned on her that Bill had asked a question. "What do you mean what haven't I learned?"

"Oh, just the matter of our house being shot up, my being attacked in our own home, Mr. Peters being killed. . .not to mention the fact that the boys and all your friends are worried. . .little things like that. I don't want you to be the next victim."

She dismissed his cautionary words and ignored the look of concern on her husband's face. She looked directly at the window of her son's office and mouthed the words, "I know you're in there."

"Hi, Mom. I see you across the street. I guess you saw Grant leave my office."

"Caught. Again. Your dad and I are eating a healthy meal. Why don't you come over and visit with us?"

"Okay. I know what that tone of voice means."

She laughed. "Okay, my smart, intelligent son, enlighten your mother."

"It means get your ass over here right now."

"Correct. So?"

"So, I'm on my way." He locked up his office and walked across the street.

* * * * *

AS HE REACHED for the door handle to enter the bakery, Rachel walked around the corner.

"Hi, Jake. How are you?" she said cheerfully.

Oh, yeah, all the little Mah Jongg ladies will find their way here today. Guess I'm in for a grilling.

"I'm great. Have you been beating up my mom playing Mah Jongg?"

"You know I'm not any good, but lately, I think my luck has changed." She laughed.

"Oh now, Rachel, never say it's luck. . . it's skill, don't you know." He held the door open for her.

"I'll try to remember that. Oh look, there's your parents. Guess we all had the same idea."

I wonder who orchestrated this gathering.

Rachel and Jake placed their orders, took their numbered receipts, and joined Lillian and Bill at their table. Just as they were sitting down, Victoria walked in.

Yep, here they come, meandering in, one at a time.

As he predicted, Victoria ordered and then joined them. She got right to the point. "Okay, Jake, I saw you and Grant running down that man after the memorial service. Who was he, pray tell?"

"He was Sheila's ex-husband," Lillian chimed in.

Jake frowned and said, "Mom, I wish you wouldn't just broadcast information. You don't know who might be listening."

Again, she ignored his cautionary comment. "Come on, son, you know we'll all learn his identity soon enough."

He shrugged but didn't say a word. Looked at his father for help.

Bill shook his head. "It's no use. She won't listen to me either."

True to form, Lillian continued, "Did you learn anything about him when you and Grant talked to him?"

"Not anything relevant," replied Jake.

"Relevance, smelevance, he wouldn't tell us anything if he had," snorted Victoria. She dismissed Jake and turned to Rachel. "Aren't we meeting at your house this coming week?"

"Yes, we are, and I hope everyone can come. I'm feeling lucky," Rachel responded. "I found some cute paper plates and napkins with Mah Jongg tiles imprinted on them. Can't wait for everyone to see them."

"I'm sure those will bring you a little luck. You'll need it. I've been practicing this week. Have the tiles on my dining table and have been playing for all four people. . .pretending the different players are we. . .and I've won every round."

"How absurd is that?"

Before Victoria could make a rebuttal, Lillian steered the conversation back to her favorite topic: solving a murder.

"Rachel, you said you were keeping your eye on the tall brunette at the memorial service."

"I did watch her."

"Did you learn anything?"

"Not really. You know, there was just something about her that I could not put my finger on."

"Like what?" asked Victoria.

Rachel rubbed her eyes. "I know I've seen her before but not with short brown hair. I think she was wearing a wig."

"Well, besides the hair, do you remember anything else about her?" asked Victoria.

Jake enjoyed listening to the women talk. As a child growing up in Dallas, he would sit quietly playing with his *Star Wars* toys on the floor and later as a teenager pretend to be reading while his mom and her friends played Mah Jongg. They often forgot he was present. He learned a great deal about life just listening to their gossip.

He did that now, hoping these women would forget about him, let him off the hook. He realized his father was doing the same, silently eating his French fries. He watched as Rachel tried to force her brain to recall lost information. A widow, she was the calm one of the group. Then, he watched Victoria who had, in his opinion, given up on her curly, unruly hair. He did not recall ever seeing her without a headband. It was pulled back with one now failing miserably to control the bouncing curls.

Jake ceased his musings when he heard Rachel say, "I am pretty sure I have visited with her at the lake, maybe as a newcomer." She paused. "Lillian, did you get a good look at her face?"

"Yes, and I agree with you. She looks like someone I know but who? I can't quite place her."

"I talked to Grant before going to the memorial today," said Rachel.

"What about if I may ask?" said Lillian.

"He asked me to meet with him before the end of the week so the two of us can go over all of my newcomer lists and files. Maybe, hopefully, something will pop out that we've missed."

"There are our numbers, Rachel. I'll get our tray," said Jake. He returned with their food, and they all sat quietly for awhile, eating. *Okay, ladies. Who's next?*

It was Victoria. "I just remembered something."

"About Sheila?" Jake asked.

"No. It's about my sister-in-law. She's planning to visit us next week."

"What's that got to do with anything?" Bill finally entered the conversation.

"I don't know exactly when she will arrive; she's always vague about that. I may have to get a sub for Mah Jongg."

"Oh, no," said Lillian. "Don't ask Sally Jane. She's just too nosey. Last time we played with her, you'd think we were playing Twenty Questions."

"Now that's the pot calling the kettle black if I ever heard it," said Bill. He and Jake both had a good laugh. Lillian just glared.

* * * * *

LILLIAN'S POSITION AT the table gave her a clear view of the street. All during their conversation, she periodically glanced out the window to make sure her dog was okay. She could not hear him bark, but when she saw Eli rise on all fours wagging his tail, she knew he had seen someone he knew.

And, my sweet boy, who is coming down the sidewalk. Whom are you eager to see?

The passerby – a tall, slender woman wearing a tight black dress and a wide-brimmed straw hat -- gave him a wide birth in order to look into the bakery's window. The dog's tail drooped. He turned around and slinked back to his post. *Disappointed, are you, Eli?*

Lillian stood. "Excuse me," she said to the group gathered around her table. "I need to check on Eli, make sure he has plenty of water."

As Lillian approached the door, she saw the woman quickly turn away from the window and sprint down the sidewalk. *I saw the frown on your face before you spun around. I wonder why you are so interested in what's going on in here.* By the time Lillian stepped outside, the woman was half a block away, back turned. Lillian took note of the elegant dress the woman wore, the three-inch heels sporting a wide, gemstone studded buckle, and the hat that obscured her hair. *Who are you?*

The dog's barks were drawing attention from other walkers, so Lillian reached down to pet him. "It's okay, Eli. Be quiet." The dog lay down but kept his head turned in the direction the woman had gone.

Lillian continued to soothe the dog long after he needed it. *I'll wait right here until you drive by. I want to get a better view of you. I feel I'll need to remember you.* Soon, a white late model car pulled out of the parking lot. The driver was a young woman wearing black, no hat. As the car passed by, Lillian made a mental note: *young, brown hair, familiar face.* Lillian returned to the table.

Bill looked up. "Eli okay?"

Lillian nodded. "Okay, guys, what did I miss?"

"Absolutely nothing," Victoria said as she brushed back an unruly curl.

* * * * *

THE MYSTERIOUS VOYEUR hurried on her way. *I'd better hurry if I plan on following that bus to Dallas.*

Chapter 18

THE CATERER WAS just leaving when Lillian arrived at Rachel's house the next day. Of course, Lillian had planned it that way. She parked Eli just inside the door and then plopped down her opened handbag beside him, knowing he would nose around in it when he was ready for his favorite chew toy.

Rachel had her living room set up for Mah Jongg. As usual, she had the affair catered by the assistant chef at the clubhouse. She had ordered popcorn shrimp with two different kinds of sauce, cucumber and cream cheese sandwiches, chips, and nuts. For dessert, she was serving cherry tarts and chocolate brownies, her favorites.

"Rachel, before anyone else arrives, I need to talk to you. Last time we played, you mentioned something about the vase of flowers in Sheila's house."

"I did, didn't I?" responded Rachel. "Okay, what's your question? I'll do my best to answer it correctly."

"Do you remember what kind of flowers they were?"

"As a matter of fact, I've been wracking my brain about that. They were big white flowers; I think we've referred to them as snowballs. The only snowball bush I know that grows here is on –" Before she finished her sentence, the doorbell rang.

"Am I late?" asked Margaret as she let herself in. "I rushed straight over here after work."

"Do you need to freshen up before we begin our game?" asked Rachel.

"No, but I could use a glass of wine before we begin."

"Red or white?"

"Do you have any Franzia boxed wine?"

"Sure do. Which do you want – red or white?"

"Red, please." She looked around the room with a puzzled expression. "By the way, where's Victoria?"

"Haven't heard from her, but as I recall, she did mention that her sister-in-law was coming to visit."

"I just hope she doesn't ask Sally Jane to sub for her," said Lillian. "I think she's a busybody."

"Oh now, Lillian, Sally is a pretty good Mah Jongg player," chided Margaret. "She's not the only person in this room to involve herself in someone else's business."

Lillian laughed and walked over to Margaret and gave her a big hug. "Point taken," she said. "Thank you, my friend, for reminding me I ought not to criticize others, especially if all of us share the same flaws."

Margaret hugged her back. "If anything, Lillian, you are honest, and most of the time, the most considerate person I know."

"I need to brew some coffee. You two make yourselves at home. Give me a few minutes, Margaret, and I'll bring your wine to you."

"Sure, take your time, Rachel," Margaret said.

"Yes, do that. I need to talk privately with Margaret for a minute," said Lillian. Rachel nodded and left them alone.

Lillian led Margaret farther away from the kitchen door. With a glow in her eyes, she spoke in a soft voice, "And speaking of being considerate – please don't think I'm being too blunt -- but, Margaret, do we need to start planning a wedding?"

Margaret blushed and whispered, "I confess Grant and I have been seeing each other for the past six months, but don't get too excited. He needs time."

"I know he does," said Lillian.

"Do you think he will ever let go of his love for Alice?" asked Margaret.

"He will, but I think he has to work out his anger toward Jake, first."

"I've noticed they aren't as close as before, but I don't understand," said Margaret. "Do you?"

"I do, but neither my son nor Grant will talk to me about it. And, Bill won't let me broach the subject to him. He thinks we need to let them work it out."

"Please tell me what you know. Grant won't talk to me and gets short with me when I ask."

"I'll try. It all revolves around Alice's death. When they work through that, you'll see Grant heal, and so will Jake."

"How does Alice's death affect Jake?" said Margaret.

"He feels that Grant blames him for Alice's death," said Lillian. "I know my son well. Eventually, and soon I hope, he will muster up enough courage to talk to Grant about it."

"That's going to be tough on Grant. We all know how Alice was after Grant left for the Middle East," said Margaret.

"Yes, we do," said Lillian, "but Grant doesn't, and we've not had the heart to tell him."

"Somebody should, and soon," said Margaret. "Sometimes, I feel as though I am competing with a ghost."

Rachel entered the room bearing the glass of wine Margaret ordered. "I hope you like boxed wine. It took me awhile to figure out how to work the spout."

"Right now, I'll like it as long as it's liquid," said Margaret wearily.

"Good." Rachel looked back and forth between the two women. She turned to Lillian. "I just remembered the name of the lady who bought the house on Louisiana. She's a beautiful blonde. I called on her when she first moved into the house."

"What's her name?" asked Lillian.

The doorbell rang again, and Rachel ignored Lillian's question. She walked over and opened the door. There stood the beautiful blonde from Louisiana Lane.

"Yes? May I help you?"

"Hello. Rachel, isn't it?"

Rachel, at a loss, just stood and stared at her. Eli's reaction to the person surprised Lillian, who was seated across from Margaret at the dining table.

Upon hearing the lady's voice, the dog ran to the door. His wagging tail and his happy yelps told Lillian he was happy to see the visitor.

I saw you act that happy on the sidewalk outside of the bakery. Could it be possible? No, couldn't be.

Her line of vision to the front door was obscured by the see-through fireplace between the living room and dining room. She heard a lady's voice say, "Well, hello, Eli, fancy seeing you here."

And how do you and Eli know each other?

The silence grew. Lillian wondered if Rachel needed assistance dealing with the person and decided to go to the door. As she stood, she glanced at Margaret who also had been listening. She was shocked. Margaret's eyes had become hard, deadly cold.

What could possibly be the problem here? Better check it out.

Then the newcomer stated, "You don't remember me, do you? When I moved into the house on Louisiana, you were so kind to welcome me to the neighborhood."

Lillian stopped and sat back down.

Is she the one you mentioned earlier? And how does she know Eli?

"Yes, yes, now I do. You're Donna Traydon, aren't you?"

Good, girl, Rachel. Your memory's beginning to click.

"I am."

"What can I do for you, Donna?"

"I hope I'm at the right house."

Invite her in, Rachel.

"I'm supposed to sub for Victoria tonight," Donna said.

If you don't, I'll have to join you at the door. It will be obvious then that I'm curious about her.

Lillian breathed a sigh of relief when she heard her friend's response.

"Well, hello, Donna. Forgive my poor manners. I'm sorry I kept you standing on the front porch. Please come in and meet the other ladies."

Rachel led Donna through the living room and into the dining room where Lillian and Margaret were seated.

"Lillian, Margaret, I'd like to introduce Donna Traydon," said Rachel. "She's subbing for Victoria tonight."

"Pleased to meet you," said Lillian. She was taken aback by Margaret's behavior.

Margaret suddenly stood ramrod straight and glared at Donna. "We've met," was all she said.

Interesting. Why so hostile, Margaret?

"Yes, we have, but it's been a while since we last saw each other." The tone of Donna's voice resonated with a deep sadness.

She rebounded quickly, smiling. "It's nice to see you again. It's been a long time."

Margaret did not respond. Instead, she turned and walked to the dining table where Rachel had the Mah Jongg tiles ready for play. She sat down, took a sip of her wine, and motioned for the others to join her.

Rachel and Lillian discreetly exchanged questioning looks. Lillian knew there was a reason for Margaret's bluntness as well as her obvious disapproval of Donna. But her southern lady upbringing took over the situation.

"Welcome to the world's least famous, unable to concentrate but always ready to talk, Mah Jongg group," said Lillian. "I guess Victoria's company arrived?"

"Company? That's not what I was told," said Donna.

"Oh?" questioned Lillian. "I thought her sister-in-law was coming to visit."

"I don't know anything about visitors," said Donna.

"How do you know Victoria?" asked Margaret with a friendlier voice, denoting the return of civility to her demeanor.

Good for you, Margaret. I'm glad you've joined in the conversation. You and I are going to talk about how you treated Donna when she first arrived. It's really not like you to be so rude.

"I don't actually know her," said Donna. "Sally Jane was supposed to sub for Victoria, but she couldn't make it."

"How come?" said Lillian.

"Sally said she had a family emergency and asked me to fill in for her."

Rachel laughed. "Lillian, I think Sally read your mind."

"I don't want to hear anything about her mental telepathy abilities," Lillian laughed.

"You just don't want to lose again." Margaret laughed along with her two friends.

She addressed the newcomer. "Donna, that's an insider joke."

Donna looked amused but, not understanding the joke, said nothing. She was still standing, purse hooked on her shoulder. She appeared lost and confused. Stay or go? Lillian was relieved when Donna commented to Rachel, "What a lovely home you have."

"Oh, thank you, but where are my manners? I don't seem to be able to keep up with them tonight." She pointed to the sofa. "You can put your purse over there."

"Would you like some refreshments before we begin?" asked Lillian.

Donna nodded and sat down.

The mention of food spurred on their hostess. "Oh, by all means. You'll find plates on the end of the buffet."

Margaret was first in line. "Where in the world did you find paper plates with Mah Jongg tiles? These are so cute."

"You know me. I always go to Tuesday Morning on Tuesday mornings. They received a new shipment last week and had just opened the box. When I saw the clerk—she was puzzled by the graphics on them—in fact, she muttered, 'What kind of dominoes are these?'—I asked her how many packages were in the box. She counted out twenty, so I bought all of them."

"You could have stopped with 'Tuesday Morning.'" Margaret continued to load her plate until it was almost overflowing.

"I was going to send some home with all of you, but your sarcasm doesn't deserve any."

"Whoops. Should not have said that."

"If I'm as lucky tonight as I think I will be, I might be generous to you. Donna, you and Lillian help yourselves to the food before it's all gone." Rachel made a big show of pointing to Margaret's plate.

"What? You know I don't have time to eat lunch. I'm always hungry by the end of the day," replied Margaret.

"I know you are. Eat up. Plan on taking leftovers home."

"Thanks."

Lillian motioned for Donna to go through the line after Margaret. *I want to see your back. Can't put my finger on it, but I know I've seen you someplace. But where?*

"What a feast you've prepared," Donna said. "Everything looks wonderful. You must have spent all day in the kitchen preparing all of this."

"Don't be impressed. I don't cook. The club's chef always caters for me. Enjoy."

The women did just that. The four of them sat contentedly chatting while they sated their appetites. Rachel kept the wine coming, and soon everyone was relaxed and ready to begin Mah Jongg.

The ladies put their plates aside.

"The tiles are already shuffled," said Rachel, "so let's get to it, build the wall."

They threw the dice. Lillian was low, so she assumed the East. She looked at Rachel. "Did you forget anything?"

"I don't think so, why?"

"Our cards? Helps to know our game plan, don't you think?"

"Can't believe I didn't put them on the table." She jumped up and after searching two buffet drawers, exclaimed, "Ah, ha, here they are. Sorry about that."

Eli, who had fallen asleep with his head on his favorite toy, jumped up, sniffed the base of the door, and began his low warning. Lillian's stomach muscles tightened. *Oh no. What now? I know that sound.* She kept this thought to herself. In a calm voice, "Come, Eli." She motioned for the dog to sit beside her chair. He trotted over and sat down. "Here." She handed him a cracker. He devoured it in one gulp. "Lie down, Eli. Everything's okay."

"He is a good guard dog, isn't he?" Rachel stated.

"Yes, he is."

"Do you think I ought to turn on the flood lights, see if anyone is outside?"

"No, Rachel. Ignore him. He probably just had a doggy dream." *I hope that's all it was.*

"Good. That's settled. Let's play," ordered Margaret. "I can't be here all night—have things to do tomorrow."

"As do I. Saturday is a work day for me," Donna said.

Conversation ceased as they examined their tiles and began to play. For the next half hour, the four women concentrated on the game. They occasionally paused to make a comment to each other. On this particular evening, Lillian noted that Margaret had been unusually quiet. She racked her tiles, ignoring the mundane chatter of the other three.

No one had been successful, so they had taken a break. Lillian reshuffled all of the Mah Jongg tiles.

Rachel was in the kitchen making coffee and getting out the dessert.

Finally, Margaret spoke. "Donna, just how do you know Sally Jane?"

When she did so, the shuffler stopped and listened. *Thank you, my friend. I, too, am interested in the new player.*

"I met her through Jason Carpenter."

"Well, I guess my next question is how do you know Jason?" Margaret wanted to know. Lillian noticed that Margaret's eyes had lost their hardened glare when she spoke.

"He does the auditing for the lake's business office where I work," said Donna. "Sally Jane came in with him one day, and she invited me to the health club where she teaches a Pilates class."

"I see," said Margaret. "How long have you worked for the club?"

"Not long, but long enough to know that this is a great place to live," said Donna smiling.

Margaret nodded in agreement, but she didn't smile.

"It is a great place to live," agreed Lillian who was feeling uncomfortable because of Margaret's interrogation of Donna. She was relieved when Rachel returned with a tray filled with brownies and coffee. "Let me help pour the coffee."

Rachel nodded, and Lillian walked to the buffet and began filling each cup.

"Now, I remember more about my visit with you," said Rachel as she passed out dessert plates piled high with brownies slathered with vanilla ice cream.

Donna laughed nervously as she accepted the plate being passed to her. "Thank goodness. You visited me when I first moved into my house on Louisiana."

"If I remember correctly, your yard has two of the most beautiful trees in Leisure Lake. They have huge, white flowers."

"Are you referring to the snowball trees?" asked Donna.

Lillian, jolted by Donna's question, stopped pouring the coffee. Fearing she might spill it and interfere with the conversation, she inhaled and exhaled to calm her jitters before passing the beverage around the table. Finished with her task, she sat down the carafe and resumed her seat.

Rachel's initial question to Donna had brought her back to her favorite sport, an activity more fun than Mah Jongg: solving a mystery, especially if it involved a crime. Lillian understood Rachel's tactic. Her friend and ally had deliberately dropped an important clue in her lap. She listened attentively to the rest of the conversation between the two.

"Yes, I am. They are, I think, some of my favorite blooms. As I told you during our visit, I am on the welcoming committee and try to touch base with all newcomers."

"I've never lived in a neighborhood like this one. It's good to feel so welcomed."

"We want everyone to feel at home here."

"Believe me, I do."

"That's always good to hear. We don't usually get much feedback from people. Oh, yes, now I remember. Do you mind if I ask a nosey question?"

"Depends on how 'nosey' it is."

"Here it is: Did you know Stella Dallas?"

Eli's ears perked up at the sound of 'Stella Dallas.' *Good question, Rachel. Let's see how honest she is. If she knows Eli by name, she should admit to knowing Stella.*

"Stella?" Donna looked confused.

"She lived down the hill and around the corner from you."

Donna paused, eyebrows drawn tight. Her frown formed two short perpendicular indentations in the center of her forehead.

"Oh, now I know the one you're talking about. I didn't know her. It's really sad, though, about the woman's death, her being murdered, you know." Shaking her head, she asked, "Why did you ask if I knew her?"

"I thought you might have met her. Like I said. I call on everyone, and when I visited her, I noticed that she had a vase of snowball blooms on one of her end tables."

Donna shrugged and took the last bite of her brownie. "Excuse me, ladies, but I can't play and talk at the same time."

"Yes, let's continue," said Margaret sternly.

They began the next round. Donna was East and broke the wall. Finally, Rachel announced, "Mah Jongg!"

"I can't believe it," stated Margaret good-naturedly.

Lillian laughed. "Believe it. We have a winner."

"Rachel has never had the privilege of saying 'Mah Jongg,' and now, she has beaten us again, Lillian."

"I know," laughed Lillian. "Rachel, you are on a roll. Two times now, you've been our big winner."

"It must be Victoria's influence on me. After all, she's the one who taught me to relax with a glass of wine. And, not to mention Lady Luck. Lately, I've felt lucky."

They all laughed. Margaret said, "Now, young lady, show us what you've got."

Rachel said, "I played a Lucky 13."

She turned to reveal her tiles: FFFF 4444 9999 = 13. For the first time that evening, Margaret laughed. "Count your tiles, Rachel. Looks to me like you've got one too many on your rack."

Rachel shrieked. "I guess I wasn't so lucky after all. Sorry, girls."

Margaret turned to Lillian and stated, "She's dead. Do you see what she's done?"

Lillian laughed, too. Donna just sat there staring at Rachel.

Good-natured Rachel stated, "What a dufus I am. Let's start another round."

"We'll do just that, but I suggest you switch back to hot tea," laughed Lillian.

Finally, at ten o'clock, Margaret yawned and said, "It's late, girls. Let's call it a night."

"Yes, it is late," agreed Lillian.

"Can we help you clean up?" asked Donna.

"Oh no, don't worry about it. It was nice having you with us. I hope you enjoyed it."

"My pleasure, indeed. Thank you for your hospitality."

She got her purse and said goodbye. With Eli following close behind her, Rachel walked Donna to the door and watched her drive away. When Rachel turned back around, Lillian recognized her friend's puzzled expression. *Oh yeah. You also know she lied. Don't worry, my friend, I'll find out why.*

Eli came and put his head on Lillian's knee. As she gave him some loving pats, she mused, *I'd swear you wish you could have gone with her.*

Margaret had her purse on her arm and prepared to leave but stopped just before she opened the door. She turned to Lillian and said, "I'd like to meet you tomorrow for lunch. There is something I need to tell you."

"Sure, Margaret. Would twelve thirty at the Corner Bakery be okay with you?"

"Perfect," said Margaret.

"It's a date, then."

After Margaret left, Rachel sat across the table from Lillian. "What was that all about?"

"I think Margaret is worried about Grant and just needs someone who will listen and not judge," said Lillian.

"Did you notice the tension between Margaret and Donna?" asked Rachel.

"Yes, I did. I also noticed that Donna was quick to say that she didn't know anyone named Stella," said Lillian. "But if she didn't know Stella, how did she know Eli?"

"Also, she sure was quick to suggest we continue our game when I asked about the snowballs."

"Did you have that in mind when you bid the Lucky 13?"

"You know me well. I thought that would solidify the clues I dropped earlier."

"Good thinking, my smart friend."

"I'd bet my pension that she knew Stella," said Rachel. "Don't you agree she lied?"

"Okay, I'm listening. I know you have more to say about that."

"You're so right. Would you believe it if I tell you I saw Donna at the funeral?"

"Really, you saw her? I didn't see her in the audience."

"Yes, I'm telling you she was there. I'd recognize her anywhere, straw hat and all."

"What? What do you mean by straw hat?"

"She had on a big straw hat. Since it was a sunny day, I assumed she wanted to protect her skin."

"I thought she lied to you." Lillian paused, thinking. "But if what she said is true and she didn't know the woman, why would she have attended the funeral?"

"Good question."

I have a strange feeling," said Lillian, making preparations to leave. Eli uttered his usual warning as if in support of her last statement.

"What kind of feeling?" asked Rachel.

"I can't describe it. It's like a premonition that something bad's about to happen, but I will say this: I fear for our safety here at the lake. Two murders now."

"I know. It's terrible."

"Be careful, Rachel."

"I will. Don't you worry about me," she said.

She hugged her friend. "Thanks for a lovely evening."

"Wait up, Lillian, until I turn on the floodlight so you can see better."

Lillian appreciated her friend's kind gesture.

Lillian walked toward her car, and Rachel was closing her door when they heard the squeal of a car's tires as it sped away into the night.

Lillian reached the other side of the dimly lit street. Eli startled her when he jumped, straining on the leash. He bounded with such force that she almost tripped as she tried to step up onto the curb. She saw a small Schnauzer running toward them. Eli pulled even harder on the leash. The other dog also was pulling on the leash its elderly, white-haired owner was holding. Like Lillian, his arm was outstretched as his dog tugged on an expandable lead.

He spoke, "Don't worry, ma'am, Zoe won't bite. Sorry if she scared you."

"She did spook me."

"Again, sorry about that." As he walked away, he turned. "You have a good evening and be careful. Strange happenings around here these days with the murder and all."

"Thanks, you also," she said as she dragged Eli away from his new canine friend and stuffed both herself and the dog in the car. In her side mirror, she watched the man as he continued to pull Zoe down the street.

Lillian sat in her car for a moment, waiting to make sure Rachel closed both her storm door and her inside door. She sat a little longer, waiting. The floodlights around the house dimmed. Darkness.

Lillian shivered. Like a panther, the blackness of the night stalked down the street and pounced on her SUV as if to pull her and her dog toward an evil that lurked in her once peaceful neighborhood. Eli growled a warning. She finally turned the key in the ignition. The motor roared to life, and she drove away.

"I'm worried," she said to her four-legged companion as she turned the corner and headed home. Eli propped his chin on her right shoulder and planted a wet kiss on her ear.

"I appreciate your moral support." She patted his head, enjoying the comfort of his soft, white, fluffy topknot.

* * * * *

THIRTY MINUTES LATER, Rachel almost had her house back in order. She tossed dirty paper plates and napkins in the trash can beneath her sink. Coffee cups and saucers, along with brownie-crumbed forks rested in the Kenmore dishwasher. Wine glasses soaked in the kitchen sink.

As promised, she placed the clean paper plates and napkins displaying Mah Jongg tiles, equally divided, into separate ziplock bags, each sealed and bearing the name of one of her friends. "I'll take these to them next week when we meet at Lillian's."

As she put away all of the leftovers, she thought, "Oh, dear, I promised Margaret she could have these. We forgot all about it. Guess I'll take them to her tomorrow." No response from a now empty house, one that of late was always too quiet to suit Rachel.

She sighed and looked up at the ceiling.

"I still miss you, you big lug. Why did you have to die and leave me all alone?" She often talked out loud to her deceased husband. "You're right. I remember what you said. Don't wallow, ever. Be happy. Enjoy life."

With that last thought, she began whistling a happy tune as she washed the wine glasses. She stopped. Did she hear something? She listened, relieved to hear only the ring of the doorbell.

"I hope that's Margaret. She'll save me a trip," Rachel said as she walked through the house to answer the door.

Forgetting Lillian's recent warning about being careful, she didn't look through the security hole before opening the door. All she saw was a gun.

Whump.

Rachel slumped down, a bullet hole right in the middle of her forehead.

Chapter 19

SINCE THE TWO murders at Leisure Lake, Bill worried about Lillian when she was out of his sight. More than once he tried to convince her to let Jake and Grant solve the murder without her help. She, of course, refused. As a result of her stubbornness, especially after someone shot out their front window, he felt his concern was justified. So, it was a relief when he heard her car drive into the garage. He met her at the door with a bear hug and a kiss.

He looked down at Eli.

"Glad you were with her, old boy." The dog wagged his tail and walked on by Bill on his way to the back of the sofa, his favorite place to sleep. "Worn out, are you?" Bill smiled at Lillian. "How was Mah Jongg, my dear? Hope you didn't lose the ranch," he said jokingly.

"Oh, it was fun, Bill. I wish you could have seen Rachel."

"Why? Was her luck with her tonight?"

"She thought so, especially after a few glasses of wine. She may have had a little too much to drink and thought she had won. It was Margaret who called her attention to the fact her hand was dead."

"I guess I shouldn't laugh since I don't have a clue about the rules of Mah Jongg, but knowing Rachel, I bet she was embarrassed."

"So much so that she became a teetotaler again."

They both had a good laugh. Bill could not quite imagine Rachel being tipsy. "I can't believe that sweet, little Rachel could ever be inebriated."

"Believe it."

"But, go on, finish telling me about the evening."

Lillian continued her story, "We had a new girl as a sub for Victoria tonight. Rachel had forgotten that she had met her, but Eli did not."

"I knew Victoria's sister-in-law was coming to visit. Who was the new person?"

"Someone you wouldn't know," said Lillian. "But, she said she works at the club in the business office."

"What's her name?"

"Donna Traydon. It was so uncanny, though."

She looked at Bill and raised an eyebrow. "You're pale. What's wrong? Are you sick?"

"No, I'm fine."

He turned away from Lillian.

She shrugged, ignored his body language and his scratchy voice when he asked, "What was so 'uncanny'?"

"I thought about it when I saw her and couldn't get her out of my mind all the way home."

"Tell me your thoughts."

"If she had brown hair, she would be a dead ringer for Margaret," said Lillian. "I even arranged it so that they would have to stand side-by-side to fill their plates at Rachel's buffet."

Bill turned back around to face Lillian.

"What's wrong?" asked Lillian when she saw the pain in his eyes.

"Sit down, Lillian. I have a confession to make, one I should have made a long time ago."

Lillian paid no attention to his command. Instead, she put her arms around his neck and gave him a quick kiss. "Oh, silly. I didn't mention Margaret's name to make you feel guilty."

"Make me feel guilty? What are you talking about?"

Lillian laughed and said, "Tsk, Tsk, I saw you the other day with Margaret. I saw you hug her in broad daylight, right there on the sidewalk."

"You saw us and haven't said a word to me about it?" said Bill. "And here I thought you were curious about everything."

"I thought she might have been talking about Grant or sharing some other kind of problem with you," said Lillian. "You're a good listener, you know."

"Well, in a way, you're somewhat correct."

"I didn't want to interfere if she was confiding in you. Sometimes, I try to be considerate."

She stopped teasing and looked at him. "This is serious, isn't it?"

"Sit down, Lillian, I have a story to tell you."

Lillian dropped her arms, pulled out a chair and sat down at the small dinette table. He took the seat opposite her. *I can't begin to guess what's so important.* She could not imagine where the conversation would take them. She looked at him, nodded for him to continue.

"Think back about fifteen years or so. Where were we living then?"

"We were both working, you with the newspaper, and I with the school district."

"You're correct. If you remember, I had my own weekly column then."

"I do remember. What happened back then? More importantly, why is it relevant now?"

"There was a very young girl, right out of high school, as a matter of fact, who came to work for us," said Bill.

"Go on."

"The young girl was Margaret." He reached across the table and placed his hands on top of hers.

"Grant's Margaret?"

"Yes, his girl and your friend."

"That means you've known Margaret for a long time."

"I have," said Bill.

"Even though it would have been a good thing to know, why is that fact so important? Did you and she have. . ."

"No, heavens no. Don't even go there. You know I wouldn't. . ."

"We've settled that point. Continue your story."

"I've been a father figure to her. You see, both her parents died in an automobile accident about a year before we moved here."

"How sad. That explains why she never mentions any of her family."

Lillian waited for him to continue. After a few seconds of silence, "That's not all you want to confess, is it? There's more you think I need to know. Right?"

"I'm afraid so," said Bill.

"It's late, and I came home tired and ready for bed, but not now. Once again, you've succeeded. My curiosity's on overdrive."

"I'm sorry. I knew you were tired, but I feel this can't wait until morning."

"Out with it."

"Margaret had a sister about two or three years older than she. By now, I know you can tell me who she is."

"Donna. I just knew there was something between those two," said Lillian. "It happened when Donna walked into Rachel's living room."

"Sweetheart, make yourself clear. What are you talking about?"

"Margaret was at Mah Jongg tonight. She looked more strained than anyone I've ever seen when Donna walked in. In fact, she looked furious."

"This was one of my biggest concerns. I hoped you would never meet Donna."

"Why?"

"I knew you would ultimately link them together. I also hoped they would never meet out here, especially because of Margaret's relationship with Grant."

"That would be impossible since Donna said she worked in the business office. She's bound to run into him."

"That's too bad for Margaret."

"Why?"

"She's worked hard to distance herself from her sister."

"Did she tell you she didn't want anything to do with Donna?"

"Not in so many words, but you have to understand Donna has not been quite as upstanding a citizen as Margaret," said Bill, "but I can almost understand why."

"Don't keep it to yourself. Tell me why Margaret doesn't like her sister."

"They had a falling out when both Margaret and I worked at the newspaper."

"Sisters always have little spats, sibling rivalry, you know." *From the look on Margaret's face when Donna walked in, there's more than sibling rivalry between them.*

"This was more than that. Donna began hanging out with the wrong crowd and turned her back on the young people her parents approved."

Lillian shook her head. "I know all about that from my years on a high school campus. Some teenagers seem to think they have to rebel against their parents for trying to choose friends for them."

Bill nodded in agreement. "Donna wouldn't listen to her parents even though Margaret begged her to do so."

"What happened?" asked Lillian.

"She rebelled even more. Margaret felt the more she tried to talk to Donna, the more she rebelled. Donna eventually became pregnant."

"Uh oh. How did her mom and dad take that? I hope they supported her, gave her the love and understanding she would need. Keep in mind that's not an easy ordeal for a young girl."

"They didn't. Instead, they pretty much disowned her until she told them that she had been raped. They tried to get her to file charges against the man, but Donna would not press charges no matter how much her parents pleaded with her. Finally, they convinced Donna to put the baby up for adoption."

"So. . ." Lillian had to know. "Did Donna ever identify the father of the baby?"

"Margaret said Donna told her his name but not her parents, and she asked Margaret to keep her secret from them."

I wonder why she would want to protect him? If he wanted to keep his reputation intact, I bet he threatened Donna. She would definitely have been afraid of him in that case.

Silence. When the minutes dragged on, Bill stood and put the tea kettle on to boil.

"I can understand you need time to digest everything I've told you. While you think about it, I'll make us a cup of tea."

They sat at the table slowly sipping the green tea. "Are you mad at me for keeping this information from you? Talk to me."

"No, I'm not angry. I'm just mentally commiserating with a family that had to struggle with the heartbreak of having a daughter raped and, as a result of the adoption, never saw their grandchild."

"I know that must have been difficult."

"Yes, I can't imagine not ever seeing our two grandchildren, can you?"

"Of course not."

"Bill," said Lillian, "did Margaret share this information with you then or just recently?"

"Guess I didn't make that clear. I knew about it then. In fact, I was the one who referred Donna to an attorney who handled private adoptions. After that, Margaret never mentioned it again, and I didn't ask any more questions. I wish that I had," he said sadly.

"Don't dwell on it. You did what was necessary at the time."

"I believed it then."

I wonder? Donna gave up a baby. Sheila adopted a baby. Could it be? No, I don't believe in coincidences.

Chapter 20

THE NEXT MORNING, Grant and Jake sat in the Corner Bakery. They had finished with their breakfast Panini, but still lingered at the table silently sipping their coffee. Grant, who had been staring out the window, sensed Jake squirming.

"Okay, out with it. I can tell you're worried and have something on your mind."

"I talked to Mom early this morning."

"You always talk to her before we have breakfast on Saturday mornings."

"Yeah, but this time, she told me something that surprised her, too. It flat stunned me."

"Are you going to share it with me or are you going to keep the surprise to yourself? I guess it'd be too good to be true if her news involved something else about Sheila, something that would help us close this case."

"That would have been nice, but you know her as well as I. She tells only what she wants you to know."

"You're right about that. I bet she knows more about Sheila and is keeping it to herself. But I digress. Exactly what did Lillian tell you?"

"She talked about her conversation with Dad last night."

"Last night? Let's see. Friday? Mah Jongg. Women. I guess she told him all about the gossip she heard. I know that was interesting."

"Kind of. But it was what he told her about Margaret."

"What are you talking about?" asked Grant.

"It seems Dad knew Margaret way back, before he retired, back when he worked for the newspaper."

"You're kidding, right?"

"I'm serious as death."

"Well, since we're very much alive, tell me. I hope it isn't as sad as the look on your face." The waitress came by and refilled their cups and moved on to the next table.

"Listen, has Margaret ever talked to you about what happened to her sister?" Jake sipped his coffee, waited for Grant's reply.

"No, I haven't talked to Margaret in a couple of days. She has been as busy as I've been, so we just haven't had time to discuss anything, not even the weather," said Grant. "And, furthermore, she's never mentioned her family, not her parents, not a sister, *nada.*"

"That's odd. You've not ever been curious?"

"It wouldn't matter if I was. We have an agreement. I don't pry into her past, and she leaves mine well enough alone. Anyway, go on. Tell me what you think I need to hear. Now, I'm curious as to what your dad knows about Margaret that we didn't."

"I'm probably talking out of turn, but since I started this conversation, I'll just go ahead with it," said Jake.

"Good idea."

"To make a long story short, Margaret worked at the newspaper with my dad. He told Mom that her sister had been raped. Had a baby as a result of it."

"Like I said, she's never mentioned a sister," said Grant. "Did your dad say what happened to the sister and her baby?"

"Margaret and Donna don't communicate anymore. According to Dad," said Jake, "Donna gave the baby away. Private adoption."

"Well, I guess Margaret will pass on that information to me when she's ready. Like I said, we leave the past where it is: in the past."

"Okay, if that's what you do, but I just thought you would like to know."

"Thanks for your concern, buddy, but right now, I have other things on my mind."

"Sometimes, I don't understand you."

"Good. We're even in that regard."

"We do have a homicide to solve." Grant motioned for the waitress to refill their cups once more. They sat silent again for a good five minutes.

He broke the silence.

"Jake, I'm completely stumped. This investigation has me thinking I'm in the wrong profession."

"I know what you mean. I've never seen anything like it," said Jake, "and there are no other leads right now."

"I haven't come up with any either, and no one at the lake has given any useful information."

"FYI: I tried to call Jonathan at the number he gave me."

"Any luck?"

"Not yet. Seems he's been ill and hasn't shown up for work the past two days."

"I'm still not sure I buy his goody, goody, I'm redeemed story," Grant said. "You need to try to work with the PD in the Dallas area. Ask them to keep an eye on him."

Jake nodded and then asked, "Did you ever follow up with Rachel? She might have information she doesn't realize she knows."

"I did. In fact, she and I are meeting tomorrow morning to go through her newcomer files. I hope we can identify just one other person, anyone who might have had contact with or might have known Sheila."

"Why just the newcomers?" asked Jake.

"The club always has a party to welcome new property owners to the lake. Perhaps there was someone at the party who might remember seeing Sheila," explained Grant. "That is, if she attended one of the parties."

"Hopefully, she did."

"If not, we're at another dead end."

"Does Rachel always attend the parties?"

"I doubt she's missed very many, except of course, right after her husband died."

"Do you think she would remember if anyone hooked up with Sheila at the party?" Jake said.

"Absolutely. She has a remarkable memory, which is good for anyone who has the job as chairman of the welcome committee," said Grant. "She never forgets a face but sometimes has to rack her brain for a name to go with it."

After a brief pause, Grant continued. "I think I'll drive by your folk's house, see how they're doing."

"Thanks. If she sees you today, Mom won't be pestering me this afternoon. I'll call you if anything turns up on this end," said Jake.

"By the way, have you heard anything else from the medical examiner? It'd be nice to see the toxicology report."

"Hope to hear from him today or Monday. He did request a rush on it."

"Good. See ya."

Needing time alone to think how he would broach an important topic with Lillian and Bill, Grant slowly drove back out to Leisure Lake. *I've got to get this out of my system he thought. I need to talk to Lillian.*

Chapter 21

THE RAYS OF the mid-morning sun reflected off the gentle waves of the small fishing lake across the road from the Prestridge's house. Lillian, lost in thought, watched two fishermen who, having caught nothing for their efforts, had given up and were rowing slowly back to the shore.

"You know, Bill, those two," she motioned to the men, "remind me of Grant."

"How so?"

"Well, they didn't catch what they set out to get, so they're giving up. Look at them. Even from here, I can tell how unhappy they are about the way things turned out."

"So how's their not catching fish remind you of Grant? I don't understand."

"I think he's given up."

"Given up on the case?"

"Of course not. He's given up on women."

"Now, Lillian."

"I don't want to hear any 'now Lillians.' Follow my line of thought here for a minute. Grant truly loved Alice. She was the catch he wanted, but she left him empty handed, just like those fickle fish over there in that lake. They've left those men with empty baskets."

"I have to admit that's a good analogy."

"He's afraid to find out about Alice and the things she did while he was away fighting in the Gulf," said Lillian.

"Yeah, I know," said Bill. "I guess what bothers me is that his fear has driven a wedge in his friendship with Jake."

"Yes, and Jake does not want to be the one to tell him, to disappoint him. He'd rather just take the blame for her death than hurt Grant anymore." She sighed. "I wish there was something we could do."

"I do, too, but those boys are going to have to come to grips with the situation, and that includes their brotherly bond. It's fractured," said Bill.

"And that doesn't even take Margaret into account."

"No, it doesn't. It's a good thing she is as understanding as she is. Otherwise. . ."

Alerted by Eli's excited yelps, Lillian looked down the street to see Grant's cruiser turn the corner.

"Change the subject. Here comes Grant now." In a stern voice, she cautioned, "Wait, Eli. Let him park before you bound down the steps. The dog sat to wait. His tail scraped back and forth on the wooden deck.

"Well, speak of the devil," said Bill.

"Hush. We weren't speaking of him and don't put Grant in that category," chided Lillian.

Grant parked his cruiser in the drive, grabbed his radio, and slowly dragged himself out of the car. The dog bounded down the steps and ran out to greet him. Grant reached down to pet Eli. He said a few soft-spoken words no one else could hear to the white ball of fluff. The poodle raced up the steps and reached the top ahead of him.

As Grant stepped up onto the deck, Bill stood to welcome him. "Come on up here, son. We're as happy as Eli to see you."

"It's a good day to sit out here," Grant said. "I've always liked to sit here and watch the ducks swim around in the lake."

"Yes it is always relaxing to see them paddle back and forth from the feeder to open water. And Lillian's homemade cranberry scones make it worthwhile. How about I get you one of those? We've got a fresh pot of tea, too."

"Sounds wonderful." Grant bent over and hugged Lillian. "You always have just what I need. I can't refuse your scones even though I've already had breakfast." He sat down in a colorful Adirondack chair next to Lillian, took a deep breath, and let it out slowly. He gripped the armrests of the chair as though he had to hold on for support.

Lillian placed her hand on his arm. "I feel you need something more than my good cooking."

"I'm afraid I do," admitted Grant. "I need advice from a woman or, to be more exact, from a mother."

"I'm here," reassured Lillian. "Do you need to talk about your relationship with Margaret?" Though she knew he needed to talk about his love for her, she also knew that until he resolved his feelings about Alice and Jake, Margaret would have to wait.

"Not exactly. But what I want to talk about will also involve her in a roundabout way," admitted Grant.

"I hope you aren't just leading her on. She is crazy about you," said Lillian.

"I assure you, I'm not leading her on," said Grant. He paused.

Bill returned with a TV tray ladened with a mug of steaming tea and a scone. Grant picked up the cup and took a big gulp. He nibbled on the scone and looked out at the lake. "The water is so beautiful today. Watching the waves ripple is restful. I can understand why you love this deck so much."

"We spend most of the early mornings out here," Bill said.

"But the lake isn't what I came here to discuss." He put down his cup and placed Lillian's hands in his. "I've come to apologize to both of you, and I intend to do the same to Jake," said Grant. "That is, when he and I have time to talk about things other than Sheila's murder."

"You owe us no apologizes." Bill pulled a chair close to Grant and sat down.

"We love you and just want you to be happy," said Lillian. She knew how difficult it was for Grant to ask forgiveness.

"Both of you know how badly I've treated Jake since I've been home." He looked at each of them and continued. "I've blamed him for Alice's death. I've been wrong in doing that. I've heard the stories about her. I just didn't want to believe them."

"Exactly what have you heard?" asked Lillian.

"Now, Lillian, whatever he's heard is just gossip," said Bill, ever the peacemaker.

"No, Bill, it isn't. The rumors are all too true," she said. "Let's be totally honest with him."

"I'm afraid you're right. The gossip is true. I know she was unfaithful to me and had begun to drink heavily. Her drinking began before I left for the war. I tried to get her to stop, go to AA. She wouldn't listen. Thought she could do it on her on."

"I know we human beings think we are the cure givers, but we are wrong. Alice needed a higher power in her life," said Lillian.

"I blame myself to some extent, though, because I should have helped her more, both physically and spiritually," confessed Grant. "I fear I let her down."

"Grant, I'm so sorry things didn't work out between you two. I know how much you loved her," said Lillian.

"I did love her. Because I adored her so much, I refused to see her flaws until it was too late," said Grant. "I blamed everyone else, especially Jake, for the mistakes she made after I left. But at the end of the day, no one could have stopped her. She made her own decisions."

"And sadly suffered the consequences." Bill shook his head.

"Unfortunately, I can't change any of that," said Grant.

"You still have the future," said Lillian.

"Yes, I do, and I intend to live it. I've had enough of self-pity," said Grant.

"Is there anything I can do to help you?" Lillian leaned over and patted Grant on the back. "You know I'll do anything for you. I don't like to see you worried or unhappy. All you have to do is let me know what you need."

"Well, talking to you has put me half-way on the right track, but I still need to talk to someone else before I can erase all of my mistakes," said Grant.

"That would be Jake," said Bill.

"Yes. Through my fear of facing reality, I've punished him enough, and I feel terrible about it."

"I know what to do now," said Lillian.

Before she could articulate her plan, Grant interrupted. "I have a plan of my own."

"Tell me. I'll do whatever you ask. I want you two back the way you've been all your lives -- brothers who care for each other."

"Can you invite Jake and me over one night soon so that I can talk to him here, at home? I want the two of us to have the opportunity to talk man-to-man."

"I can arrange that," Bill said.

"How?" asked Grant.

Bill spoke to his wife. "Lillian, you arrange a girls' night out for you, Jessica, and Margaret."

"Sure. We haven't done that for awhile now," agreed Lillian, disappointed that she would miss out on seeing the two boys she loved most re-establish their friendship.

"That'll work," said Grant.

"Let's make it for tonight. I'll call Jake. Be here around six thirty," said Bill.

Eli began to howl seconds before the sounds of sirens once again broke the peaceful atmosphere of Leisure Lake. As they grew louder and closer and more intrusive, Lillian groaned. "What now?"

Chapter 22

ALMOST IMMEDIATELY AFTER the first wail of the sirens, Grant heard the voice of a security officer speaking on the radio he kept clipped to his shirt. An incident had occurred on Oak Grove Lane. Security had called 911. An ambulance was on its way. Lillian and Bill heard it, too.

"That's the street where Rachel lives." Lillian jumped up and made for the door. "I'm getting my purse and going over to her house."

"No, you don't." Grant caught her by the arm.

"Something may have happened to Rachel. I have to go," said Lillian.

"Bill, keep her here," said Grant. He rushed down the deck's steps and ran to his car.

"Done," said Bill. He put his hands on her shoulders, pulled her to him, wrapped his arms around her, and began to talk to her with a soothing voice.

"Calm down, darling. Take a deep breath. Everything's going to be okay."

"You're right. I know I'm overreacting, but if Rachel's in trouble, I need to be there for her. "

"Let's give Grant time to check things out. Let him do his job."

"I guess he doesn't need my getting in the way."

Bill smiled lovingly at his wife. "Remember the last time Rachel called 911 and said she needed an ambulance?"

Lillian began to laugh. "Yes, there was a cat in the oak tree in her backyard. She couldn't coax it down and decided to climb the tree to get it."

Both of them chuckled.

"Rachel suffered a lot of cuts and scratches, not all of them from the tree, as she wrestled with the cat trying to "save" it. I think she ended up with several stitches as a result of that fiasco," said Bill.

* * * * *

GRANT UNDERSTOOD THE urgency in his employee's voice. He parked in front of Rachel's house. Two paramedics and two of his security officers stood on the walkway to her front porch. He saw a motionless form crumpled, lying in the doorway.

He jumped out of his car and met one of his men who was hurrying down the driveway to meet him. "What've we got?"

"Looks like she was shot when she opened the door. Single bullet to the forehead," Todd said.

"Have you been inside?" asked Grant.

"No, we waited for you."

"So, no sign of a forced entry?"

"None that I can see without a closer look."

"Must have known the culprit."

"Looks like it."

"We'll know more later."

The paramedics were standing on the porch. Grant walked up, nodded to one of them, who said, "Looks like we were too late again, Mr. Perryman."

"Who placed the call to you?" asked Grant.

"Same guy who called security," said the officer who stood beside one of the paramedics. Neighbor across the street. Said he had walked out to the end of his driveway to pick up the paper, saw the opened door, and decided to check on (he looked at his notes) Mrs. McAnally."

"Do you have his name?"

"Yes. It was a Mr. Wolver, first name Thomas."

"Which house?"

"Across the street, two doors east."

Grant got out his notebook and wrote down the information. "Have you called the M.E.?" asked Grant.

"Yes sir, we called Will Ogburn after we determined there was nothing we could do for the lady," said the paramedic. "We'll just wait around until Mr. Ogburn arrives if you don't mind."

"Thanks, appreciate it," said Grant. "He'll need your help to transport the body."

Grant surveyed the scene. He looked up at both of his officers and in a gruff voice gave them instructions. "Todd, Robert, I want this street blocked off. Now. No one enters or leaves until we've questioned every homeowner on this cul-de-sac. Understand?"

"Yes, sir," Robert said. Todd didn't respond but ran to his truck to get the supplies he needed to follow Grant's orders. He retrieved four barriers from the back of the security truck and set them up across the middle of the street. He stood guard at the entrance to the cul-de-sac while Robert took yellow crime tape from the glove compartment. Robert also grabbed several wooden stakes from the supplies he kept in his truck. He pushed them into the ground, stapled the crime tape to them and thus sealed off Rachel's entire yard.

Grant watched their efforts, and satisfied with their security measures, examined the door. *No damage. Just as I thought. Looks like Rachel herself opened it.*

He reached into his shirt pocket for his notebook and jotted the following:

Ask Lillian who played Mah Jongg here last night. What time did each woman leave? Did they see anything unusual on their way to their cars or home? Don't alarm them, but make sure they understand they might be in danger.

He walked around the house to see if there was anything that looked out of place. *No evidence of a forced entry to windows/back door.* Noticing the wet grass, he knew the sprinkler system had evidently kicked on during the night, so he looked for footprints in the soft ground around the windows. He found none. By the time he completed his search and walked back around to the front of the house, he saw Will Ogburn getting out of his vehicle.

Through clenched teeth, Grant said, "Looks like an execution to me, Will. Look at her and let me know if you agree with me."

Will began his on-sight examination. After a few minutes, he stood and nodded, "Well, it looks to me like this lady opened the door for someone and probably never knew what hit her."

"My thoughts, exactly," agreed Grant. "Can you give me your best estimate of time of death?"

"Just a guestimate, mind you. I'd say sometime between ten-thirty and twelve-thirty last night, but I'll know more after I do the autopsy."

"Thanks, call me when you have additional information," said Grant.

"Is it all right with you if we remove the body now?"

"Go ahead." Grant looked down at her and then at the paramedics. "Be gentle, will you?"

"Always are."

Grant took out his handkerchief and wiped the sweat off his face and neck. *How in the world am I going to break this to Lillian? Rachel was her best friend.*

Grant had his phone out dialing the sheriff's cell number when Jake drove up and parked. Grant closed his phone and walked down to meet him at the end of Rachel's drive. The two men shook hands.

"My God, what happened?" Jake asked as he watched the medical examiner and his assistant load the body in the county's vehicle. "Whose body is Will taking?"

"It's Rachel."

"Damn. You know how close Mom is to her?"

"I do. And dread telling her."

"We'll do that together."

"Thanks."

"Who reported it?"

"Neighbor across the street. He called the ambulance and then security." Grant repeated what he knew and identified the neighbor's house.

"Well, let's divide up the street and talk to the neighbors. Which side do you want me to take?" said Jake.

"I want both of us to conduct the interviews together. We can alternate with one of us asking questions and the other observing and taking notes," instructed Grant. "I'm especially interested in the house directly across the street, the one with the green shutters. That's the neighbor who called security."

"What's his name?"

"Thomas Wolver."

"I suggest we start with him. Chances are, the others saw nothing," said Jake.

"Sounds good. Let's go," said Grant.

Chapter 23

AS AGREED, JAKE and Grant walked across the street to Thomas Wolver's house. Grant knocked. They heard a small dog barking fiercely behind the door. When Wolver opened the door, he held a Miniature Schnauzer, who growled at the men. He recognized both of them.

"Come in, come in."

"Thank you, Mr. Wolver. We'd like to ask you a few questions if you have time," Grant began.

The dog barked louder.

"Of course, I have time. But wait here. Zoe doesn't like strangers. Let me put her in her carrier. I'll be right back."

"Sure," said Jake.

When Wolver returned, he asked, "Can I get you guys a drink?"

"No thanks. Like I said, we need to ask you a few questions about what you saw across the street."

"Have a seat, gentlemen. I'll try to help as much as I can." Wolver sat on the sofa and motioned toward two chairs across the room for them.

They each took a chair. Jake began. Grant took notes.

"Mr. Wolver, you're the man who called security, is that right?"

"Yes, sir. I did."

"What caused you to feel you needed to do that?"

"Well, I always sleep late, especially if I stay up to watch a late movie on TNT. I walk Zoe first thing every day. We have our little routine every morning."

"Exactly what time did you walk her today?"

"I'd say around nine-thirty or so, give or take a few minutes. Zoe kept trying to cross the street. She usually likes to go over to Ms. McAnally's house when she sees her out in the yard."

"So, that's why you went over there today?"

"No, and yes. I noticed that her storm door was ajar, so I decided to walk over and close it for her. That's when I saw her lying there on her front porch."

"Did you touch her?"

"Yes, I did. After calling her name and getting no response, I reached down and checked her carotid artery for a pulse. Am I in trouble for that?"

"No. Did the dog—Zoe—touch Ms. McAnally?" asked Grant.

"Oh, no. When I saw the lady, I picked up Zoe."

"When did you last see Ms. McAnally alive?" asked Jake.

"Last night. But I saw all the other ladies, too."

"Can you give us their names?"

"Yeah, sure. In fact, Sheriff, your mom was here. I saw her when she was leaving. Zoe and I were out for our last walk of the night. I was surprised, and so was she."

"Did she have a white poodle with her?"

"She did. Zoe and her dog tried to make friends."

"What time was that, Mr. Wolver?" Grant asked.

"I'd guess it was around ten-thirty. The other ladies had already gone."

"Can you identify them?" asked Jake.

"Let's see, besides your mom, there was the lady who works in the county clerk's office at the courthouse. Can't remember her name."

"Could it have been Ms. Snyder?" Grant asked.

"Yes, she's the one."

"How do you to know her?"

"Had to file some papers down there after my wife died. You know, probate stuff."

"Go on."

"Then, there was the other woman. I don't know her. Never seen her before."

"Could you describe her?" Grant prodded.

Wolver thought for a moment.

"Yes. She was tall—almost as tall as that Ms. Snyder—with brown hair."

"Anything else you noticed about her?"

"No. Sorry. Those ladies sure like to play their games, don't they?"

"What do you mean by that?" asked Jake.

"Well, I know they play Mah Jongg every Friday night, and last night was Ms. McAnally's turn to be hostess."

"How do you know that?" asked Jake.

"The caterers were there. They always cater her parties," he explained.

"Do you remember the name of the caterer?" said Grant.

"Yes, Mrs. McAnally always uses the club's chef."

"Mr. Wolver, if you think of anything else, please give me a call," said Grant. He handed him his card. Jake did the same.

"I'll do that, Mr. Perryman." He looked at both cards and placed them in his shirt pocket.

"That man is as curious as Lillian." Grant said as soon as he thought they were out of earshot.

"It's surprising he knows their routine so well. Makes me wonder who else in this neighborhood does."

They walked to the next house.

As soon as they stepped up on the porch, the door flew open, and an elderly lady stepped out onto the porch. "Young men . . . oh, Grant, that's you. . ."

"Hello, Mrs. Larson. We need to visit. . ."

He didn't have a chance to finish his sentence. Mrs. Larson talked so fast, she sounded like an auctioneer. "I've been watching the goings on here for the past four hours. I know you're questioning everyone. Rachel is dead."

"Yes, ma'am. We have a couple of . . ." Once more, the woman interrupted.

"Talk to Mr. Nosey next door. He knows everything about everyone. I need your permission to leave cause I have a doctor's appointment, so I'll tell you everything I know about what happened across the street last night."

"Thank you, ma'am. That would be extremely helpful. What exactly do you know?" asked Jake.

"Nothing," was the terse reply. The door slammed shut and then opened. "Mr. Grant, you okay with my leaving?"

"Sure, I'll clear you."

He spoke into his two-way radio and told the officer at the roadblock to let Mrs. Larson pass. That done. He told Jake, "I hate to keep people sequestered when I know that they know nothing."

"Me, too. Let's split up. You take this side, and I'll take the next side of the street."

"That's a plan. People can go about their business sooner. Besides, there are only three houses left."

"Yeah, and I'm sure they won't know anything useful."

It took less than an hour to talk to all of the neighbors in the three remaining homes on the cul-de-sac. They regrouped in Grant's car and reviewed their notes.

"We didn't learn a thing," said Grant, "but the hardest job for today is yet to come."

* * * * *

BILL WATCHED LILLIAN try to stay busy in the house. It was clear to him that she had Rachel on her mind. She would start one task, leave it, and start another. Finished none of them.

Finally, Lillian said, "I'm done with all of this busy work. Grant should have called me by now."

"No, he shouldn't have called you. I'm sure he's busy. He can take care of things by himself."

"I'm going to call Jake. He'll tell me what's going on."

"You can't do that."

"Why not? Oh never mind that question. I know why."

"You know he's with Grant."

"I don't have a good feeling about Rachel. If all was well, she would have called me by now. She might need me," said Lillian.

Bill looked at his wife and saw the concern etched on her face. He knew she would not stop worrying until she knew Rachel was okay, so he said, "Lillian, I'll drive you around to Oak Grove so that you can see for yourself that everything is all right."

Her shoulders relaxed. "Great. Thank you. I'll get my purse."

Eli saw Bill take the car keys off the hook by the back door. He raced ahead of them and jumped in the back seat when Lillian opened the door for him. Bill pushed the button, and the back passenger window went halfway down, giving Eli enough room to hang his head out the window.

"There you go, buddy. Enjoy the ride."

Bill drove slowly to the other side of the lake.

Before he reached the turn taking them to Oak Grove, he said, "When I stop in front of her house, I don't want you jumping out of the car."

"Why?"

"I want you to promise me you'll wait to see what's going on."

"I will," she promised.

They turned the corner. The officer held up his hand. They stopped.

"Why do you think the street is closed, Bill?" said Lillian.

"I don't know, but it can't be good."

The officer walked over the driver's side of the car. As Bill lowered the window, Todd recognized him.

"I'm sorry, Mr. Prestridge, can't allow you to enter here."

"Why? What's happened, Todd?"

"We've had an incident, but at this time, I'm not cleared to discuss it with anyone. The sheriff will make it public when we know more."

"Yes, sir." Bill made a U-turn and drove away.

Angry for being denied access, Lillian ordered, "Stop this car right now. I'll walk to Rachel's if I have to. I need to talk to her, see if she's okay."

Bill kept driving, "We're going home to wait to hear from Grant and Jake."

Lillian pressed her lips into a thin line, drew her eyebrows together, making a worried frown. She stared at Bill and crossed her arms in defiance.

"Wait? You want me to wait when I know Rachel needs me? You know better than that."

Bill said nothing, just kept driving.

Wait? He says 'wait'? That word is not in my vocabulary, especially when a friend needs me. If Rachel's hurt, and he just keeps driving – well, he'd better be ready to defend his actions.

Bill drove Lillian back home. He took the long route. As he passed the first tee box on the front nine, he waved at one of the guys waiting to tee off.

"Why don't you drop me off at the house and then join them?"

"Until we know what's happened over on Oak Grove, I don't want you home by yourself."

"I'll be all right. I won't be alone. I've got Eli." Upon hearing his name, the dog pulled his head back into the car. When no commands were meted out to him, he continued his perusal of the passing landscape, whiskers and ears peeled back by the cool, autumn wind.

"Are you sure?"

Lillian could tell Bill wanted to play with his buddies.

"Yes, I'm positive. I promise I'll stay there and wait to hear from Grant and Jake." Lillian saw Bill hesitate.

"There's nothing you can do here but sit and watch me worry, and that makes me more nervous. Go on. Enjoy yourself," she said, smiling.

"I will, but remember your promise: Stay here and wait for Grant's call."

"I promise."

Bill parked in the garage. Opened the door for Lillian and Eli. He grabbed his clubs and backed into the street.

Well, it didn't take you long to head for the golf course. I guess a round of golf is more important than my friends.

* * * * *

"**COME ON, ELI.** Let's you and I go out on the deck, soak up some sun."

Lillian was wearing a broad-brimmed straw hat and sunglasses when she saw Jake and Grant standing at the bottom of the driveway. Finally, they headed her way. She watched them, her eyes hidden behind the dark glasses. She dreaded to hear the news they brought. They both looked weary, shoulders stooped, heads down.

As they reached the top step, Jake held out his arms, and his mother stood and hugged him. He patted her on the back for quite some time. Finally, she pushed away from him. "I knew last night something bad was going to happen. I just felt it. I warned Rachel."

She studied the faces of both boys. Jake's was solemn, clearly concerned about his mother. Grant's was red. The veins on his neck bulged. He was angry.

So was Lillian.

"Tell me the truth. Rachel's dead, isn't she?"

"Yes, Mom. I'm so sorry."

"When did she die?"

"The medical examiner gave us a preliminary time. He said it could have been around ten-thirty to twelve-thirty last night."

"Oh, no. I left there a little after ten o'clock."

"Lillian, did you hear or see anything out of the ordinary?" asked Grant.

"No, but as I started to leave, both Rachel and I heard tires squeal."

"Did you see the car?"

"No, Grant. The only one I saw was a gentleman walking his dog."

"We know about him. When we questioned him, he told us about meeting you."

"I hate to ask, but I have to know. How did Rachel die?"

"Mom, brace yourself."

"Tell me."

"A single shot to the forehead. I don't think she ever knew what hit her."

"Did someone break into her house?"

"No. She had opened the door for someone. Mr. Wolver and his dog found her, lying in the front doorway."

"Then she would have seen the scumbag who shot her." Lillian turned her back to the men and looked at the lake. *Rachel, I promise I'll find the person who shot you. Whoever killed you will pay. I won't rest until he or she is found.* When she faced Grant and Jake, she said, "Enough is enough. I don't intend to lose another friend." She pressed her lips together and took a deep breath. *No time for tears. They won't help Rachel.*

"Lillian, I swear to you that I'll find the vermin that did this." Grant's voice didn't sound human. Instead, it was guttural, more like Eli's growl.

"I know you will, and I also know I'll do everything in my power to help."

"Right now, Mom. Your safety is our biggest concern. By the way, where's Dad?"

"I sent him to the golf course."

"I don't believe it," snorted her son. "Just wait until I –"

Grant held up his hand, and Jake clamped his mouth shut.

She saw his warning to Jake and decided it was time to refocus.

"Let's sit down," she said as she bent to pick up the straw hat that had fallen off when Jake hugged her to him. "Grant, do you think Rachel's murder could be connected to Sheila's somehow?" she asked.

"I do," said Grant.

"What makes you say that?" said Jake.

"I don't believe in coincidences," said Grant.

"Neither do I," agreed Jake.

"That makes three of us, but tell me specifics. Why do you say that right now?" she said. *I'll not mention my thoughts about the adoption theory. Let them tell me what they know. Besides, I don't know if Grant knows anything about it.*

"The fact that I had planned to meet with Rachel this morning to review all of her newcomer files. We wanted to see if there could be any information in them that would connect someone with Sheila," Grant explained.

"And the fact that someone made sure you couldn't keep that appointment makes me feel that someone just didn't want you to make any connections there," said Jake.

Lillian, who had been listening to the exchange, asked the obvious question. "But who knew you two were going to meet?"

"Interesting question," said Grant. "I'm wondering that myself."

"I knew about it," said Jake. "Rachel could have mentioned her appointment with you to anyone."

"I doubt it. She knew I wanted to keep the investigation closely guarded," said Grant.

Both men looked at Lillian.

"Mom, did you know about the meeting?"

"She didn't tell me," said Lillian, "and she knew that I was helping you with the investigation." Both Jake and Grant glanced at each other, both slightly smiling.

"If it hadn't been for you taking the documents out of her house, we would not have known anything about Sheila's real identity or the fact that she had been married and had adopted a child," offered Grant.

"So, if she didn't tell me, her best friend, then I wouldn't think she told anyone else. Hmm." Lillian frowned. "Now, I'm mad. Whoever thinks he can come into my world and kill my good friend had better watch out."

"Now, Mom, Grant and I don't want you hurt. Promise me that you will not meddle in this case anymore. In the first place, you're too emotionally connected to it," said Jake.

Lillian did not verbally respond to Jake's plea. She just lowered her head in acknowledgment of his request.

Don't think for one minute, boys, that I'm staying put for long. I will carry my thirty-eight with me from now on. I will capture Rachel's killer, and that's a promise I intend to keep—for me and for Rachel.

Jake said, "Mom, Grant and I need to go now. Are you sure you're okay?"

"Don't worry about me. You two get busy on finding the criminal who thinks he can disrupt our lives and murder one of my best friends."

* * * * *

GRANT AND JAKE left Lillian sitting on the deck, Eli beside her chair. They stopped when they reached their cars. Grant stopped and leaned against his vehicle. Jake stood beside him.

"Do you think your mom will keep that promise?" Grant asked.

"Hell, no. Did you hear her say she would?"

"No."

"Well, be prepared. She's going to be dangerous." Jake looked up to see his mother standing by the railing. She waved at them and then sat back down in her chaise.

"I've seen that fire in her eyes more than once, and it's there now, just hidden behind those sunglasses."

"We need to work fast. Three murders in less than three weeks."

"Yeah, this community is going to be in a state of panic if I don't clear things up fast. I dread the next homeowner association meeting. I may not have a job."

"If it makes you feel any better, the county commissioners aren't too happy with me right now either," admitted Jake.

"Do you remember I told you that I don't believe in coincidences?"

"Yes, I do. Coincidences usually aren't what they seem to be. What are you thinking?" asked Jake.

"I'm thinking there is someone who knew about my meeting with Rachel," said Grant.

"Who?" asked Jake.

"Besides the security dispatcher, who always knows where I am, it could be the new girl in the office," said Grant.

"The new girl?" said Jake.

"Yes, wait a minute." Grant listened to the message coming through on his radio. "Tell him I'll be right there."

"Tell who?" asked Jake.

"A gentlemen who claims to be a friend of Rachel's just tried to enter the gate. If he is who I think he is, he will be sad to hear about her," said Grant. "I'll talk to him and get back with you." Grant turned to go.

"Ten Four." Jake looked up and waved to his mom, then climbed in his vehicle and drove away.

Lillian smiled and waved.

* * * * *

LILLIAN HAD WATCHED the exchange between the two as they stood in her driveway. *It's a good thing I read lips. Grant, you didn't tell Jake the name of the new girl, but I know who she is. And, if she told the truth about not knowing Sheila, why would she care if Grant met with Rachel?*

Chapter 24

GRANT WALKED INTO his office. There stood a tall, gray-haired gentleman who was talking on his cell phone. He quickly finished his call when he heard someone come into the room. David Nix turned around, reached out, and shook hands with Grant.

"Hello, Grant. I haven't seen you for a while," said David.

"Seems like a long time, but I seem to lose track of time these days," said Grant.

"It has been at least six months since I was here to see Rachel."

"That long?" asked Grant.

"When I stopped at the entrance to the lake, I noticed you have new security personnel. I gave them my name, and they told me to park my car in the parking lot of the business office. I was ushered in here. I don't understand why."

Grant nodded slowly.

"I told the people at the gate to send you to me. I need to talk to you. It's not good news."

"Why do I dread hearing what you are going to say?" said David.

"I have some sad news to give you. Have a seat, David," said Grant.

"It's Rachel, isn't it? Is she sick?"

"No, she's not sick. It saddens me to tell you that Rachel is dead," said Grant.

David reacted the way Grant expected upon hearing about the death of a long-time friend. He gave David time to process the sudden news before proceeding. He knew that David would have questions, but he had some of his own to ask.

Mighty convenient that Robert's old business partner shows up the morning after Rachel's murder. I bet her death will be a great advantage to him.

"How did she die? I just talked to her two days ago, and she seemed okay. She was in a good mood, her usual happy go lucky, sweet person attitude," said David.

"Sounds like her. Did she say anything that would make you think she was stressed or worried about anything?" Grant ignored David's question.

"No, she didn't. She never worried about the business."

"I know," said Grant. "In fact, I've heard her say that of all the business partners her husband could have had, you were the cream of the crop."

"After Robert's death, I've pretty much run the business by myself. Of course, I've kept Rachel as a full partner."

"Did she ever have questions about the company?"

"No, not really. She trusted me to keep it going and to make a profit."

"That's probably a challenge right now."

"It is, but as everyone in the oil and gas industry knows—just hang on—the price per barrel always fluctuates."

"You and Rachel go way back, don't you?"

"We do. Both she and Robert. We've been friends since our college days."

"I didn't realize you knew each other then," said Grant.

"It was my fiancé Lori who introduced Robert and Rachel."

"They were pretty close, weren't they," said Grant.

"More than close. They were by far the happiest couple I've ever encountered, totally devoted to each other and their children," said David.

"Robert and Rachel were excellent role models for young couples. They were both active in the church here, you know."

"They enjoyed counseling young couples before they tied the knot and had some good stories to share with them," said David.

"So, you said that you talked to her two days ago?" Grant pulled him back to the present.

"Yes, Rachel and I have been conducting our business over the phone," explained David, "but there are some papers for the corporation that need Rachel's signature, so I flew in last night to meet with her."

"How long did you plan to be here?" asked Grant.

"I had planned to meet with her this morning, get her signature on the documents, and then fly back to Houston this afternoon. We planned to drive into town and eat at some new sushi restaurant. . .can't remember the name," said David, his voice getting softer as his brows knitted together.

It was obvious that he was fighting to maintain his self-composure. Grant decided that David needed something to do, so he decided to solicit his assistance regarding Rachel's children.

"We have not contacted Rachel's children yet. Just found her this morning," said Grant.

"Found her, you say? Please, Grant, explain. We've danced around the subject long enough. I need to know exactly what happened," pleaded David.

"Well, David, to put it bluntly, Rachel was murdered sometime last night," said Grant.

"Oh, no! How? Who would do such a thing?" asked David, obviously shaken.

"Right now, I can't answer that, but I assure you that I will do everything in my power to find and hold accountable the person who did this," said Grant.

"You just don't think of this sort of thing happening here at Leisure Lake, a gated community, and with all of the security you have. . . it just doesn't seem possible," said David.

"I know, but what you don't know is that this is the third murder we've had recently," said Grant.

"Good Lord! What's happening here?" It was obvious David's shock was wearing off and being replaced by another emotion: anger.

"David, can you compose yourself long enough to call Rachel's children?" asked Grant.

"Can I go out to the house to get telephone numbers?" asked David.

"I'll drive you over," offered Grant.

"Thanks," said David.

* * * * *

GRANT DROVE SLOWLY through Leisure Lake taking the long route to Rachel's house. Even though he had given Ogburn permission to move the body, he wanted to make sure the M.E. had had sufficient time to do so. When they finally parked in the driveway, Grant saw the county medical examiner's van drive around the curve on its way into town. Grant heard David take a deep breath. Grant mentally counted to ten before he said anything to David.

"David, I have to warn you," he began.

"What about?" asked David.

"I don't want you going through the front door or into the living room for that matter. There's quite a lot of blood. Don't think you'd want to see that," said Grant kindly.

"You're right. I don't," agreed David.

Grant continued, "And before we go into the house, you will need to slip these surgical slippers over your shoes and wear these gloves." He reached into the back seat and grabbed a black bag that until recently he had never really needed. "Wait until we step inside to put them on." David nodded, took the slippers and the gloves, and followed Grant.

"If we enter through the kitchen, you'll have access to Rachel's desk in her computer room situated in an alcove just to the right of the breakfast area." Grant led him around the house to the back door.

"Okay."

"David, understand that I'm breaking protocol here," said Grant.

"How so?" said David.

"I shouldn't let anyone in Rachel's house until forensics has completed its investigation, so promise me one thing," said Grant.

"Anything. I want to help find who killed my friend and partner," said David.

"Don't touch anything unless I give you permission," said Grant.

"I won't."

As they approached the back door, Grant reached for the knob and then suddenly drew back. "I forgot. It's locked, and I didn't bring the key."

"I have a key. Let me open it." David pulled a key ring from his pocket and opened the door.

Okay, thought Grant, *interesting. Why would he have a key to Rachel's house? Why would he need it? Was there more than just business between these two friends?*

It was as if David read his mind. He explained, "Rachel trusted me with every aspect of her life. She wanted me to be able to get in the house whenever I came and gave me keys to her house and Robert's old car so that I could use both if I needed to be in East Texas when she was out of town." Grant nodded. They entered the house.

"May I look in Rachel's desk for an address book? The telephone numbers of her children should be in it," said David.

"Yes, but remember: don't touch anything else without my permission."

With Grant looking over his shoulder, David opened the center drawer. It contained the usual pencils, paper clips, staple remover, things one would expect to find. Grant then motioned for David to open the drawer on the right side of the desk. It was neatly organized with hanging files, all of which were labeled.

Grant looked at each tab. Most of them had topics indicating they held business documents. He then motioned for David to open the bottom drawer on the left side of the desk. Again, a row of neat files were nestled in the green hanging folders.

David indicated a file labeled "Last Will and Testament." Grant reached over David's shoulder and removed it.

"I guess this document is one that needs to be given to the DA," said Grant, "but first, let's look through it. See what we can find."

"I already know what it says," admitted David, "and this is only a copy. The original is in Rachel's safe deposit box."

"Oh?" Grant raised his eyebrows.

"The four of us, Robert and Rachel and Lori and I, used the same attorney to draw up our wills," said David.

"Tell me about them," said Grant.

"If I had predeceased Robert, then he would have served as the executor for me just as I have served as executor for his estate. We both agreed to take care of Lori and/or Rachel in the event of either of our deaths," explained David.

"What happens if either Lori or Rachel were to die? Did your wills take that contingency into account?" said Grant.

"Yes, they did," countered David.

"How?" said Grant.

"Right now, as soon as Rachel's will is probated, her children will be taken care of by a trust that will continue to be funded from the profits of the company," said David.

"I suppose you're the trustee?" Another question followed an affirmative nod from David. "And will the children share equally?" asked Grant.

"I know what you're thinking," said David, "but all of Rachel's children are quite successful in their own right. They adored their mother and would not have caused her any kind of worry or physical harm."

Grant mulled over this information for a few minutes while David continued to look for Rachel's address book.

Finally, he said, "David, I think Rachel's children will be more receptive to your breaking the news to them. Sounds as though the two families are quite close. When you do so, I'd like to ask a favor of you."

"Sure, Grant, what is it you want me to do? Oh, wait a minute, I think I know," said David.

"Good. Tell them to contact me when they arrive. I'll need to talk to them. I want to make sure I leave nothing out of our investigation, find out where they were yesterday and last night around ten-thirty. I want to rule out all possibilities."

"I understand," said David. "I will give them that information without it sounding like they'll be facing an interrogation."

"Thanks, David. You know money has a way of bringing out the beast in some folks."

"Sometimes, we think we know people, but we don't," said David.

My question right now is: Do I really know you?

"Ah ha! Here it is," said David proudly as he extracted the book from the top left-hand drawer of Rachel's desk.

"Copy down their names, addresses, and telephone numbers," instructed Grant, "we can't take the book out of the house just yet." *But I can and will*, thought Grant, *when I come back.*

Grant took David back to the clubhouse.

"Give me a call, will you, when you've contacted all of the children," said Grant.

"Will do," said David as he got into Robert's old white Lexus.

* * * * *

AS DAVID DROVE away, Grant wrote down the license plate number. He decided to go back through Rachel's house. *There's got to be something I'm missing. Rachel's death follows Sheila's murder too soon. And then, there's Mr. Peters. Did they have a connection that I haven't found yet? And there's David and that white Lexus. Did he lie to me when he said he hadn't been here during the last six months?*

Grant drove back to Rachel's house and parked in the driveway. Jake pulled in right behind him, got out of his car, and climbed into the passenger seat beside Grant. The two looked at each other, and without saying a word, prepared themselves to search Rachel's house.

As they walked up the drive, Grant said, "Rachel's death is too soon after Sheila's murder, don't you think?"

Jake nodded. "Rachel knew something, or someone thought she did."

"Let's search this house. There's got to be something, some kind of clue we haven't found yet," said Grant.

"Rachel must have opened the door without checking who was there," said Jake.

"That was my first thought, but what if someone had a key, someone like her business partner, David Nix?"

"Could be. Both you and I have a key to mom and dad's house."

"People share their keys. Unfortunately, everyone around the lake has a false sense of security," said Grant.

"That's because you do your job so well," countered Jake.

"Well, be that as it may, let's get to it," said Grant, "but before we do, I need to tell you I let David Nix in the house."

"Why?"

"He volunteered to call Rachel's children but needed their contact information. I let him look in her desk."

"I see. That's all he touched?"

"Yes."

They walked around to the back door and into the kitchen. Jake noticed the green light on the dishwasher. Jake opened the door and then pushed it completely closed to turn off the light. "Looks like Rachel had been cleaning the kitchen. The dishwasher completed its cycle."

Grant had his clipboard and was taking notes. He walked over to the sink, filled with cold soapy water. "She obviously was in the process of washing wine glasses. There are two in the dish drainer, and two are still in the sink," he said.

"She was definitely interrupted by someone at the door," said Jake.

The men walked through the rest of the house. Nothing seemed to be out of place. The card table was still set up in the living room. The Mah Jongg tiles were neatly stacked in the leather case where Rachel kept them. The case was open and still rested on the card table.

"Doesn't look like a burglary," said Jake.

"No, the person who rang that bell had an agenda: to kill Rachel," said Grant. "I'm going back to her desk and see what I can find."

"You mentioned you had set up an appointment to meet with her and go over the file she keeps on newcomers," said Jake.

"Yes, I did," said Grant.

"Other than the new girl and the dispatcher, do you know if anyone else knew about your meeting?" asked Jake.

"No. I wish I did. I'm convinced that someone found out about it and made sure she couldn't keep it," said Grant.

"Do you have any ideas?" asked Jake.

"Not at present, but one is forming," said Grant.

"Would you like to share it?"

"I intend to question everyone in my office come Monday," said Grant. "Jake, would you look through the rest of the house with me?"

"Are you looking for something in particular? If I know what it is, perhaps, I'll have a better chance of locating it," said Jake.

"I want to look through Rachel's newcomer file if it's here," said Grant. "It may have some information we can use. See if you can find it."

"I'll start in the living room."

Fifteen minutes later, Jake walked over and put his hand on Grant's shoulder and said, "Grant, listen to me. You're not responsible for Rachel's death."

Grant looked up. "I'm head of security. It's my job to protect the residents at the lake. If I'm not responsible, why do I feel so guilty?"

"I don't know the answer to that question. When I figure it out, then maybe I can forgive myself for my own mistakes," said Jake as he turned to go into the dining room.

Chapter 25

JAKE CONDUCTED A thorough search of the house while Grant read the documents in every file folder Rachel kept in her desk. He did not find anything that would resemble the newcomer file Rachel kept. Jake walked back into the computer room and saw Grant staring out the window.

"I take it that you didn't find the file," he said.

"It's got to be here somewhere," said Grant. "Did you find that large bag she always carried around with her?"

"I didn't see it," responded Jake, "but I'd bet my paycheck that's where we'll find the file."

"Maybe, she left it in her car," said Grant.

"Might as well check it out. We've done just about all we can do here," offered Jake.

Rachel's car was parked in the carport behind her house, unlocked of course. Grant walked around to the driver's side and opened the door. He reached down to pop open the trunk.

Jake whistled when he saw the trunk open. "Hey, you were right. Here it is."

Grant rushed around to the back of the car, picked up Rachel's bag, and extracted the file. He motioned toward a table on the patio.

The two men sat down and began to read Rachel's notes about the people on whom she had called. She was very thorough in her description of them as well as her impression of their homes and how they had decorated them.

"I remember hearing Rachel say you can learn a lot about a person just by the way she decorates her home," Jake said.

"Wait a minute," said Grant as he picked up two pages that had been clipped together. On the front page was a post-it note. On it Rachel had written, *these two women know each other but don't like each other.* He showed the documents to Jake.

"Does Rachel's note mean anything to you?" asked Jake.

Both men stopped talking when they heard footsteps on the gravel drive. Grant did not have time to answer Jake's question, but nodded in the affirmative and closed the file. He put it back in Rachel's bag. Both men stood up to face the intruder.

* * * * *

"I KNEW YOU two would be here. Have you found any clues?" asked Lillian.

"I have a better question. Didn't you just promise to stay out of this case?"

Lillian shrugged her shoulders. "Technically?"

"Never mind, you two," said Grant. "Bickering won't help us."

"I agree." Lillian smiled at him and then looked at her son. "Jake, none of the girls know about Rachel. Did you or Grant talk with them?"

"I'm surprised you haven't called them," Grant said.

"I'd rather be shot than have to break this news to them. You know they loved Rachel like a sister."

Jake said, "You don't have to do it alone, Mom. We'll help."

"I do have a suggestion," said Lillian.

"Let's hear it," said Grant.

"I'll call and ask Victoria and Margaret to come over for coffee. Then we can break the news to them at the same time."

"Good idea," said Jake. "They were very close."

"Yes, they were. We know Rachel hosted Mah Jongg last evening. The girls may have seen something unusual, maybe some information we can use," said Grant.

"Mom, when you call, tell them you have some news they need to hear in person."

"Okay. I'll go home now and make the calls. I'll ask them to meet me at the house in about thirty minutes."

After Lillian left, Grant pulled out his cell phone and called his officer on duty. "Todd, I want you to keep those detour signs up. For the next couple of days, block off the main street leading to the crime scene. Do not let anyone other than those who live there drive past the signs. Take down all license numbers, too."

"Sure thing, boss," said Todd.

Grant said, "Just don't want those two coming in and deciding to pick up Rachel on their way to your house."

"Good thought," said Jake. "We'd for sure lose control of the situation if they did."

* * * * *

AFTER LILLIAN CALLED her friends, she walked into the kitchen to make coffee. As she poured the water into the appliance, her eyes tried to tear up, but she brushed them away with the back of her hand. "I don't have time for this weepy nonsense," she said to the coffee pot when it began to drip. She heard a tap on the front door and opened it.

Both Margaret and Victoria stood there. "Come in, girls. We need to talk."

"Let's wait for Rachel," said Margaret. "I'm sure you called her, too."

"No, I didn't call her."

The three ladies turned when they heard the door open again. Jake and Grant walked into the room. Jake walked across the room to stand beside his mother. "Please sit down, ladies."

He guided his mother to the sofa and indicated places for the other ladies to sit.

As they seated themselves, Grant looked at Jake.

"You tell them, Grant. They will appreciate hearing the sad news from you."

Lillian nodded for Grant to proceed.

"Victoria, Margaret, Lillian didn't call Rachel because Rachel, because Rachel. . ." Grant's voice trailed off as he choked back tears.

"Grant, just tell us. Has Rachel been in an accident or something?" said Margaret.

"Not an accident. Rachel has been shot, and it was fatal," said Lillian. She watched the reactions of the other two ladies. She nodded to Bill who had come in the back door. He walked over and stood behind her chair.

Margaret cried softly, trying to maintain her composure. Grant went to her, cradled her in his arms and patted her on the back. While Victoria wiped tears from her eyes, Lillian stood and walked over to the window to gaze at the lake.

Eli jumped onto the back of the sofa. He crept along the back until he reached Grant still comforting Margaret. The dog put his head on Grant's shoulder.

Lillian finally turned away from the window. She squared her shoulders and turned to face the others.

"Jake, Grant, this has gone on long enough. Three murders within a month. I've had it," she announced. "From now on, I'm on the case." As the men in the room stared slack-jawed, she ordered, "I don't want to hear one word from any of you."

"Now, Mom, don't let your temper get the best of you," said Jake.

"It's not going to get the best of me, but here is what we are going to do," she said in her best *I'm in charge now* voice.

"Just wait on giving us your instructions," said Grant. "We need to talk, all of us. Jake and I have exhausted our resources just trying to solve Sheila's murder, and now we have two more, one too close to all of us."

"Yes, it is too close for comfort," agreed Victoria. "I'll do whatever I can to help you. It goes without saying that I'll also do what Lillian tells me to do."

"We'll get to that later. I need to ask you ladies some questions, but if you aren't up to it right now, I can wait," Grant said.

"No waiting," said Lillian. "I can't speak for Victoria or Margaret, but I'm mad, mad as all get out. Ask me anything, and I'll try to be objective, but I'm mad. Rachel didn't deserve this."

Soft spoken Bill entered into the conversation. "I'll pour some coffee. I think all of us could use a dose of caffeine right now. Might help clear our heads." He left to carry out his mission. He rummaged through the pantry looking for some kind of snack.

Grant pulled out his notebook and began writing a list of questions he wanted to ask. Jake walked over and peered over Grant's shoulder, read over the list thus far, and indicated that he would like to add a question. Grant handed him the notebook.

Jake wrote his question and handed the notebook back to Grant, who nodded his agreement.

"Ladies, Jake and I have put our heads together and have come up with a few questions. If you're ready to begin, we'll do so."

Bill walked in with a carafe of coffee and a plate of cookies he had found in the pantry. He set them down on the sideboard, and the ladies poured coffee for themselves. No one took anything to eat. All of them sat around the dining room table. Grant took a deep breath and began.

"First of all, as Jake and I walked through Rachel's house today, we noticed the Mah Jongg tiles still on the card table," Grant began.

Before he could ask his question, Lillian chimed in, "Yes, they were there when I left. It was Rachel's turn to host Mah Jongg last night."

"What time did the group break up?" asked Jake.

"Hmm, let me see, we finished earlier than usual, didn't we, Margaret?" said Lillian.

"Yes, in fact, I know we finished before ten o'clock because I was home and in bed by ten-thirty."

"Who played last night?" asked Jake.

"Besides myself, Margaret, and Rachel, there was a substitute for Victoria," said Lillian. She saw Margaret stiffen her back. *You don't have to say anything else. Leave it.*

Margaret said, "Lillian's being nice." Her hardened facial expression mirrored the sarcastic tone of her voice.

"That's right. I asked Sally Jane to sub for me," said Victoria.

"Sally couldn't make it, so she had a sub, too. Lillian failed to mention that it was my ne'er-do-well sister who ended up being your substitute."

Victoria, left eyebrow raised, looked confused but said nothing. She stood, walked to the buffet, and chose a cookie.

Lillian watched Grant as he wrote in his notebook. When he looked up, she directed her next comment to her son.

"Jake, I have some questions to ask you and Grant before you continue with yours." *I can tell by your faces, you welcome a diversion right now.*

"Ask away. Maybe your questions will spur all of us to remember something we didn't think we knew."

"Here goes. Was there a break-in, a burglary?"

"Good question," Grant answered. "From our walk around the house, Jake and I determined that was not the case."

"So. . .you think she knew the person who shot her?" asked Victoria.

"We do," answered Jake. He paused and looked at each woman before continuing. "That is why it is so important for you ladies to think about last night. Any little thing, no matter how insignificant it may seem, could be just the one thing Grant and I need to find the culprit."

"When was she found?"

Neither Grant nor Jake answered, so Lillian continued.

"Who found her?"

"A neighbor found her," Jake said

Lillian directed her next question to Grant.

"Was it that grumpy Mrs. Larson?"

Grant shook his head.

"Then, I bet I can tell you who it was," said Lillian with a defiant tilt of her chin.

"Mom, I don't think you need to know that information right now."

"Why, are you afraid I'll pester Mr. Wolver?" *Surprised, are you? When will you learn that your mother is always a step ahead of you?*

Grant smiled. "You might as well be honest with her, Jake. After all – "

Jake nodded. "Mom's going to snoop until she learns everything we know. Isn't that what you were going to say?"

"You know her as well as I do."

"Let's go back to my first question you two ignored."

"Which one?"

"This one: When was she found?"

"This morning. We got the call between nine and ten o'clock," Grant said.

"I know the M.E. has already determined the time of death, hasn't he?"

"Yes, ma'am," Grant responded.

"Mom, I don't think you want to know that detail."

"Tell her," Victoria ordered. "All of Rachel's friends have a right to know."

"No, don't. Your reluctance to say tells me everything I need to know," Lillian said.

Victoria began to wipe the tears streaming down her cheeks. "She was there all night."

"How awful." Margaret's voice quavered.

"Straighten up, Victoria," Lillian commanded. "Margaret, that goes for you, too. Rachel wouldn't want you to fall apart," Lillian said sternly.

"One more question, ladies," Jake said to keep the conversation flowing. "Did Rachel appear to be worried or preoccupied about anything last night?"

Victoria responded, "I didn't notice anything unusual about her demeanor. Did you, Margaret?"

Margaret shook her head. "No, I didn't either."

When Jake looked at his mother, she shrugged. *I'll keep her conversation about the business to myself for now. It may or may not be relevant.*

Chapter 26

LILLIAN LOOKED AROUND the room. Everyone was tired. She could tell that Jake and Grant were emotionally drained. Grant had gone to the buffet for more coffee. He brought the half-empty pot and refilled the cups. Lillian indicated with a wave of her hand she didn't want anymore and said, "I suggest we should call it a day. All of you look as exhausted as I feel."

"Wait a minute." Victoria perked up and looked at Margaret. "You mentioned a sister. You've never mentioned having family. Tell us about her."

Margaret looked down and then glanced up to face her friends. "This will be difficult for me."

Grant placed the coffee pot on the buffet, gave a slight nod, and softly said, "Go on."

Margaret swallowed and tried hard to choke back tears. She didn't have much success. Her voice gave way. Bill came to her rescue.

"Margaret, I think it is time I broke my promise and stepped in here to explain some things, don't you?" said Bill.

Margaret nodded.

Bill continued. "Margaret does have a sister, one who has never appreciated what her sibling tried to do for her." He addressed the women. "I have to confess, I've known Margaret longer than I've known you."

"How so?" Grant moved to the empty dining room chair next to Margaret. He took her hand in his, put his arm around her, and pulled her close to him.

"When I worked for the *Star Telegram*, Margaret was just out of high school and was working part-time to pay for her college classes. We became friends, more like father/daughter friends if you know what I mean." He looked at Lillian who smiled at him.

Okay, Margaret. Time to come clean. Let's see if your story matches Bill's, thought Lillian.

"I don't know what I would have done without Bill. You see, my family was in quite a turmoil over my sister," said Margaret.

"What had your sister done?" asked Victoria.

"My parents were upset with her because she had begun to date an older man and would not tell them who he was. She insisted on seeing him even though my father had strictly forbidden her to do so," said Margaret. "My sister was three years older than I and should have graduated from college in the spring."

"Let me guess," said Victoria. "She dropped out of school, got pregnant, and was abandoned by lover boy."

"You are so right. Not only was she abandoned by lover boy but also by our parents who would have nothing to do with her. They were so disappointed with her."

"So, Dad, how do you fit into this scenario?" Jake said.

"It was I who suggested to Margaret – after she told me about her sister's predicament – to contact an attorney who handled private adoptions."

"I did, and my sister decided that would be best for the baby. She didn't think she could take care of a child by herself," said Margaret.

"What happened, then?" asked Victoria.

"I lost contact with her. After she gave the baby up, she really went off the deep end, perhaps from guilt, perhaps from feeling abandoned by the baby's father. I don't know. But I know she was deeply hurt because of our father. He disowned her, and our mom just stood by and did not stand up to him."

Margaret looked at Grant who had not taken his eyes off her and said, "I'm so sorry I've not told you any of this before. Can you ever forgive me?"

"There's nothing to forgive, my dear. We all have a past of some kind. Just remember, I love you," said Grant who leaned in and kissed her on the forehead.

Jake reached over and picked up Grant's notebook, read over Grant's notes, and asked. "Victoria, was there a reason why you weren't at Rachel's house playing Mah Jongg as usual?"

"My sister-in-law had come for a visit, so I asked Sally Jane to sub for me. I don't know why she couldn't or why she had to ask someone to sub for her, but I intend to find out," said Victoria.

"Go easy on her," said Margaret. "She had no idea that the person she asked to sub would have any connection with any of us."

"Did Rachel know her?" asked Grant.

"I believe she did," said Margaret.

"And how do you know that fact?" asked Grant.

"Rachel mentioned she had called on her when she first moved into the lake area."

Lillian sat forward in her chair. *Grant, you haven't asked the key question yet. You are in for a surprise.*

"Okay. Well, I think I've got a clear picture of what happened. There's just one thing you've not told me," said Grant.

"What's that?" asked Margaret.

"Her name," said Jake. *Good job, my boy.*

"Oh," said Margaret, "it's Donna, Donna Traydon. She works in accounting at the club. At least, that's what I think she said."

* * * * *

AT THE MENTION of the name Donna, Lillian noticed Grant and Jake quickly exchange glances. *I'll talk to them privately and tell* *them what I suspect. Could it be that Donna returned and – can't let Victoria know what I'm thinking. If she knew I consider Donna as a murderer, they would have to arrest Victoria, and I just can't lose anyone else I love, not right now.*

Lillian stood up.

"Well, I hate to break up this group," she said, "but I think we've all had enough for tonight."

Grant turned to Margaret, "I'll take you home."

"No, I can drive myself. You have your work to do."

"You'll do no such thing," said Victoria. "I have a suggestion to make."

"What are you thinking?" asked Jake.

"The way I see it, this house is not safe. As I recall, someone's already shot out the front window. Obviously, Rachel's house wasn't safe either."

"So, what are you getting at?" said Grant.

"I don't think Margaret needs to be alone, nor do I think Lillian is safe here. I want both of you to come to my house for a couple of days," said Victoria.

"And what makes you think we'll be safer with you?" asked Margaret.

"I have a gun," said Victoria.

Lillian laughed at her stubborn friend. "Guess what? All of us have guns. And I, for one, am not afraid to use mine."

Grant spoke up quite sternly, "Victoria, I don't want to have to come after you. Go home. Lock your doors. I suggest that Margaret stay here with Mom and Dad. She can sleep in Jake's old bedroom, and I intend to stay here as well. You see," he said patting his gun, "I've got one of those, too."

"I'll have to go home to get my toothbrush and pajamas," Margaret said.

"No, you don't," said Lillian. "I have everything – night clothes, brand new toothbrush, and any other toiletry you may need – in the guest bathroom."

Bill laughed. "Lillian is always prepared for out-of-town guests. I guess you could qualify for that since you live in town."

"Okay, that takes care of Margaret. So Victoria, I'll follow you home, make sure you get there safe and sound," said Jake. He then hugged his mother. "I'll be back out first thing in the morning."

"Thanks. I have some thoughts on this," Lillian whispered in his ear as she hugged him goodbye.

* * * * *

EARLY THE NEXT morning, Margaret was up and dressed quickly so she could drive by her house and change into her work clothes. Shortly after her exit, Jake drove into the driveway. He walked up onto the deck and rang the buzzer. Lillian opened the door, pulled him inside, and hugged him.

"You're just in time for breakfast. Your dad and I were about to sit down and eat. Come join us," said Lillian.

"Only coffee. Jessica fed me well this morning."

Grant walked in. "Me, too. Coffee sounds real good right about now."

"Did you sleep well?" asked Lillian.

"As a matter of fact, I didn't. Just kept thinking about Margaret and her sister. Sad," said Grant, "sad that Margaret and Donna could not have worked things out."

"It is," said Jake, "but sometimes brothers make the same mistake."

"I guess you're right about that," said Grant, "and speaking of which, Jake, I want us to be right with each other from now on."

"Man, oh man, what good news," said Lillian, beaming.

Jake grabbed Grant and gave him a big bear hug. "I have wanted to do that for a long time, but I need to explain some things to you."

"No, you don't," said Grant. "I've blamed you for Alice's death, but I knew her before I left for the Gulf War, and I knew what she was capable of doing."

"I do feel like I let you down," said Jake. "I did promise to look out for her while you were away."

"You could not have saved her. She was a budding alcoholic before I left, but I refused to see it. When I was in the Middle East fighting, I worried about her. It's not your fault she drove her car into that tree," said Grant.

Jake bowed his head, overwhelmed by Grant's words of forgiveness.

Grant continued: "The Lord has a way of taking care of us. If Alice and I had married, I'm afraid my life would have been one living hell."

"Let's pray that Alice had a chance to know the Lord before she died. At any rate, you have indeed been blessed. Margaret truly loves you," said Lillian.

"And I love her," said Grant.

"Well, what are you going to do about that?" asked Bill who had silently walked into the kitchen and had been listening to the conversation.

"Simple," said Jake. "He's going to marry her."

Grant laughed. "Jake, that's the smartest thing you've said all morning." He picked up the blue mug Lillian had placed before him. "You know I've changed my mind. I'm suddenly hungry. Think I will have some of those pancakes."

"Coming right up." Lillian bowed her head and prayed, "For all of your blessings and mercy, Oh Lord, we are grateful."

An amen was said by all.

Conversation ceased as the diners stacked pancakes, butter melting between them, on blue willow plates, and drizzled syrup over them.

Jake broke the silence. "Grant, I think we ought to re-canvas the neighborhood and see if Rachel's neighbors can remember anything out of the ordinary now that more than twenty-four hours have passed."

"They've had time to think about it for awhile. I need you to run a license check and a criminal background check on one Donna Traydon," said Grant.

"Didn't you already do that," asked Jake, "when the lake employed her?"

"We ran her name through DPS but did not do a comprehensive criminal background check," said Grant.

"I'll call it in right now." Jake opened his cell phone. When he ended his call, he said, "We'll have the results by the end of the day."

"Good. Thanks. Let's drive over and begin knocking on doors. See what we can learn, if anything, from those who should have known Rachel best," said Grant.

"Before you leave," said Lillian. "I need to talk to you about Mah Jongg at Rachel's."

"Okay, what can you tell us?" asked Grant.

"First, Rachel did indeed know Donna and had visited with her when she first moved to Leisure Lake," began Lillian. "And I think Stella had also visited with her."

"What makes you think that?"

"It was something Rachel said when she was talking to Donna, but for the life of me, I can't remember what it was."

"When you do, give me a call." Jake turned to Grant. "How well do you know Donna?"

"Not well, mostly just in passing when I'm in the clubhouse. She's always friendly. Smiles and speaks when she sees me," said Grant. "My first impression about her was she was extremely shy. But now I think she's just a reserved type, the kind who opens up only after getting to know you."

"Mom, you're a good judge of people. What's your opinion of Donna?"

"Well, I can tell you that she was Miss cool, calm, and collected at Rachel's last night," said Lillian. "But it was obvious that she and Margaret had no love for each other. Now, I know why."

"Anything else?" Grant wanted to know.

"I think you'd be wise to run that criminal background check. There's something about her. . ."

"Tell me what you're thinking," Jake said.

"You know I don't believe in coincidences," Lillian said.

Both men nodded.

"So, what are the chances of Donna, who gave up her baby, and Sheila, who adopted a baby, both living here so close to each other?"

"Where are you going with this, Lillian?"
"Think about it, Grant. Who knew both ladies?"
"Rachel." Grant looked at Jake.
"And she's dead," said Jake.

Chapter 27

GRANT AND JAKE stood to leave. "Let's go over our notes, and then revisit Rachel's neighbors if we come up with more questions to ask them," suggested Jake.

Grant nodded.

"Before you leave," said Lillian, "I have another thought. Have you notified Rachel's children?"

"No. I met with David yesterday. He volunteered to contact them," Grant said, "and as soon as the medical examiner releases the body, which should be later today or sometime tomorrow, I will meet with them. But first, I want to give them time to make funeral arrangements."

"Where will they stay? At Rachel's?" asked Lillian.

"No, they can't stay there. It's still a crime scene in an ongoing investigation," said Jake.

"Do you have David's telephone number?" asked Lillian.

"I do," said Grant.

"If you will give it to me, I will call him and suggest where he and the children can stay while they wait for the medical examiner," said Lillian.

"What are you thinking, Mom?" asked Jake.

"Well, you do want to keep Victoria out of trouble, don't you? I think she needs to feel useful, and her taking care of Rachel's children just might fill that need," said Lillian.

"Great idea," said Grant. He pulled his notebook out of his pocket handed it to Lillian. "Here, copy down David's number."

"I'll call Victoria and set it all up this morning. But first, I have to drive into town. I have some errands to run."

"Would you check on Margaret for me if you happen to go by the courthouse?"

"I'll be glad to do so, Grant." *Yes, my dear, that's exactly where I'm going. If I'm as good a judge of character as you two think, I'd bet that Margaret held out on us last night. She knew more about Donna and Rachel than she let on.*

* * * * *

LILLIAN CIRCLED THE courthouse looking for a good place to park. As she drove by the employees' lot, she looked for Margaret's car. *I wonder where she parked it.* Lillian found a vacant spot across the street. She put three quarters in the meter and, dodging a white car, ran to the other side of the road.

She rode the elevator up to the second floor to the clerk's office. There were three assistants behind the counter. As soon as the first one finished with the client she was helping, Lillian stepped forward.

"I'd like to see Margaret, please."

"I'm sorry ma'am, but Ms. Snyder isn't in this morning."

"Do you expect her later today?"

"No, ma'am. Would you like to make an appointment for tomorrow?"

"That won't be necessary. Thank you." Lillian left the building. *I'll drive by Margaret's house. Last night may have been too much for her. She might need a day of R and R.*

* * * * *

MARGARET'S BRICK, RANCH style house was situated on the corner of Tremont and South Broad. Lillian parked in front and climbed out of her car. Walking down the curved sidewalk, she admired the well landscaped front yard. *I wonder if Grant helps her maintain this beautiful lawn.*

As Lillian reached the door, she saw Margaret standing there waiting for her.

"Hi, Margaret. May I come in? We need to talk."

Margaret motioned for her to enter.

"I've been expecting you."

"I went by the courthouse, but when I found out you didn't go to work, I decided to drive by and see if you are okay."

"Thanks, Lillian, I appreciate your concern."

"Things have been a bit rough for all of us these past two weeks." *Are you going to invite me in, or are we going to continue to stand here in your foyer?*

"Yes, they have." Margaret led Lillian into the living room. "Please sit down. Would you like a cup of tea?"

"Thank you. That would be lovely."

"Coming right up," Margaret said and headed for the kitchen.

Left alone, Lillian wandered around the room looking at the works of art on the walls as well as the eclectic mix of contemporary and antique furnishings

Margaret has good taste. Lillian thought as she noticed the Louis V desk dominating the space below the large leaded glass window facing the street. *Expensive. I didn't know a county clerk's salary paid enough for all of this. Perhaps, she inherited from her parents.* Lillian remembered Bill had known Margaret when she was much younger, before she moved to East Texas. *I'll ask Bill. He may know. Maybe she's been married before. Hope Grant isn't getting involved with someone he knows nothing about.*

As she glanced down at the desk, she noticed a check. *One hundred thousand dollars -- that's a lot of money.* Then, she saw the name of the person who had endorsed it.

That's odd. Why would he give that kind of money to Margaret, but more importantly, what's his connection to her?

Margaret returned with a tray. On it was an antique Repousse solid sterling teapot with a beautiful pastoral theme. Margaret had chosen plain white contemporary teacups.

Lillian tried not to stare at the serving pieces. To hide her interest in the tea set, she said, "I've been admiring your taste in furniture – it's quite different – refreshing, actually."

"I love to mix different periods." Margaret poured the tea and handed a cup to Lillian.

"You've done a great job."

"Thank you. You said we need to talk."

"Yes, I wanted you to know about mine and Bill's conversation."

"Have you had an argument with Bill about my meeting him?" asked Margaret. "I saw you across the street and know you saw me with him in front of the courthouse. I've wanted to talk to you about that."

"Bill's already confessed why he met with you," said Lillian.

"Confessed? What are you talking about?" asked Margaret. *Why would the word 'confess' bother you?*

"Well, as you know, Bill keeps secrets if someone asks him to do so," began Lillian. "Bill told me a little about your past together at the newspaper. What he said last night was for the benefit of everyone else."

"Oh, I see," said Margaret.

"No, you don't. Let me say, Margaret, that I'm glad you trust Bill. He is a good father figure and always wants to help others when he can," said Lillian.

"Yes, he does, and I will always be grateful to him for helping me advise my sister," said Margaret.

"I hope your sister has had a good life."

"To tell you the truth, I really don't know or care one way or the other."

"You were surprised to see her at Rachel's, weren't you?"

"I guess that was pretty obvious to everyone. That's the first I knew she lived at the Lake."

"I've never seen you treat anyone that way. I've been worried about you."

"Why?"

"I think family is important. Perhaps, you could try to get together with her."

"Don't go there. Donna has caused me too much heartache."

Lillian placed her teacup on the tray and spoke authoritatively. "Be that as it may, I do have some advice for you regarding Grant. I suggest you pay attention to me, young lady. That is, if you don't want to lose him."

"I'll listen, but I'll not make any promises to follow it."

"Be patient with Grant. Let him have time to process everything you told us."

"That advice I can take."

Lillian stood to leave.

"I'll see you later."

She did not wait for Margaret to answer, nor did she look back as she walked out of the house. Lillian started her car's engine and drove to the corner. Turning right, she noticed that Margaret's garage door began to slowly open. *Interesting,* she thought. *Where are you going now? To work, I hope.*

* * * * *

ON HER WAY home from Margaret's house, Lillian – without taking her eyes off of the road – reached toward the dash of her car and pushed the speed dial. Victoria picked it up after the first ring and began to talk.

"I thought you would never call," she said.

"I have something I need you to do."

"Just tell me, and it's a done deal," said Victoria.

"Rachel's children, along with David Nix and his wife Lori, will be coming in to make the funeral arrangements for Rachel. Since my house is full right now, do you think they could stay with you?" asked Lillian.

"Of course, they can," said Victoria.

"Good, I've got David's telephone number. If you have pen and paper handy, I'll give it to you."

"Hold on a second," said Victoria. She rummaged through her desk. "Okay. I'm ready. Shoot," she said.

After writing down the number, Victoria promised, "I'll call David as soon as possible and extend the invitation to him and Rachel's children."

"You're a lifesaver."

* * * * *

A MEMORIAL TO celebrate Rachel's life occurred two days later. Lillian, Bill, Margaret, and Victoria sat in a back pew of the First Baptist Church. They stood as Rachel's family exited the sanctuary. Lillian had not heard one word of the eulogy. Instead, she scanned the audience, looking for any suspicious characters, someone who could be a murderer. *This is nonsense,* she thought, *surely the culprit would stay far away from here.*

The minister dismissed the congregation. One by one, everyone filed out of the sanctuary.

On the sidewalk in front of the church was a bicycle rack. Lillian had secured Eli's leash to it so he could wait for her. He had walked around and around the apparatus. His leash was so tangled that he couldn't move. When the dog saw her approach, his yelp was one of pure pleasure.

"Eli, what have you done to yourself?"

She intended to speak with David Nix to express her condolences, but he passed by while she was bent down trying to free Eli. When she stood and turned toward the street, she saw David get into his car.

I'll have to talk to him later.

Eli strained against his leash. Lillian turned in the direction the dog was pulling and saw a young woman approaching. As she reached Lillian, she extended her hand and spoke.

"You're Lillian Prestridge, aren't you?"

Lillian nodded and shook hands with the lady.

"I'm Rebecca, Rachel's daughter. I know you were a good friend of my mother."

"I was and still am a good friend. I'm so sorry for your loss. If there's anything I can do, please don't hesitate to ask me."

"Actually, there is. I went to the bank to retrieve Mother's will from her safe deposit box and found her diary."

"Her diary, you say?"

"I would like to meet with you and give it to you to read – that is, if you have time. I glanced at it, but I couldn't understand the meaning of some of her entries. I hope you can."

"I would love to read Rachel's diary. She may have written something that means nothing to anyone else, but might help me understand her death."

"Can you meet with me tomorrow?"

"Yes, let's meet at the lake's clubhouse around noon. I'll treat you to lunch,"

"See you then. I'll bring the diary and some other papers I'd like you to see."

Lillian patted Eli. "You must have liked Rebecca. You didn't growl or bark. Good, boy."

She and her faithful white, fluffy guardian walked to their car where Bill stood waiting. Lillian was quiet during the drive.

Why would Rachel keep her diary in her safe deposit box? Did she fear someone would destroy it. It had to be important enough for her to put it there. I hope her entries will give me some insight so I can solve this mystery.

* * * * *

"ARE YOU ALL right?" Bill asked as he parked the car in their garage. He climbed out of the car and walked around it to open the passenger door for Lillian.

"You're too quiet. Penny for your thoughts."

"I've been thinking about Rachel. While you were waiting at the car for me and Eli, I met a beautiful young lady named Rebecca."

"Who's she?"

"Rachel's daughter."

"I knew she had a son and a daughter but never heard Rachel mention their names."

"Rebecca and I have a lunch date tomorrow."

Bill nodded. "That's good. I know if anyone can cheer her, you can by telling her some good stories about her mother."

If you only knew why we're meeting, you wouldn't be so encouraging.

Bill shrugged off his suit jacket and loosened his tie as they entered the back door. "I'll see you later."

"Let me guess. The fairways are calling." Lillian smiled.

"You don't mind, do you?"

"Of course, I don't. Go. Enjoy. I'm going to call Victoria. See what she thought of the memorial," she said as she kicked off her shoes and opened the refrigerator. "I'm thirsty."

Lillian poured a glass of ice tea, walked into the living room, opened the drape covering the large front window, and sat down on the sofa. She propped a pillow against the armrest and leaned back. She lifted her legs and stretched them out on the sofa. Eli jumped up and took his favorite spot straddled on the back.

Lillian set her glass on the coffee table and retrieved her cell phone from the pocket of her pantsuit. She scrolled the contact list and stopped on Victoria's name.

Victoria answered on the fourth ring.

"Hi, Lillian, I hoped you would call. It was a nice service don't you think?"

"I think so. The reason I called is to thank you for being so hospitable to Rachel's family and to David."

"I was glad to help," Victoria assured Lillian.

She paused, then continued, "We just have to find out who is committing these murders. I think the same person who killed Sheila and Mr. Peters, killed Rachel."

"I think the same thing," said Lillian, "and I'm determined to find out who did it. But promise me you will be extremely careful. You and I may be next on the culprit's list."

"Do you really think we are in danger?" asked Victoria.

"I do. I think whoever killed Rachel did so thinking she knew more than she should about Sheila."

"How does Rachel's knowledge of Sheila affect us?" said Victoria.

"I'm thinking that the murderer may believe Rachel told us something."

"Why would someone even make the connection between the two? Remember, Rachel had to wrack her brain to remember anything about visiting Sheila."

"Yes, I know, but I think she may have been lying to us. Or, perhaps she knew but didn't want to say anything in front of the others."

"I hadn't thought about that."

"Don't you think Eli could have been warning us when he suddenly, without any reason, began to growl?"

"Now that you mention it, he did act odd when we were at Rachel's. Didn't you get up and go look out the window because of the way he was acting?" Victoria asked.

"I did. I remember that, but I didn't see anything suspicious I thought it may have been some kind of nocturnal animal."

"Perhaps, he could have seen someone outside her house, maybe someone listening to our conversation? Just thinking about it gives me the shivers."

No response.

"Lillian, can you hear me? Are you there?" Victoria sounded panicky.

"Yes, I'm here," said Lillian.

"Thank goodness. I thought we had lost our connection."

"Let's think back about Rachel. Could she have said something in warning that we didn't catch at the time." And then, "Oh my gosh! She did!" exclaimed Lillian.

"What?" yelled Victoria.

But Lillian had already hung up the phone. She hurriedly dialed Jake's cell phone number, but her call went straight to voice mail. She left a message for him to call her right away and then dialed Grant's cell number, but got a busy signal. *Oh dear, I've got to get in touch with them right away, she thought. Eli must have seen or heard someone outside the window. How stupid of me. Rachel gave me a clear signal. No wonder she's dead.*

Chapter 28

JAKE AND GRANT parked in front of Rachel's house. Both men got out of their cars and surveyed the cul-de-sac.

"Since Rachel's house is pretty much on the corner," Grant said, "I think we need to visit all of her neighbors and not worry about what they need to be doing today. They, especially Mr. Wolver, might just remember something now that didn't seem important at first."

"Let's get to it."

They walked across the street, and Grant stepped up to the front door of the red brick cottage with black shutters. He rang the doorbell. A short, gray-haired gentleman opened the door.

"Hello, sir, I'm Grant Perryman, Chief of Security here at the lake, and this is Jake Prestridge, County Sheriff."

"I know who you are. I guess you want to ask me about what happened to Ms. Rachel," said the man.

"I do, but first, could you give me your name," said Grant.

"Sure, I'm John Gentry," he replied.

"Mr. Gentry, could you tell me whether or not you saw or heard anything out of the ordinary that night?" asked Grant.

"Well, Miss Rachel had her usual group of lady friends over to play Mah Jongg," said Gentry.

"Did you notice what time the ladies left her house?" asked Grant.

"Not exactly. I don't usually pay that much attention to what Miss Rachel and her friends do, but I remember thinking they finished earlier than usual."

"Could you give me your best guestimate about the time?" asked Jake.

"Well, I'd say it was before ten o'clock, maybe closer to nine-forty or so."

"Did you hear or see anything else that you can think of?" asked Grant.

"As a matter of fact, I can. I always walk Oscar, my bulldog, just before we go to bed. Either I have to wait until Wolver walks Zoe or I go first. That Schnauzer of his causes all kinds of trouble if she sees another dog on the sidewalk."

"We'll talk to Mr. Wolver also, but let's get back to what you saw, if you don't mind," urged Jake.

"Well, as I was saying, I was walking my dog around the circle when I heard a car crank up and speed away," said Gentry. "Don't know why the driver had to make such a ruckus, peeling rubber. Must have been a teenager."

"Could you describe the car?" asked Grant.

"It left so fast I couldn't tell you the make, but it was white. I do know that," said Gentry.

"About what time was that?" asked Grant.

"Oh, by then, I guess it was closer to ten-thirty, give or take a few minutes."

"Mr. Gentry, would you agree to testify in court if we need you to give an account of what you saw last night?" asked Jake.

"Sure would. I'll do whatever I can to help you prosecute whoever killed Miss Rachel."

"Thank you. We appreciate your help."

Both Grant and Jake shook hands with him and left.

As the two men walked away, Jake's cell phone rang. He listened, took out his notebook, and made a couple of notes.

"You might be right about Donna," he said. "Guess what kind of car she drives."

"I bet it's a white one."

"A white Lexus to be exact," said Jake.

Before Grant could respond, his cell phone rang. It was the medical examiner. "Hello, Will. Do you have something for us?" he asked. He held his phone so that Jake could also hear the medical examiner.

"I can now pinpoint Ms. McAnally's time of death to be right around ten-thirty."

"Did Rachel have any defensive marks on her?" asked Grant.

"None. She must have opened the door and was shot point blank."

Jake felt his cell vibrate. He pulled it out of his pocket and noticed he had received a voice mail. He listened to the message with a frown on his face. He immediately tried to call Lillian. Busy signal. He tried again. Busy again.

"What's wrong? Who are you calling?" Grant asked.

"Let's get back over to the house. Mom just left a frantic message."

"What did she say?"

"I couldn't understand it all, but she sounded desperate. Hurry!"

Both men raced to their cars and took off in the direction of Lillian's house. Grant picked up his two-way radio and called the office. "Lois, put me through to Donna."

"She's not in today, sir."

"What? Why? Did she call in?"

"She did. She said she was ill and would not be in today."

"Thanks, Lois. You know how to reach me if you need me."

"Ten-four."

* * * * *

GRANT AND JAKE parked in Lillian's driveway and ran up the steps of the deck. They reached the front door just as she opened it.

"Come in, boys, I know what the connection between Sheila and Donna is."

"And how did you figure that out?" asked Jake, always amazed at his mother's intuitive nature.

"When we were playing Mah Jongg at Rachel's, she kept mentioning flowers," said Lillian.

Jake sighed. "Okay, Mom, tell us about the flowers."

"She said she had admired Sheila's flowers. You know, the flowers in her vase that was broken," said Lillian. "Remember, when you caught me peeking in the window, there were flowers on the floor."

"I remember catching you contemplating breaking and entering," said Grant, "but in the forensic's report, there was no mention of flowers."

"Don't you know what that means?" asked Lillian.

"What, Mom?" said Jake.

"It means that whoever killed Sheila could have returned to the house and removed the flowers, probably the person I heard trying to get inside when I was there alone."

"That's how he or she knew your identity and tried to scare you by shooting out your window. Bet anything, he was hanging around your house that night," said Grant rubbing the back of his head.

"He was probably the same person who knocked you unconscious," said Jake. "You were right, Mom, Grant wasn't drunk the next morning."

"I know that. You two could never lie to me."

"Let's get back to that vase and the flowers," said Grant. "Why do you think they are important?"

"It took awhile for me, but based upon Rachel's description of them, I believe they were flowers from a snowball bush," said Lillian. "And I know who gave them to her."

Lillian looked at Grant. *Come on, you know where they grow. Think. It'll come to you.*

"There's only one snowball bush in Leisure Lake," said Grant.

"Where?" asked Jake.

"On Louisiana Lane," said Grant. "Lillian, I remember you mentioned the vase when we reviewed your notes, early in our investigation, but it totally slipped my mind."

"Let's find out who lives there and see if Rachel had anything in her newcomer file notes we found yesterday," said Jake.

"On it. Lillian, would you pour us a drink, please," said Grant. "I'll be right back." He walked out to his car and retrieved Rachel's bag, brought it to the table, pulled out her file folders, and spread them out on the dining table. "Both of you take a folder. Let me know if anything pops out at you."

Grant sipped a glass of tea Lillian had poured for him. Each of them picked up a folder and read the notes Rachel had jotted down after each of her new member welcome visits. Twenty minutes later, Grant found what he was looking for.

He handed the folder to Jake who began to read aloud:

Visited with Stella Dallas today, on Pecan Street. Seemed very nice, but was very shy. Seemed to be uneasy about letting a stranger in the house. I emphasized our twenty-four/seven security here at the lake. She relaxed somewhat as I described all of the clubs and organizations here. I admired the vase of snowball blooms, and she said that another newcomer had given them to her. I asked her for the person's name and said that I would like to call on her as well.

She gave me the name: Donna Traydon.

On the second sheet in the same folder, Jake read:

Drove over to Louisiana Lane to meet with Donna Traydon. Did not get to talk very long with her because she had an interview with the club manager. Said she hoped to get a job at the club.

"So, she did know Donna," said Grant. "I'm afraid Margaret's sister is right in the middle of this case."

"But that doesn't prove Donna had anything to do with her death," said Jake.

"I agree with Jake," said Lillian.

"You're right," said Grant. "But at least, we have another lead that may be of help."

"Mom, what was your true impression of Donna?" asked Jake.

"I think she's an honest person. At Mah Jongg, she said she gave Stella some flowers."

"Why didn't you mentioned that before we looked through these documents?" Jake look perturbed.

"I wanted to know what Rachel had written. I'm glad she and Donna are in agreement. But I digress. You asked for my opinion of

Donna. At first, she seemed to be very friendly and looked forward to meeting the rest of the Mah Jongg ladies. She was very talkative. But when she saw Margaret, her demeanor changed."

"How so?"

"She seemed more subdued. I guess that would be a good description."

"Well, I obviously need to talk to her," said Grant as he slowly stood. "Come on, Jake. Let's leave your car here. Might be safer for your mom if we do. We can both ride in my car."

"Wait a minute," Lillian ordered. "I need to go with you. I have some questions for her."

"No. You stay here and wait for us," Jake said. "We'll bring you up-to-date ASAP."

There's that word again. Wait. They're crazy if they think I'll sit here and twiddle my thumbs.

* * * * *

IT SEEMED TO Grant that all of the evidence pointed to Donna since she had known both Sheila and Rachel. *Could she be the murderer? Why? What motive could she possibly have for killing them? If she did, this will be hard on Margaret.* Grant felt that it was imperative that he talk to Donna. *What we've got is only circumstantial. I've got to find concrete evidence, something that can be used in court to prove her guilt. I know Jake is right. So far, what I've got is only supposition.*

Jake interrupted his thoughts. "I think I'll call my office to find out if they have completed the extensive background check on Donna."

"Please do," said Grant.

Jake used his cell phone to call his deputy, "Have you come up with anything on Donna Traydon?" Pause. "Nothing yet?" Pause. "If you do, call me on my cell phone."

"Let's drive over to Donna's house since she hasn't shown up for work today," suggested Grant.

"How do you know that?"

"I checked with the office. She called in sick."

He drove the obligatory twenty-five miles per hour through the narrow and curving streets that surrounded the lake, past the beautiful scenery of meticulously manicured lawns. A late morning sunlight glittered through the trees.

As the cruiser twisted and turned through the neighborhood, Grant could not resist an occasional glance at the reflection of the sun off the gentle waves of the lake. Combined with the sun's dancing between the leaves of the trees, the view promised a peaceful environment.

"I always enjoyed driving through Leisure Lake," Jake commented as they eased around another curve.

"Reminds me of the toy kaleidoscope I had as a child. Your dad gave it to me. The colors always cheered me when I missed my parents."

The turn onto Louisiana ended their talk about the scenery. Donna's house was on the corner at the end of the street. Grant eased into the circular drive in front and parked. He and Jake climbed out of the car and walked up the sidewalk to the front door. Before either of them could ring the doorbell, a white Lexus sped out of the drive onto the side street.

"What the. . ." Grant interrupted.

"Come on! Let's stop her."

Both men rushed back to the car, jumped in, and raced after the Lexus.

"She's driving like a maniac," Jake said.

Grant drove as quickly as he could, maneuvering the car around the narrow curves of the two-lane road. He reached for his radio as he skidded around a corner.

"Damn. You lost her."

"Calling all gates, all officers. Come in."

Multiple 'yes, sirs' could be heard through the open line as the lake's security personnel responded.

"I'm in pursuit of the driver of a white Lexus. Stop any white Lexus trying to exit."

"Ten-four."

By the time Grant made the last turn toward the main gate, he saw Todd and Robert, his best security officers, standing in the middle of the exit. Both men had their hands up signaling the white car to stop. At the last minute, they jumped out of the way of the speeding vehicle. The driver of the Lexus ignored their attempts, sped through the gate, and turned out onto the highway, and quickly picked up even greater speed.

Grant turned on his siren and raced through the gate. He made a circle motion with his left hand as he passed Todd and Robert. They jumped in their patrol cars and followed.

"Don't get suckered into a high-speed chase in this old car," Jake said. "Let me use your radio. The second that car drove through that gate, she left your jurisdiction. Now, she's in mine."

"Sure," said Grant. "I'll just keep her in sight. Donna ought to know better."

"Best call off your guys, too."

Grant nodded. "You use the radio. I'll get Todd on my cell."

Todd answered on the first ring. "Yes, sir."

"Stand down. We're out of our jurisdiction."

"Ten-four."

"Todd, did you get a look at the driver of the car?"

"No, sir. I was too busy jumping out of the way. Sorry."

Grant ended the call. *I hate to think Donna would try to run over a co-worker, but I guess it wouldn't be the first time she did something stupid.*

Jake called the dispatcher and gave a description of the car, including the license plate number. Grant's old cruiser could not compete with the speed of the newer car. The distance between his car and the Lexus kept growing wider. Soon, they heard another siren. A state trooper who had been parked beside the interstate entered into the chase.

About fifteen miles down the road, they saw flashing lights from two state troopers' cars. The white Lexus had been pulled off the road. Grant drove up behind the cars and parked. The troopers stood beside the car.

"Did she give you any trouble after you stopped her?" Jake asked the troopers.

"No, sir," the younger of the two troopers said. We asked him to stay in the car, and he did so."

"He?"

The trooper looked puzzled but made no comment.

Grant shook hands with the trooper. "I appreciate your assistance. It was a good thing you were close by."

"Glad to be of service. If you don't need us, we'll be on our way," the senior trooper said.

"Thanks. We'll take it from here," Grant responded and then turned to Jake who opened the driver's door, leaned down, and ordered the person out of the car.

Both Grant and Jake were surprised.

"David?" Grant asked. *Thank you, Lord,* Grant thought. Then the thought occurred to him, *I hope Donna is okay.* He scowled. "What are you doing driving Donna's car?" He demanded.

David raised his eyebrows. He looked confused. "This isn't her car. It's mine when I'm in town. Remember, I told you Rachel lets me drive Robert's old car."

"What were you doing at Donna's house?" Grant asked.

Before David answered Grant's question, Jake fired another one to David.

"What in the world were you thinking?" asked Jake. "Why didn't you stop? Didn't you see the flashing lights on Grant's car?"

"That's just it. I wasn't thinking. I panicked."

"Perhaps, you'll enjoy having time to think on your ride back to Leisure Lake. Come on," Jake said, taking him by the arm.

As Jake led him to Grant's cruiser, David asked, "What about Robert's car? I can't leave it here on the side of the road."

"I'll call a tow truck," Jake said.

"They'll charge me a small fortune," complained David.

"Too bad. That's your problem." Jake opened the back door on the passenger side. The captive bent his head down and climbed into the car.

Chapter 29

GRANT COULD NOT decide whether or not he was relieved or frustrated about the identity of the driver of the car. At any rate, he called security to inform them the culprit had been caught and to make a request. Todd answered the call.

"Yes, sir, did you catch up with the speedster?"

"I'm on my way back to the lake with our man who likes to see if he can outrun the police. Where are you right now?"

"I'm still at the entrance," said Todd. "I'll wait here for you."

"Ten-four."

 Jake turned to Grant.

"Drop me off first so I can get my squad car."

"I'll meet you in the conference room."

"Where are you going?" asked Jake.

"I'll be there after checking on Donna. I want to make sure she's safe. Call me if he tries to give you any trouble."

"I don't think he'll be a problem, but I'll wait for you to join us before I begin questioning our suspect."

"Let him stew for awhile."

Grant drove through the entrance gate and waved for Todd to follow him. He dropped Jake at his car and then proceeded back to his office. Todd met him at the door.

"Put this guy in the conference room. Stay with him. The sheriff is on his way."

"Yes, sir." Todd grabbed the man by the shoulder and led him down the hall.

Grant walked by accounting, and as usual, looked in. He was surprised to see Donna at her desk.

He walked in and stopped in front of her desk. *I can't believe I've never noticed the resemblance between her and Margaret before.*

She looked up and smiled, "Hi, Grant."

"Donna, can you come into my office? I need to talk to you," said Grant.

"Sure, just give me a moment to put away what I'm working on right now," she responded cheerfully.

Grant had placed two cups on the circular table he used for conferences in his office.

Donna walked in and he asked her to have a seat. "I'm not being fired, am I?"

"No, why would you ask that question?"

"You look and sound pretty serious. Have I done something wrong?"

Grant didn't answer her question. Instead, he asked, "Would you like a cup of coffee?"

"Yes, I would," said Donna as he poured both of them a cup.

"I have to ask you some questions," Grant began.

"What about?"

Grant took a sip of his coffee and sat the cup on the table. He spoke softly. "It has just come to my attention that you and Margaret Snyder are sisters," he began.

"We are, but unfortunately, we have not seen each other for several years," Donna confided.

"When did you last see her?" asked Grant.

"Actually, we saw each other last night quite by accident."

"Where?" asked Grant. *I'm relieved you're telling me the truth.*

"At Mah Jongg at Rachel McAnally's house. And I can tell you this. Both of us were shocked to see each other," admitted Donna.

"Why were you surprised to see Margaret?"

"It's personal. I don't talk about my family."

"I understand. Families can be tedious." Grant decided to let that topic rest for a few minutes and continued. "How long were you at Rachel's?"

"Let's see. I left a little before ten o'clock, I think it was."

"Did you happen to go back to her house for any reason?"

"No. Why would I?"

Grant ignored her question and continued, "You called in sick this morning, but now you're here."

"I had a doctor's appointment at nine-thirty, so I had to take a couple of hours of sick leave," said Donna.

"What time did you clock in today?" asked Grant.

"Not long before you arrived, maybe ten minutes ago."

"Could you give me the name of your doctor so I can verify that you were in his office?" said Grant.

"I can, but why are you asking me all of these questions?" asked Donna. "I hope you don't put everyone who takes sick leave through this type of interrogation." She straightened her back.

Grant observed her body language and reminded himself. *She's right. This shouldn't feel like an interrogation.* He relaxed his shoulders and continued.

"Since you weren't here when the call came in, you probably don't know Rachel was murdered last night right after you ladies left her house," said Grant.

Donna paled. She reached for her coffee cup, but her hand shook so badly she withdrew it. She bent her head down for a few moments, and when she looked up, tears were streaming down her face. Grant stood, walked over to his desk, picked up a box of tissues, and offered it to her.

Donna pulled out two and began to dab at her eyes. "I'm so sorry to hear that. Rachel was so kind to me last night. She didn't know I was subbing for Sally Jane prior to my showing up at her doorstep," said Donna.

"Did you notice any conflict or tension between Rachel and the other ladies?"

"No, the only tension was between me and Margaret." She paused. "I just wish. . ." Her voice trembled so that she could not finish her sentence.

"You wish what?"

"I'd rather not say." She looked down. "Like I said earlier, I don't discuss my family."

"Donna, look at me."

She wiped her tears and followed his command. Grant spoke softly. "I have to confess that I know what caused the rift between you and Margaret."

"You do?"

"I do. It's my job. You can think I'm too nosey if you choose, but when this situation is cleared up, I think you and Margaret need to clear up your differences," said Grant.

"Why are you so interested in Margaret and me?" asked Donna.

"I intend to marry Margaret," said Grant, "and I would like for her only relative to be at the wedding."

"I'm not sure she would agree with you, but I'm willing to try," said Donna.

"I'll make sure you have that opportunity, but right now, let's get back to the night you subbed for Victoria," said Grant. "When you left Rachel's, did you notice anything unusual?"

Donna took a sip of coffee and thought for awhile. Suddenly, a broad smile crossed her face. Her eyes lit up.

"Why, yes, I did," she said. "I thought it unusual at the time."

"What was it?"

"At the end of the cul-de-sac, I noticed a lone car parked at an odd angle."

"What do you mean by 'odd angle'?"

"The front faced out, and it wasn't parked in a space."

"What kind of car?"

"That's what caught my eye," said Donna. "It looked just like mine, a white Lexus."

Grant didn't respond right away.

"Is that important? Will it help you?" said Donna.

"You bet it will," said Grant. "You've been a big help."

"I'm glad. I really liked Rachel."

"One more thing," said Grant. "I want you to go with Robert to your house to check on things."

"Why?"

"While you were at the doctor's office today, you may have had an intruder," said Grant.

"Who?" asked Donna.

"Someone who drives a white Lexus," said Grant. He felt sorry for the woman. She was already pale having heard bad news, but he had never seen someone go so white and look so scared. He tried to reassure her.

"You're safe right now. We have him in custody."

"May I ask who it is?" said Donna.

Grant thought for a moment and then decided not to tell her. Donna looked puzzled. *She can wait to learn his identity.* He pushed the intercom button on his phone. Robert answered. "I'd like for you to take Donna home so she can check on her house. Make sure everything's all right." Then to Donna, "Report back after you and Robert have inspected everything."

"Yes, sir."

Robert stood at the door waiting.

Chapter 30

AS SOON AS they left, Grant walked down the hall to the conference room. Todd was alone. "I thought I told you to wait here with Jake and the prisoner," Grant growled.

"I'm sorry, sir, but the sheriff felt the prisoner needed to be put in a more secure place. He took him downtown to lockup."

Grant's face turned red. He clinched and unclenched his fists. *He said he would wait for me. He had no right to take David out of here without my permission. This is my jurisdiction.*

Grant took a deep breath. "Guess I'll drive to the jail," he said before turning to leave.

"Sir, one more thing."

Grant stopped and looked back. "Yes?"

"He said to tell you one word."

"What?"

"*Stew.* Strange. Do you know what he was talking about?"

The frown on Grant's face turned into a smile. "Got it."

* * * * *

GRANT PARKED HIS car in a reserved parking spot in front of the courthouse. The security guard recognized him and let him in the building. He decided to go by Margaret's office first. The door was locked.

Forgot it's Saturday. It's work day as usual at Leisure, but the Clerk's office is closed. Today of all days, my sweet Margaret needs a day to recoup.

He walked on down the hall to Jake's office. When he opened the door, he saw Jake sitting at his desk, a file folder opened, calmly reading.

"Stew," Grant laughed. "You really confused Todd."

Jake grinned and then looked serious. He closed the folder and put it aside. "I didn't think you'd mind if we let him stew down here. Are you ready to walk over to the jail?"

"Ready. Finish up what you're doing. I'll wait in the hall."

"Thanks, it won't take me long." Finished, Jake stood, put on his hat, and picked up the keys to his office. He closed and locked the door.

Grant was talking on his cell phone when Jake met up with him. "Let her stay at the office if she feels safer there." He ended the call and said, "I've been thinking."

"Me, too. I can't imagine what David could have been doing at Donna's house."

"It's a puzzle to me."

"Is Donna all right?" asked Jake.

"Shook up but okay. Robert just called. He walked through her house with her. Nothing missing."

The two waved at the guard as they left the courthouse.

They walked two blocks and entered the jail. An elderly woman was complaining about her neighbor's dog barking all night. Grant was amused when he heard her say, "I want something done about that noise. My bridge ladies can't concentrate."

Grant chuckled and shook his head. "I see you have the same kinds of problems here that we have at the lake."

Jake and Grant passed the reception area, leaving the desk sergeant to handle the gray-haired geriatric demanding justice.

Jake smiled and pushed the elevator button. "At least, she didn't say Mah Jongg ladies."

"Let's hope she's not like Lillian. By the way, I'm surprised we haven't heard from your mom."

Jake's cell phone rang. He looked at the caller ID. "You spoke too soon." He put the phone back in his pocket. "She'll leave another message. This is just the tenth call I've ignored since our high-speed chase."

"I know she's dying to know if we caught the culprit." Grant laughed, then stopped as his cell began to ring. He groaned

"Your turn."

Grant didn't answer. "Let's talk to him. If nothing else, we can give him a citation for speeding."

"You first," Jake said as he opened the door to the squad room. He spoke to the officer seated at the first desk. "Bring the prisoner to interrogation, please."

Grant followed him into the observation room. Behind the glass, they watched the deputy lead David into the room. He told the man to sit down, and then the officer unlocked one of the handcuffs and fastened it to the table.

"He looks terrified, don't you think?" asked Grant. "Have you run a background?"

"He's squeaky clean."

"We'll see. Since we're in your jurisdiction, you go first," Grant said.

"Anything in particular you want me to ask, besides the obvious, of course?"

"Ask him about his relationship with Rachel. I'd like to see if he tells you the same thing he told me when I informed him of her death."

Jake left and entered the interrogation room. He turned on the tape recorder as soon as he sat down. Before he could speak, the door opened. In walked a well-dressed man carrying a briefcase.

"Thank God," the prisoner said. "I thought you'd never get here."

"I came as quickly as I could."

"Who are you?" Jake asked.

"Richard Woodfin. I'm David Nix's attorney." He handed Jake his card, then placed his briefcase on the table and sat down beside his client. "I have to ask: Do you treat everyone who receives a traffic violation like this?"

"Mr. Woodfin, your client committed a felony when he ran from law enforcement officials and endangered the lives of several people in a high-speed chase on a major highway, not to mention those who could have been injured in a private, gated community. We've detained him for questioning."

"Have you written him a citation for speeding?"

"Not yet, but -- "

"What do you claim he did in the so-called gated community?"

"The Chief of Security has not charged him with anything as of now."

Mr. Woodfin stood. "So, you've merely 'detained' my client. You haven't made an arrest? Am I correct?"

"Sir, I suggest you sit down and let me talk with your client. He may have information we need to – "

"Release my client now, sir, or charge him. We will see you in court."

Grant ground his teeth as he watched the smug arrogance of the attorney. *That sounds like a good idea to me. I'm thinking, Mr. Woodfin, your client may be guilty of more than a traffic violation. Just wait. We'll meet again. You won't be so cocky then.*

Jake looked at David, then removed the handcuffs.

"You may go for now, but understand you may be subpoenaed regarding a homicide at Leisure Lake." Jake quickly glanced at the mirror and gave a slight grin to Grant.

"Homicides? I haven't killed anyone."

David was obviously shaken.

Grant smiled and thought, *Nice work, Jake. He said homicides. So, he knows about more than one. You dropped that bomb just right.*

"Don't say anything else," Woodfin ordered.

"Shut up, Richard. I may break traffic laws now and then, but I'm not a murderer."

"I'm advising you, David, to keep quiet," his attorney said.

"No, Richard, I won't. I'm not going to sit here quietly and be accused of murder."

Jake smiled at the attorney and then directed his attention to David. "I know you had an appointment with Rachel."

"How do you know about any appointment my client may or may not have made with –" Woodfin paused, "the person you called Rachel?"

"For your information," Jake ignored Woodfin and said to David, "Rachel had your name penciled on her calendar for the day after her death. Perhaps, you decided to go to her house early, and the two of you quarreled. Maybe, your temper got the best of you. During the argument, you killed Rachel accidentally."

"I'd never hurt Rachel. Jake, you've got to believe me."

"Don't say anything else," Woodfin ordered.

David ignored him. "Jake, I swear, I didn't kill her."

Woodfin put his hand on David's shoulder and said to Jake, "Sir, unless you have evidence to the contrary, my client is innocent, and we are leaving now. Come on, David, let's go."

Grant listened to David's plea of innocence. *I wonder if Rachel mentioned having a problem with David to Lillian?* He made a mental note to ask Lillian that question.

Jake turned off the recorder he had begun at the start of their conversation. He looked at the two men facing him. David looked contrite. Woodfin glared at him.

"Go. Get out of my sight, but don't fly back to Houston until I give you permission," Jake ordered. He opened the door so the two men could leave. "Stop by the desk. Pick up your wallet and keys before you leave."

Grant joined him in the hall. His phone rang. It was Lillian. He didn't answer. Grant watched as David signed for the envelope containing his belongings.

"Unusual talisman," the desk sergeant said.

"What are you talking about?" asked David.

"The gold charm."

Grant walked over to the desk. "Hold up a minute. David, let me see that."

David's attorney stepped up. "You don't have to show him anything, Mr. Nix." He glared at Grant. "If you want to see anything that belongs to my client, get the judge to sign a subpoena." And then to David, "Collect your stuff, and let's get out of here."

Jake's cell rang. He sighed. "Hello, Mom."

"Finally. I decided that I'd have to call the sheriff if you didn't answer this call."

"I am the sheriff."

"Minor detail," said Lillian. "I've tried and tried to reach you. I know you've been busy, but the reason I called is . . ."

Jake interrupted her. "Let me guess." He put his phone in speaker mode. "You want to know all about the high-speed chase."

"No, I'm not calling about that at all. I hope David stopped before anyone was hurt."

"Did you talk to security?"

"No."

"Then how did you know it was David we were chasing?"

"You just told me."

Jake ended the call without saying goodbye. Immediately, Grant's phone rang.

Grant shook his head. "Hello, Lillian, you shouldn't do that to your son."

"I should have known. You two are always together."

"What can I do for you?"

"I've been trying to get in touch with you two about dinner Monday night. Talk to my son, and if he isn't too mad at me, tell him I'm preparing dinner for you two. Bring Margaret. Be here around six-thirty."

"I'll do that. Thanks."

"Why are you thanking her?"

"Your mom says we are to be at her house for dinner day after tomorrow. Six-thirty sharp."

"Great." Jake's voice showed no enthusiasm for seeing his mother.

Grant laughed and slapped him on the back. "She's your mom. Live with it." He laughed when Jake made a face. "See you Monday.

Oh, by the way, don't forget to bring Jessica. I've had enough for today."

The two men went their separate ways.

* * * * *

HOME AT LAST, Grant settled into his recliner. He placed his favorite beverage, a Miller Lite, on the table by his chair. After picking up the remote to the TV and roaming through the channels, he chose the local station. Grant closed his eyes listening to the weather report and soon fell asleep. The steady drone of voices faded on the television.

However, when he heard, "We interrupt this program to bring you breaking news," Grant jerked awake. He watched the newscaster describe the scene behind her. "We've been told by the state trooper, who responded to a 911 call, that an unidentified man was found lying on the side of the road by two young brothers riding their horses along FM 2401. The victim had been shot. One of the first bystanders to arrive at the scene told this reporter it looked to him as if the man committed suicide. At this time, authorities say they do not know how the victim died and won't know until their investigation and an autopsy are completed. Stay tuned. As we receive updates, we will pass them along to you."

Grant's attention shifted from the newscaster to the activity occurring around the parked car. In the distance, he saw Jake talking with two constables. They stood beside a white Lexus. *I've seen that car before,* Grant thought. Will Ogburn's van could also be seen in the background.

Grant reached for his cell phone on its first ring. On the TV screen, he saw Jake reach for his.

Bet that's Jake calling me.

"Hello, Grant. Are you watching TV?" Lillian asked.

"Just woke up. I see Jake talking to Ogburn."

"Recognize that car?"

"Sure do."

"If you talk to Jake, tell him to call me."

"Will do." Grant closed his phone.

He had also seen the mile marker sign alongside the road. When the news flash ended, Grant got in his car. *Jake may need my help.*

* * * * *

GRANT PARKED HIS cruiser behind the traffic cones the state troopers had set up to direct traffic around the scene. As he dodged a reporter, Grant waved. Jake beckoned for Grant to join him and the officers who were taking notes and photographs of the tragedy.

"Thanks for coming by," Jake said. He nodded toward the reporters from two area television stations. "I won't ask how you heard about this incident."

"Breaking news," said Grant, "disturbed my nap. I recognized the car. It's the one David's been driving, right?"

"Correct," Jake said. "Look at the scratches on the driver's door."

Grant walked closer to the car. "I'd say he had a run-in with a poodle by the name of Eli." Grant bent down and looked into the driver's side window. "The news reporter mentioned suicide?"

"Does it look like he took his own life?"

"I'd say David Nix was executed," Grant said.

Will Ogburn commented, "It's hard to commit suicide by shooting yourself in the back of the head, don't you think?"

"I would agree with you, but until we know for sure what happened here, we're not saying anything about it to the media."

"Got you." Will asked, "May we move the body?"

Jake nodded. "If forensics has all the photos they need."

"I agree," said Grant, "let's keep away from the media."

"I had him pegged for the murders," Jake said.

"He may not have been guilty of murder, but I'd sure bet he was guilty of something. It's a shame his attorney had to interrupt our interrogation of him."

"Unfortunately, he can't answer any questions now."

Jake received a thumbs up from forensics and turned to Will Ogburn. "We're through here. He's all yours."

"Thanks. I'll get my report to you as soon as I can," the medical examiner said.

Jake and Grant walked away from the scene. They reached Jake's squad car and climbed inside. Jake's cell phone rang.

"It's probably your mother. She called me before I left the house. Told me to tell you to call her."

Jake looked at the caller ID. "Not my mom – the district attorney."

Grant said, "Well, don't just look at it. Answer it."

"Sheriff speaking." Jake put the phone on speaker so Grant could hear the D.A.

"I've been watching the television and see you have a situation on your hands."

"Yes, sir, you and the rest of the county saw the news."

"I don't know who that young reporter is, but I intend to call the station manager. We don't need a reporter who takes one look at a scene and tells the community her thoughts or a bystander's opinion."

"Yes, sir, I understand. She quit reporting and started creating the news, but despite what she said, the victim, David Nix, did not commit suicide."

"David Nix?"

"Yes, sir. That's the identity of the victim."

"That's odd," said the D.A.

"How's that?" asked Jake.

"I have sitting on my desk, a complaint signed by a Ms. Rachel McAnally accusing David Nix of embezzling monies from her oil company." Silence. "Jake, I'll call you first thing Monday morning. Go home now. Be with your family." The D.A. hung up.

Grant looked at Jake. "Sounds like David had a good motive to kill Rachel."

"Yeah, but who had the motive to kill him?" Jake asked.

Chapter 31

MONDAY EVENING, PER Lillian's invitation, Jake and Jessica, Grant and Margaret greeted each other as they arrived simultaneously to Lillian's dinner party. Bill met them at the door and ushered them into the living room.

Eli bounced up and down, making strange noises. He barred the door with his enthusiasm until each of the guests acknowledged him with either a pat on the head or a scratch behind the ears.

As they entered, Lillian, as well as Victoria and her husband Tony, stood up to greet them. Two more people were there.

Margaret stopped, hesitated briefly, and then walked over and hugged her sister. "Welcome home, Donna," she said.

"You don't know how long I've waited to hear you say that."

"You don't know how long I've wanted to say it."

Lillian stood beside Bill. She watched the body language of the sisters. *One is sincere, and as I expected, the other one is calculating.*

"Okay, now that that's over, let's enjoy being together," said Bill. "Oh, wait a minute, forgive my manners. Does everyone know Jason Carpenter?" Bill put his hand on the shoulder of a tall, red-haired, freckle-faced young man wearing round tortoise-shell glasses.

Jason grinned. "Hello, everyone, especially you two," and shook hands with Jake and Grant.

"Of course, we do. Remember, Jason graduated with us," said Jake.

"And he does our taxes every year," added Grant. "Best CPA in East Texas."

"And I know all their secrets," said Jason jokingly. "Lillian invited me." He winked and then said conspiratorially, "She's playing matchmaker tonight."

Donna joined in, "We didn't have the heart to tell her that we've already met."

"How long have you known each other?" Margaret wanted to know.

Jason responded. "I audit the books for Leisure Lake. Donna is a top-notch accountant."

"We have a lot in common, both CPAs," Donna added.

"Impressive," said Margaret.

"Come on in, everyone," said Lillian. She did not smile. "Bill's been working all day."

"And I've just made the best bar-be-que ribs you'll ever eat," announced Bill proudly. "Come on out on the patio, and let's get started."

They all trooped through the house and out the back door. In addition to Bill's famous bar-be-que and sauce, Lillian had prepared homemade potato salad, baked beans, and a condiment tray filled with deviled eggs, pickles, and sliced tomatoes. Each person filled a plate.

Lillian thought, *God has indeed blessed me.*

She looked lovingly at her husband of fifty years, her son and his wife, her "other son" and his fiancée Margaret, and finally Donna and Jason. *Enjoy the moment, my dear ones. Sadness will soon descend upon you all. Hearts will be broken.* Jake broke into her thoughts.

"Mom, you said you wanted to talk to all of us."

"I do, Jake, but what I have to say can wait a little longer after everyone's eaten."

Conversation ceased as the group began to devour the feast Bill and Lillian provided. It was obvious to Lillian that the recent events were still on everyone's mind. *I wonder which one of you will be the first to speak?*

It was Jake who broached the subject as he sipped his iced tea. "David sure did destroy some lives, didn't he?"

"Not to mention mine and your mother's life. I still get angry about his shooting out our windows," said Bill.

"I don't understand that," said Jason.

"He thought. . ." Jake began.

"Let me answer that, son." Lillian interrupted. She looked at those assembled around the patio. "Does everyone remember Mr. Peters?"

Grant said, "He's the elderly man who lived across the street from Sheila. He saw me let you into her house, and he saw the person who scared you away.

"Correct," said Lillian. "He did a good job of scaring me. I hate what happened to Mr. Peters. He didn't deserve what happened to him."

"Are you accusing David of shooting out your windows, Mom?"

"Exactly. Your dad and I came to that conclusion today."

"Why would he do that?" Victoria asked.

"Think about it," Lillian said. She waited for her friend to come to a conclusion.

"So he could search through Sheila's house. Since what he wanted wasn't there, he guessed you had taken the documents he needed." Victoria said.

"Just as I figured," Grant said. "He also had to be the one who killed Mr. Peters."

"Yes, he probably did, but you and Jake will have to question him and prove that," Lillian said.

"That will be rather difficult now," Grant said. He looked at Jake who nodded.

"Why?" asked Jason.

"Remember the unidentified victim who was found dead in his car this past weekend?" Grant asked.

"I saw the news report, but authorities have not released the name of the victim pending notification of next of kin," said Bill.

Lillian knew whatever Grant's news might be, it would definitely affect at least one person. She quickly glanced around the table to gauge the reactions of the others when they heard what he said.

Grant looked at each person before saying, "The victim was David Nix, Rachel's business partner."

Lillian caught her breath.

Thank you, Grant. That's the confirmation I need. Almost all of the pieces of the puzzle are in place. She listened to Jake.

"I have a subpoena to search his plane and house in Houston. More than likely, he's already disposed of the gun."

"Jake's team has already compared the bullet that killed Rachel with the bullet that killed David," said Grant.

Jake nodded.

I just need to ask one more bit of information.

"And I'm sure they didn't match," said Lillian. Neither Grant nor Jake responded.

"Why were the documents so important?" asked Jason, getting the conversation back on his wavelength.

Lillian smiled when she saw Donna's reaction to Jason's question. She made eye contact with her. "Why don't you answer that question, dear?"

Donna nodded. "He wanted to destroy all evidence that would link him to me and his unwanted son."

Donna took a deep breath and exhaled.

"You see, he was the one who raped me while we were on a date. I didn't know he was married until later."

"I guess he thought that perhaps the adoption papers had the biological name of the father," mused Lillian. "But he was certainly wrong on that account, wasn't he, Margaret?"

"New birth certificates are issued, and files are sealed. Not everyone knows that."

"If he had hung around long enough, he. . .Oh, well, that's in the past," said Donna softly and sadly.

Jason reached over and took her hand. "Yes, but the future is still yours."

"I don't understand men like him. He had it all, a good wife, children, a loyal business partner," said Jake. "Just wasn't happy with what he had, I guess."

"And cheated on all of them," added Lillian. "Got a sweet little girl pregnant and deserted her. Didn't even offer to provide child support. He easily could have done so."

Grant looked over at Donna. "Donna, Margaret, I hope we aren't upsetting you."

Both women shook their heads in the negative. "I've learned to live with my past," said Donna. "I only wish my baby could have had a full life."

"That's not your fault," said Margaret as she reached over and patted Donna on the shoulder. "You had no way of knowing that Jonathan Davis was so cruel."

"If I had. . ." began Donna, who paused and then continued with a whisper, "I wonder if Sheila told David about the baby's death. If she did, maybe that's why. . ."

She did not finish her thought.

"Don't give him that much credit. Greed got David in the end," said Lillian. "Guess he thought he would never be caught. And wouldn't have if Rachel had not figured it out."

"What are you talking about?" asked Jake.

"You're the sheriff. Surely, by now, you've learned he was embezzling from the oil company Rachel and her husband had created," Lillian said sternly.

"How do you know Rachel uncovered the theft?" Grant asked.

"She mentioned it in her diary."

"What diary, Mom? Grant and I didn't find a diary when we searched her house."

"I visited with Rachel's daughter Rebecca when she was here for the funeral. We met at the club house for lunch the next day, and she shared her mother's diary with me. Rebecca asked me to read it and share my opinion about three of the entries. She read it but didn't understand the allegations Rachel made against David. "

"I didn't know Rachel kept a diary," Margaret said. "Rebecca must have known where her mother hid it if Grant and Jake didn't find it."

"They couldn't have found the diary because Rachel didn't keep it at her house. Rebecca had access to Rachel's safe deposit box. That is where Rachel kept her important documents. Rebecca read the diary but couldn't understand some of Rachel's comments, so she wanted my opinion about some things her mother had written."

"What was in the diary?" Margaret asked.

"Rachel wrote about her meeting with the D.A. and her claim against David. Rebecca gave all the documents, including the original of Rachel's will, from the safe deposit box to Rachel's attorney. He turned the diary over to the D.A."

Jake looked at Grant. Lillian saw their brief eye contact and continued. *I'd bet you've talked to the district attorney and already know what I'll say next.*

"According to the diary, Rachel had put two and two together about his indiscretions a long time ago. She knew he had been cheating on his wife. She also knew he had been doing some quirky accounting regarding the company's receivables." Lillian saw Jason nodding his agreement. "Jason, I know Rachel visited with you. Do you have something to add?"

"David had also begun to cheat Rachel regarding her share of the profits," said Jason. "She came to me six months ago and asked me to give her my opinion. After a forensic analysis of the documents and after secretly questioning David's assistant, we determined that the financial statements he had been producing and on which her income was based were incorrect."

Lillian chuckled. "David didn't know that Rachel's undergraduate study was in accounting. Go on, Jason."

"She let him go on for awhile. Finally, at my suggestion, she sought legal advice," said Jason. "She intended to press charges."

"Her big mistake was letting him know she knew what he had done in the past and how he was cheating her," Lillian said. "She demanded he bring all of the company's books up to date and show her accurate spreadsheets."

"That explains his murdering Rachel, but I don't understand," said Donna. "How did he learn about Sheila? I met her only by accident one day when I took a walk."

"I can answer that," Grant said. "He admitted that he had followed you there one day when you took her the snowball flowers. Do you remember where you two sat as you visited?"

"Yes, after I put the flowers in a vase, we walked out to the patio and sat beside her pool," said Donna.

"And what did you talk about?" asked Lillian.

"We talked about Michael, about my son. My heart broke when I had to give him away, but it broke all over listening to her talk about him."

Margaret had inched her way closer to Donna and put her arm around her sister.

"I'm so sorry, Donna."

"I am too. Sheila really loved him. She showed me his pictures. He was beautiful," said Donna trying not to cry.

Lillian said, "You were at Sheila's funeral, weren't you?"

"Yes," Donna admitted.

"And you peeked in the Bakery's window to make sure we were all there, didn't you?"

"Yes. I was so afraid you recognized me."

"I did, but explain to the others why you did that," Lillian said.

"I saw Grant and Jake pick up Jonathan and take him to the courthouse. I had seen his picture when I visited with Sheila. I thought if he could kill an innocent child, my baby, then he had killed Sheila, too. So I followed Jonathan all the way back to Dallas after Sheila's funeral."

"Why?" asked Margaret.

"I had my gun. I was ready to kill him, but I'm glad I chickened out."

"Why?" Jason asked.

"We had a long talk. He convinced me he had turned his life around."

"I'm afraid I would have used the gun if I had followed him," said Victoria. "He didn't appreciate that baby or his wife. He doesn't deserve any sympathy."

"Now, Victoria, we agreed you wouldn't spout off at the mouth," said Tony

"Oh, okay, I'll behave for now," said Victoria.

Lillian continued her story.

"So, when David found out that Donna was living here at the lake, too, and that Rachel had visited her, he began to worry. His past sins had caught up with him. He didn't want anyone to know. He probably followed Donna and Rachel everywhere."

Tony said, "I don't understand." Victoria elbowed him. He shrugged.

"David was so afraid Rachel would learn about Donna's connection to Sheila. His biggest fear was that Rachel would tell Lori, his wife, he had raped a young girl. If word got out, it not only would destroy his marriage but also ruin his professional reputation."

"Are you saying David shot Rachel?" Victoria asked.

"I didn't say that. You're getting ahead of me," Lillian said.

"I'm just glad we were at Mom and Dad's when he decided to shoot out the windows," said Jake. "He thought his warning shot would keep all of us confused."

"But the Lexus he drove was one of the keys to solving the murders," said Grant. "I chased that Lexus more than once."

"Oh, good grief," said Victoria suddenly.

"What's the matter?" Lillian asked her friend.

"The thought just occurred to me that I had a murderer right under my roof. When he and Rachel's children stayed with us prior to the funeral, he seemed so nice, so compassionate during that time."

"And at the funeral, his grief seemed so sincere," Tony said.

"Would you pour me another glass of wine?" Victoria held her glass out for her husband to take. He complied and took it to refill.

"Oh, you were safe as long as Rachel's children were there. He had to continue his bereaved *I've lost my best friend act*," said Jake.

"Unfortunately, we all lost someone we loved," Lillian said sadly. She let them all sit in silence for awhile. *You're trying to understand his greed and let the information you've just heard take form. I know, I've wrestled with it also. But, there's more.*

"So, what happens to the business?" asked Jason.

"Rachel's children and David's wife and children are now the sole owners of the business, and I bet they will need an honest CPA," said Lillian who had read all of Rachel's diary and knew exactly how much Rachel had trusted Jason's discretion, but being the professional, he, too, kept that information to himself.

"I've heard enough," said Grant. "Bill, would you get the ice cream and dip it for us."

"I hope it's homemade," said Jake.

"Of course, it is," said Lillian. "Anybody like peaches?" She received an applause.

After dessert, I break the last bit of news to them. Complete the puzzle.

Chapter 32

AFTER THE ICE cream had been served, everyone looked so relaxed that Lillian almost hated to break the mood. *But I will. Rachel's murderer will pay. I promised Rachel I'd find her killer.*

When all the bowls were empty, Lillian stacked them on a tray. She said, "Everybody, let's go inside for coffee. I don't know about the rest of you, but the mosquitoes are biting me."

She waited until everyone entered the house. Then, she picked up her tray and followed, stopping long enough to lock the inside deadbolt on the door. She dropped the key in her pocket and followed the group into the living room.

"Have a seat, everyone. I have an announcement to make."

"I hope it's a good one," said Bill.

Lillian shook her head. "Grant, I have some news that you won't like to hear."

"I'm listening," he said.

"Margaret, describe your white car for us."

Margaret looked strained. "What are you talking about? Everyone knows I drive a beige Honda Civic. Why should I describe my Honda?"

"Not that one, dear. The other one, the white one in your garage that you didn't want me to see."

Lillian handed a slip of paper to Jake. "Son, call in that number and see whose name is on the registration." He looked dubious. "Just do it, son. Humor me."

Jake opened his cell and dialed. "Hello. This is Sheriff Prestridge. Could you run this tag for me?" Pause. "It's DM9 X 226." Everyone looked at him. "Thanks."

He put his cell in his pocket and turned to Margaret. Everyone else looked at her.

"Tell everyone what kind of car that is," Lillian instructed Margaret.

"Why don't you since you seem to know already," Margaret demanded.

"It's a white 2012 Lexus sedan," Jake said. He turned to Grant.

Grant said nothing. He put his arm around Margaret and pulled her closer to him.

"Lillian, I think your little parlor game has gone on long enough," Grant said.

"No, dear, there are more riddles to solve," Lillian stated. "And it saddens me to reveal their answers."

"Mom, if you want to solve riddles, talk so we can understand you."

"Okay, I'll be direct and ask this question: Who had reason to kill David?"

"Yeah, who would want to do that?" said Tony. "Stealing and killing are two different things. I'm still having trouble believing he would kill anyone, especially if I judged him by his visit to us."

Victoria nudged her husband.

"Don't defend him. Stealing from a widow is terrible, but if he killed Rachel, I'll ask the question we've already heard: 'Who killed him?'"

"That's a good question." Jake thought for a moment and then responded, "I'd say either Donna or Margaret had a motive."

"Be careful, Jake," Grant warned. "Don't make accusations you can't prove."

"I warned you, my dear," Lillian said softly and walked over to place her hand on Grant's back.

He shrugged off her touch and looked at Lillian. "I don't think you ought to go there, Lillian. You know Margaret almost as well as I do. She's your friend. She wouldn't harm anyone."

"Margaret had reasons to hate him."

"So did I," said Donna. "But we aren't murderers."

"You're correct," said Grant. "I resent your insinuations, Lillian. This time, you've gone too far in your amateur sleuthing. I can't and don't believe the woman I love –" He paused.

I know I hurt you., Grant. I hope you will forgive me someday, Lillian thought.

"Grant, you don't think. . ." Margaret did not finish her sentence.

"He doesn't want to think, my dear, that you could be so cruel."

"What are you saying, Lillian?" Victoria stood, looking at the two sisters. Her gaze settled on the younger one.

Margaret made a dash for the door and frantically tried to open it, but the knob would not turn.

Eli raised his head, but when Grant, too, walked over to Margaret, he settled back down in his favorite spot on the sofa.

Grant stood and walked over to Margaret and put his arm around her. "Sweetheart, you don't have to run. We know you wouldn't hurt anyone." He glared at both Jake and Lillian. "Don't we?" They didn't answer him.

Margaret ignored him and again tried to open the door. It was locked. She turned around and screamed at her sister. "You and your despicable bastard ruined our family. My parents never recuperated after you brought so much shame to our home. You let them down so much I couldn't stand the hurt they suffered. If it weren't for me, they would have withered away. I constantly had to boost their spirits." She took a step toward her sister. Grant gently touched her arm. She pulled away but stopped suddenly when she heard the dog.

Eli, alert and listening from his perch, growled menacingly when Margaret yelled. He jumped down and charged at Margaret. She attempted to kick him away, but Grant interceded and pulled Margaret back.

At the same time, Lillian gave a stern command. "Sit, Eli." She walked over, took him by his collar, and led him away from Grant and Margaret.

To her husband, she said, "Here, Bill, hold onto him. He's as mad as I am."

Donna replied softly to her sister, "Oh, but they did recover. Of course, you would never know that. Boost their spirits? How could you make that claim? You left all of us behind. You never visited our parents."

"You cost them everything," Margaret said as she successfully pulled away from Grant, whose face revealed his conflicting emotions.

Lillian thought, *You're surprised by your fiancée's animosity toward her sister, aren't you, Grant?*

Fearing Margaret would attack Donna, Lillian motioned to Jake. He walked over and stood between the sisters.

No longer speaking softly, Donna said, "Only a college education. That's all I cost them. How do you think I got my degree?"

"Your degree is no concern of mine."

Donna continued. "Daddy paid my tuition. I worked and paid for my apartment and everything else."

"I don't believe it. He would have told me."

"He didn't tell you because he didn't want to listen to your griping about me."

"Okay, girls, enough," Lillian broke into the argument. "Both of you sit down."

Donna obliged, but Margaret returned to the door even though she couldn't open it.

Lillian spoke to Margaret. "I know you killed Rachel."

"You're crazy, Lillian," Grant spoke loudly. He turned to Margaret. "You didn't kill anyone, did you?" Her silence and the smirk on her face told him everything he didn't want to know.

"What?" Victoria said. She lunged toward Margaret, but Tony and Jake grabbed her arms and held her back. Victoria continued to sputter.

"How could you?" Donna asked. Margaret didn't respond.

"She was about to ruin everything," Lillian said to Donna. "I'll explain. Jake, Grant, you'll be interested in hearing this, too."

"Go ahead, Lillian. I believe you are going to give us a solution to Rachel's murder." Lillian noted the sadness in Grant's voice. "Even though I don't want to hear it."

"I told you it would be bad news."

Bill, who had been silent, said, "Get it over with Lillian."

Lillian cleared her throat. "Margaret killed Rachel because of Rachel's association with David. You see, Donna had revealed the father of her baby to only one person: her sister. Margaret knew David was married at the time. She has systematically blackmailed him for years."

Margaret sat down, propped her elbows on her knees, and held her head in her hands. She finally looked at Lillian. "How did you figure it out?"

"When I stopped by your house last week, I saw the back of your expensive automobile before you closed your garage door and wondered how you could afford it. But, while I was alone in your living room, I also admired your antiques, especially the Louis V desk."

"What about the desk? How did it give her away?" Grant asked.

"It wasn't the desk. It was the copy of her bank statement. Way too much money for a county clerk. Then I saw something else."

"What?" asked Victoria.

"A check for one hundred thousand dollars." Lillian paused for emphasis. Everyone waited for her to continue. "It was signed by David Nix. Then I knew."

Margaret grimaced. "You nosey old broad. I knew I shouldn't have let you in."

"Blackmail is a serious charge, Mom." He loosened his grip on Victoria. "Hold her, Tony."

"But murder is more serious," said Victoria straining to get away from Tony.

"Not one murder, but two," said Lillian, who still held Margaret in her gaze. "What happened? Did he tell you he couldn't pay anymore because Rachel had discovered he was stealing from her to pay you? So, once he mentioned her name, Rachel's life had to be forfeited also?"

Margaret snorted. "Killing Rachel was so easy. She didn't hesitate to open her door to me." Eyes wide, Margaret laughed hysterically. "I thought about killing David and framing Rachel for his murder, but I decided it was safer to kill two birds, so to speak."

Grant walked over to the woman he loved and kissed her passionately. He turned around, reached behind him for handcuffs, and handed them to Jake. "Book her."

He looked at Lillian sadly and spoke barely above a whisper. "Will you unlock the door, please?"

Lillian did as he requested. She watched him drive away.

Jake read Margaret her rights and took her out the door she had not been able to open.

Silence.

* * * * *

THE HOUSE HAD emptied quickly after Lillian revealed her solutions to all of the murders at Leisure Lake. Exhausted, she had plopped down in her recliner.

Poor Grant. He's lost too much: his parents, Alice, and now Margaret. I hope he can heal and be happy.

Bill left Lillian alone while he cleaned up the kitchen. Finished, he returned to the living room to find her sound asleep. Eli lay on the floor beside her chair. Bill covered her with an afghan and tiptoed out.

Chapter 33

THREE WEEKS LATER, Bill carried a bottle of wine and two wine glasses out to the deck where Lillian sat and watched the golden glow of the autumn sunset on the lake.

Lillian smiled when she saw him approach, a big grin on his face. "What's the occasion?" she asked.

"Remember our last dinner party a few weeks ago?"

"How could I forget it?" Lillian said.

"Well, I had an announcement to make that night, but since yours topped it, I thought it best to wait until things settled down."

"What did you want to say?"

Bill filled the glasses, handed one to Lillian, and raised his in a toast. "My sweet wife's been so busy with this case that she has completely forgotten our anniversary."

"Oh no, I haven't," she said. "I thought you had."

"For fifty years," he continued, "I have done everything I can think of to please you, but I think this time, I've outdone myself. You are going to love my gift."

"I've always loved your gifts," Lillian said.

Bill held up a picture of the new Forester RV he had bought for Lillian.

She was shocked.

"Oh, Bill, it's perfect," she said. "When do we leave?"

"Tomorrow too soon?" he asked.

Lillian hugged him and whispered, "Perfect, my dear." And then in a loud voice, she raised her glass, "I'll give you my gift when we spend our first night in it."

Eli barked. He picked up on the joy the couple shared and pranced around the room. "He's a clown," Bill said and laughed.

* * * * *

BILL AND LILLIAN had packed everything into the RV. Lillian walked back through the house one more time to make sure that she had not forgotten anything. They planned to be in the motor home for the next six months. She noticed Eli, who was curled up on the sofa watching all of the activity of packing and carrying things out to the RV. She reached down and put a hand on his head, "Eli, do you think we'd forget you?"

He wagged his tail in response. "Well, come on, you sweet thing. Let's go." That was all the invitation he needed. Eli grabbed his favorite toy and headed for the back door.

Bill laughed when he saw the dog race out the door and hop into the RV. "Eli, you do pack lightly, don't you?"

He looked at the only sweetheart he had ever had, "Lillian, are you ready?"

"I will be as soon as we have our devotional. I just feel we need to have one before we hit the road," she said.

"I thought you would want to do that," said Bill, "so I have just the right scripture for us to read this morning."

Lillian sat down at the patio table, and Bill began to read: *There is a time for everything, and a season for every activity under heaven: a time to be born and a time to die, ...a time to weep and a time to laugh, a time to mourn and a time to dance,. . . .*

He closed the Book.
He looked at his wife.
He stood in front of her and bowed.
He held out his hand.
"May I have this dance?"
She took his hand.
Eli barked.

Chapter 34

GRANT STOOD ON the pier that led out to the lake. From his vantage point, he saw Lillian and Eli climb into the new Forrester RV. Bill started the engine and eased the vehicle out of their drive. As they drove away, Grant waved goodbye at the RV's rear window. Alone, Grant closed his eyes and took a deep breath. *Goodbye, you two. Stay safe.*

The soft, slap, slap sounds of the gentle waves drew his attention back to the lake.

Watching the watery reflections of the wizened, ancient oaks dressed in their golden finery, he thought, *If only Sheila had not moved to Leisure Lake, four people would still be alive. I might even be married.* He shook his head. *No, don't think about that. Marriage isn't in the picture for me, not with Alice, not with Margaret.*

The ring of his cell phone broke his solitude.

"Hello."

"Grant," said Jake on the other end of the line. "I've been wondering how you're doing."

"I'm fine," Grant responded listlessly.

"You sound as though you are outside. Where are you?"

"I'm standing where it all started – on the dock – thinking."

"What are you thinking?" Jake sounded worried.

"This is where it will end." Grant said.

"Hold on, Grant, I'm on my way. Don't do anything foolish. We need to talk. Wait right there for me. I'll be there in fifteen minutes."

Grant laughed. "Don't worry, Jake. I'm not going to hurt myself."

"That's reassuring, but I don't understand. What's going to end?"

"My job. I quit. I'm taking a vacation. I need a change of scenery."

"Where are you going?"

"I'll decide when I drive out the main gate."

"Promise to stay in touch?"

"Ten-four." Grant closed his cell phone and threw it in the lake. *I don't want to say goodbye anymore.*

If you've enjoyed Pirtle's *The Mah Jongg Murders*, you are invited to read a sample of Book 2 of *The Games We Play Series*

Coming Fall, 2016

Deadly Dominoes

Chapter One

"You'd better be careful."

Lillian, lost in her own world, mentally checked off the items she had just purchased and hoped she had not forgotten anything. She barely heard the advice of the young man who was busy placing into the back of her Jeep the burgeoning sacks of groceries she and Bill, her husband of fifty years, would need while camping at Caddo Lake along with their white Standard Poodle, Eli.

For the first time, Lillian paid attention to the six-feet tall, muscular, dark haired young man who stood before her waiting for a response. "I beg your pardon...uh..." She glanced at the name tag pinned to his shirt. "Brandon, what's that you say?"

"I said 'you'd better be careful' ."

"Why would you say that?"

"Crazy things been happening out at that RV park at Caddo Lake."

Lillian smiled and decided to give him a pop quiz, "Okay, Brandon, just how do you know that I'm RVing and, to be more precise, RVing at Caddo?"

"Well, ma'am, there's that sticker on the front windshield of your Jeep...and," he paused, "if I hadn't seen it, I could guess you're RVing by what I just packed in these sacks. Most folks who go there, stock up on mosquito spray, suntan lotion, quick and easy snacks, milk, eggs, bread, corn meal to coat the fish they plan to fry, cooking oil. And since you've bought dog treats, I assume. . ."

"Okay, okay, I get it. You don't have to recite my grocery list. I'll have to say that you are an astute young man. I envision you as a detective someday."

Brandon laughed with Lillian. "Perhaps, you're the detective, ma'am. I'm enrolled at Sam Houston State University. My major is criminal justice."

"I should have known. You remind me of my son, Jake, and my adopted son, Grant. Both attended Sam Houston where they received their degrees in criminal justice. Maybe, you'll have the opportunity to meet them while my husband and I are at Caddo. That is, if I can coax them to drive up for the day."

"That would be nice. I'd like to talk to someone other than a school counselor who could give me some advice, someone in the real world."

"Oh, they'd be glad to do that. Well, I've got to go. Bill's waiting." Lillian prepared to leave, but for some unknown reason, felt drawn to the young man. "I'm sure I've forgotten something. Since this is the closest store to the lake, we'll be seeing more of each other. Next time we meet, do me a favor."

"Sure, ma'am, anything. Just let me know what you need."

"Dispense with the *ma'am* and call me Lillian."

"You got it."

Lillian started to get in the vehicle, stopped, turned around, and extended her hand to the ambitious young man. Slipping him a twenty dollar bill, "Brandon, I wish you well, and I thank you." She put the key in the ignition, started the motor, and proceeded to pull out of the parking lot.

Before heading back to the lake, however, she glanced in her rearview mirror in time to see Brandon walk back into the store. *Hmm, I must be losing it. I didn't even ask him what kinds of crazy things are happening at the park. Bill would be so proud of me. Should I go back and quiz Brandon a little more? No, I promised Bill that we would have a real vacation. Besides, I'll be seeing him again soon.*

*****

Tall, slim, gray-haired Lillian, a retired educator turned busybody snoop, parked beside the new brown and white Forester Class C motor home Bill had given her for their fiftieth wedding anniversary. The motor home had all the conveniences of home, albeit on a much smaller scale. With a separate bedroom, a full bath, a small kitchen and sitting area, it was just right for the two of them and Eli.

Deep in thought and curious about Brandon's cautionary statement to her, Lillian had not seen Bill and Eli walking away from the pavilion situated by the entrance to the park. She glanced in her rearview mirror and saw both man and dog hurrying to catch up with her. As soon as she stepped out of the Jeep, Bill grabbed her in an embrace. "Hi, Sweetie, what took you so long?" Bill helped her unload the groceries.

Lillian reached down and gave Eli a love pat on his topknot and smiled at her husband. "You know, you still look quite handsome, even distinguished with that salt and pepper hair."

She laughed when Bill, a former investigative journalist, looked at her, and then to no one in particular said, "Ah, yes, she evades the question. What has she been up to?" He reached into the back of the SUV and grabbed the sacks. He carried them into the motor home and sat them on the small kitchen table.

Eli bounded up the steps and sniffed each of the bags as Bill set them down.

"Eli, I bet she bought you some treats." Bill rummaged through one of the bags and pulled out a bag of chew bones. He held one up. "Sit. Shake hands." Eli lifted his right paw and eagerly, but gingerly, took his reward from Bill's left hand.

Lillian followed him into the RV and placed the non-perishables in the small pantry below the refrigerator and the cold items in the fridge. "Bill, you should have been with me. I met the nicest young man at the store."

"Oh?"

"Yes, and he said the strangest thing. A warning really. But he was so charming that I forgot to ask him what he meant and didn't realize it until I was on my way out of the parking lot."

"Now, Lillian, you know what you promised."

"Yes, I remember what I said, but...

"No buts...anyway, we've been invited to a game of dominoes this evening."

"Dominoes? We've never played dominoes. I don't even know how. Who invited us and, more importantly, I can't imagine why in the world you would even accept such an invitation."

"The Archers asked us to come."

"I see. While I've been grocery shopping, you and Eli have been socializing. By the way, who are the Archers?"

"They are the couple in the white Cruise America motor home across and down the street from us."

"What time do they want us? Did you ask what we could bring?"

"We will meet them and a few others at the pavilion. It seems that is quite the gathering place here. And we need take only what we want to drink. There is a grill there, and the Archers plan to cook hot dogs for everyone."

"Sounds like fun. I guess this is what RVing is all about. Relaxing, meeting new people, playing games. What do you think about that, Eli?"

Upon hearing his name, the poodle looked up, too busy chewing on his treat to answer her question.

Chapter Two

Relaxed for the first time in weeks, Lillian held onto Eli's leash as she walked with Bill on the way to the Pavilion. She gazed across the lake and wrapped herself in the sounds and smells that surrounded them. It was the time of day when the glow of the sun turns a muted orange in the western sky. The reflection of the trees on the water mirrored the glow of the Indian Summer sundown, and the Spanish moss dripping from their limbs gave the impression of oddly shaped golden tentacles on the water's surface. The waves on Lake Caddo had calmed to a slow ripple. Even so, the waves remained strong enough to gently rock the boats moored to the T-shaped public pier which stretched twenty feet across the surface of the water. The gentle slap, slap of the water against the boats blended with the distant sounds of laughter. The gravel crunching beneath their feet gave rhythm to the peaceful, harmonious cantata of water and distant voices.

"Bill, do you realize that for the first time in many months, we have nothing to do and plenty of time to do it?"

"Yes, and I'm glad to see you happy for a change," Bill responded.

As they entered the Pavilion, Lillian hesitated. She felt Bill protectively place his arm around her shoulders to guide her steps. Eli began a low growl, a sound she had become to know as a sign of danger.

Lillian stiffened.

There before her was an elderly man with short gray hair, rather unkempt, unshaven. The open collar of his worn, faded, khaki shirt revealed a silver cross attached to a black woven band of elephant hair. *I've seen a cross like that before, but where?*

Bill dropped his arm and placed his hand in the small of her back to nudge her forward. She ignored his efforts and walked over to the man. But before she could say anything, he looked her in the eye, nodded his head ever so slightly, turned and walked away. *Do I know you? Those dark eyes of yours are piercing. Creepy.*

"Lillian, come on," said Bill, "I want to introduce you to the camp director."

Hesitating still, Lillian allowed Bill to lead her to a man who was positioned on the far side of the Pavilion where he had just fired up the grill. As they approached, Albert looked up, stopped what he was doing, and smiling, walked over to greet them.

"Welcome, Bill, I'm glad you could come." The two men shook hands.

"Thanks, Mr. Archer. I'd like to introduce you to my wife, Lillian."

Albert reached out to shake hands with Lillian but dropped his hand when Eli jumped between them. His growl told Albert to back away, and the man followed the dog's advice.

"Nice guard dog you have, Lillian. I hope he won't pose a problem for the other guests here at the park."

"He won't hurt anyone. Sit, Eli. Stay."

The dog followed her command and sat close beside her and continued his warning in a little softer tone.

"See, Eli is well behaved. Say hello to Albert, Eli."

The poodle stopped his low growl and looked up but did not speak his usual friendly bark. Instead, he gave a loud snort and turned his head.

It was obvious to Lillian that Albert took note of the snub. He gave the animal one last, disgusting glare.

Recovering quickly, he looked at Bill and said, "I hope you two will enjoy your stay here at Caddo." Then, he exchanged his frown for a superficial smile and spoke to the dog, "You, too, Eli."

"Oh, I'm sure we'll have fun, Mr. Archer. We always love an adventure," said Lillian who had to gently tug on Eli's leash to make sure he stayed put.

"Now, wait up a minute, you two. There's to be no 'Mr. Archer' around here. People who know me would think I'm putting on airs. Call me Al," he said jovially.

Lillian responded, "You've got it, Al," and laughed along with him.

Lillian saw a woman approaching the table with a stack of wieners and buns. She placed her tray of food on the table and joined Al. She smiled and said, "Hello, you must be Bill and Lillian."

Milly and Al could have passed for brother and sister, five-feet, eight inches tall, auburn hair, freckles. Both were probably somewhere in their forties. By a quick glance at their waistlines, Lillian knew right away they enjoyed eating. Both faces were filled with laugh lines, happy wrinkles all. The two ladies exchanged greetings and, along with Eli, moved away from the men.

"Milly, do you need any help setting up for tonight?" asked Lillian.

"Oh, no thanks, we keep everything simple. Al and I usually provide hot dogs or burgers. Everything else is just pot luck. First timers are guests and aren't expected to bring anything."

"That's good because Bill didn't say anything about food. He just mentioned dominoes."

"Yes, Al and I like to play straight dominoes each Friday night with any of the RVers who show up here at the Pavilion. Some of the guests prefer forty-two, but usually, we play regular dominoes."

"Well, you will have to teach me. I've never played dominoes in my entire life."

"You're kidding," said Milly. She laughed and then asked, "or rather, is this the big hustle?"

"No, I'm not kidding. My Leisure Lake friends and I play Mah Jongg…." Lillian said wistfully, remembering the loss of one of her Mah Jongg friends who had been murdered a few weeks ago by another of ther Mah Jongg companions.

She took a deep breath and exhaled to erase the sadness enveloping her. "But I'm ready to learn a new game."

"Good."

Lillian turned to find Bill still talking with Al.

She smiled and spoke to some of the other guests who had arrived, some in pairs. All of them greeted the friendly dog accompanying her. Those who had brought food to share placed their contributions on the table and began to mingle. She joined the men and hooked her arm around Bill's.

Al said, "Come on. I'll introduce you to some of the other campers tonight. I see you've already met Simon, our handyman."

"Well, I wouldn't say we met since he made tracks when Lillian walked over to him," said Bill.

"Oh, just forget about him," said Milly.

"I agree," said Bill. "We are here to enjoy ourselves, so let's get to it."

Al took a head count and walked to the center of the Pavilion and in a loud voice gained the attention of those present.

"Okay, folks, I think we have enough people here to get started with the games. Everything you'll need is on your table."

Milly joined Al.

"I'd like to introduce all of you to our two newbies, Lillian and Bill. Eli barked. "Oh, yes, I almost forgot you. Everyone, this is Eli. I won't ask you to tell them who you are right now, but before the evening is over, perhaps you can come by and say hello to them. They'll be at our table tonight."

A man with a New Jersey accent yelled, "Okay, Milly dear, we will. Right now, let's play."

The chatter in the open pavilion became a low hum as everyone took their seats. *Well, here goes,* thought Lillian. *These people seem to know each other by the way they've chosen partners and tables.* Almost simultaneously, the dominoes tumbling from their containers clacked onto the tables, and slid into the slow rhythms of their shufflers.

"Lillian, pick seven dominoes. Bill, I'm assuming you've played before," said Al.

"Yeah, I have. As a kid, I played with my grandfather." Bill smiled. "He was quite a shark. By the time everyone had played twice, he knew what each player had in his hand."

Al started the game. He played the double five. "Ten," he said and turned to Lillian who was still considering what she had drawn and trying to line up her dominoes in some kind of order.

"Lillian, if you have a five, just play it. If not, you'll have to pass." He looked surprised when Lillian picked up one of her dominoes.

"Ten," Lillian announced as she plopped down the blank five. "We're even, Al."

"Yep, for now, but don't expect it to stay that way, Little Lady," he responded.

Milly looked at Al's red face. "I think Al's just been hustled. Are you sure you've never played before?"

Lillian shrugged her shoulders and laughed along with the other three. She noticed that Al laughed the loudest. *Hmm. Too loud. I don't trust you for a minute, Al. Neither does my dog. 'Little Lady' my . . . Lillian, ole girl, let it go.*

For the next hour, she concentrated on the strange and somewhat confusing game. All that could be heard in the Pavilion was the clack of the dominoes being slammed on the tables followed by either laughter or a groan, dependent upon the win or loss by the different teams.

Finally, after Milly had finished tallying their scores, Al stood up and yelled, "Okay, folks, when you finish the round you're playing right now, stop. Let's take a break and eat. There's a feast on the table."

"Whew, I thought you'd forgotten us," said one of the men. "I'm starving."

"I'll have these dogs ready in a minute," said Al.

"Let's mingle," said Bill.

"Yes, let's," agreed Lillian. She stood and hooked Eli's leash to the leg of her chair.

"Eli, you stay here by the table. I'll sneak an extra hotdog for you." He licked his lips in anticipation of the treat to come.

The two made their way around the room shaking hands and introducing themselves to the other players. Suddenly, a loud explosion replaced the laughter and camaraderie of the Friday night domino competitors. Its force caused the Pavilian to sway right to left, rattling the chairs and tables while dominoes skated off the tables,

Eli ran toward Lillian, dragging the chair with him.

Made in the USA
Coppell, TX
19 September 2023

21757538R00160